Status: MI

D.W. Maroney

MW00477386

eBook ISBN-13: 978-1-7327839-2-8
Print ISBN - 978-1-7327839-3-5
Published in the United States of America
State of Mind Publishing
Copyright ©2019 by D.W. Maroney
All Rights Reserved
This book is a work of fiction. While reference might be made to actual historical events, places, or things, the names, characters, places, and incidents depicted herein are either the product of the author's imagination or are used fictitiously. Any resemblance to actual persons, living or dead, business establishments, events, or locales is entirely coincidental.

DEDICATION

To the 239 souls aboard Malaysia Airlines flight MH 370. Peace be with you.

ACKNOWLEDGMENTS

M y profound thanks to Sarah Maroney for dropping a nuclear warhead on my favorite excuse for not writing this story. Because of her, I took a step into the unknown. Sarah, you inspire me every day.

There are times when internet research is enough. Then there are times when it isn't. Many thanks to Dustin Lientz for sharing his incredible knowledge of aviation with me. You made my pilots come to life. Sorry I killed a few of them off!

I also have to thank Geoff Symon for answering a multitude of forensic questions that helped shape the direction of this story.

I owe a debt of gratitude to several people who were kind enough to take a look at the manuscript in its various stages. Lyla Bellatas, your words of encouragement early on gave me the push I needed to keep moving forward.

Kathy Bennett, you have been my rock throughout this process. Your confidence in my ability to conquer this project has sustained me through countless dark moments.

Don Muncy, your time and comments were greatly appreciated.

Desiree Holt, your faith in my ability to write in this genre gave me a much-needed push forward.

Diane Nelson, Jean Joachim, and Rose C. Carole, I can't tell you how much I appreciate your time, your comments, and your encouragement. Writing can feel like being stranded on a desert island but thanks to your friendship, I know I'm not alone. A special thanks to Jean for telling me my original title sucked. It did. I fixed it.

Special thanks to my fearless editor, Laura Garland. She's a miracle worker of the first order. Any errors you might encounter are entirely my fault, not hers.

Last, but not least, I have to thank my entire family for listening to me talk about this story for years then standing behind me once I finally decided to write it.

Major Megan Sloan
Washington, D.C.
Monday 07:30 Zulu (03:30 EDT)

I didn't dare look behind me or slow down. An attacker coming out of the pre-dawn shadows of D.C. didn't concern me. I could handle those with both arms tied behind my back. The monsters lurking in the shadows of my past had driven me out of my warm bed, where shop windows as black as my soul felt like old friends and streetlights were nothing more than matchsticks, their light flaring brightly one moment and snuffed out the next before they revealed too much.

Exploding out onto the National Mall, I hauled ass past the World War II Memorial, climbed the slope to the Washington Monument, circled the marble obelisk, and rushed headlong down the other side. Ducks sleeping along the reflecting pool scattered as my feet kicked up gravel on the walkway leading to the Lincoln Memorial. I took the steps two at a time to the top, saluted the marble statue, and, without breaking stride, plummeted all the way to ground level as if the hounds of hell were on my heels.

If I'd learned anything during months of training and years in the field, it was that routines kill more spies than bullets. I veered off my pre-planned route and into an alleyway between two buildings and came out on a street running parallel to the one I'd just left. I'd seen no one, save a couple of homeless dudes in the usual places: doorways and beneath awnings that would provide shelter from the weather. Many of them were veterans, and I took out several dollar bills I kept tucked into the waistband of my running shorts, dropping them carelessly as I passed. It was the one habit I refused to give up, even if it compromised my own safety.

It was rare to see a car this early, but not unheard of. Shit happens in D.C. I'm convinced political staffers are alien beings who sleep standing up. Then there were the members of the intelligence community. They never sleep. Ever.

Too many demons, both real and imagined, dogging their heels.

I should know. Wasn't I out here trying to outrun mine?

Cars lined the streets of my neighborhood. I scanned every one as I zigged and zagged my way toward the century-old brownstone I'd called home for the last few years. I'd bought the crumbling edifice before gentrification had begun in the neighborhood and spent a small fortune to gut and rebuild before moving in. I'd slept in enough hovels on the job. I damned sure wasn't going to sleep in one in the heart of D.C.

I entered my street several blocks down from my house. Where once the curbs had been lined with derelict vehicles, expensive late-model cars now awaited their owners who slept snugly in their king-sized beds. Attuned to every sight, every smell, I felt the hairs on the nape of my neck stand on end as I closed in on my block and the smell of auto exhaust grew thicker, obscuring the faint floral scents coming from the colorful flowers my neighbors seemed to love. Every house except mine had some sort of planting—a basket, a pot, or bright blooms around the base of a tree. I wasn't home enough to keep a plant alive, and I didn't know my neighbors well enough to ask them to do it for me.

"Well, shit." A block and a half from my stoop, I spied the source of the foul odor—a black sedan with tinted windows was double-parked in front of my house, its big engine pumping out enough carcinogens to kill every plant on the block. I stopped behind a large oak that likely had survived since the days when Teddy Roosevelt occupied the most famous residence in town. Pressing my shoulders against the rough bark, I willed my heartbeat to slow before daring a look around the trunk. *Yep. My house.* A familiar figure stood on my stoop, facing the street, his head swiveling as he scanned the area.

For a split second, I considered reversing direction but dismissed the idea almost as fast as it had come to me. The car and its occupants weren't going anywhere without me, and if I didn't show soon, they'd come looking for me. I might be able to outrun the demons lurking in my soul, but I couldn't outrun my employer. I stepped out and resumed my run. At the next cross street, I knew I'd been spotted.

I hooked a left then a right into the alley and entered my house through the back door. The alarm system beeped a reminder to deactivate it. I punched in the same code I used for the front door, only backward, then reset it.

Sanchez could wait while I showered and changed clothes.

Taking the rear stairs two at a time, I stopped in the doorway of my room on the third floor. It didn't appear my latest mistake had noticed my departure or the doorbell. Facial muscles slack, his breathing even, Marcus slept the sleep of the innocent, and, if I had my way, that would never change.

I'd told the well-known civil rights attorney I worked for the Transportation Safety Administration (TSA)—had even gone so far as to make up a more or less accurate story about investigating ways terrorists might breach existing security measures. None of it was true but close enough. Going to work at the Freedom Center, TSA's operations center near Dulles International Airport, added authenticity to the story. Calling my work *classified* kept the questions at bay—mostly. In my experience, people outside the realm of clandestine operations didn't understand the need for secrets. To them, the world was one big, happy neighborhood where everybody got along and farted rainbows. I knew better. And I had the scars to prove it.

I'd been a field operative for nearly a decade. Then an unfortunate incident in the capital city of a country most Americans couldn't find if it was outlined in neon on a map had landed my ass stateside. I kept mostly to myself these days, coming out to scratch my itch against the safest post I could find when the need hit me. Thank God it didn't hit very often, and when it did, Marcus always seemed willing to let me rub up against him. He'd quit asking me questions, which was fortunate because I hoarded my secrets like a martyr hoarded virgins. A word to the right wrong person and years of work would be for naught. Lives could be lost.

I didn't exactly creep into the en-suite bathroom, but I didn't make any unnecessary noise either. I'd excelled at Stealth 101, and the lessons had stuck with me. I shed my running clothes and cranked the mixing valve on the shower all the way to cold before stepping under the spray. In less than five minutes, showered, dressed, and my still damp hair secured in a high ponytail, I swung the front door wide. Sanchez stood beside the idling car, holding the door open.

The neighborhood had gentrified, but the area was far from civilized. This was the heart of D.C., after all. I keyed in the ten-digit code to the electronic lock before turning away from what I'd hoped would be a very pleasant morning spent in bed with a man who came damn close to knowing how to rock my boat. As usual, I'd left a one-time-only four-digit code that would let Marcus leave, but anyone, invited or otherwise, who tried to exit the premises after the door shut again could only wish the cops would show up. The silent alarm would go directly to my security service—an outfit run by a former Green Beret who shared my paranoia and skillsets. With a silent apology to Marcus for leaving without saying goodbye, I swept past Sanchez. I recognized the driver and gave him a little smile as Sanchez scooted in beside me and closed the door.

"Good morning, Paul. Sorry to keep you waiting."

His gaze met mine in the rearview mirror. "No problem, Major Sloan, but you'd better hold on. Jude said to stop for nothing."

Intelligence work was 99 percent boring research that could drag on for months, if not years, and more often than not ended with nothing more exciting than the slap of a binder cover closing. Rarely was time of the essence. Hearing his orders put every cell in my body on alert.

Beside me, Sanchez said, "No time to waste."

My gut clenched. "What's going on?" If I still believed in God, I would have sent up a prayer, but since I didn't, I called on the universe to do me a favor. *Please don't let it be another plane.*

"Jude thinks he has something."

Jude Chan was an electronics wizard for a major defense contractor before an offer of a guaranteed paycheck and the opportunity to test his skills convinced him to jump into Uncle Sam's smoldering cauldron of alphabet soup. Congress had voted down appropriations for his employer, so, as head of research and development for the bloodsucker, Jude's head had been on the chopping block. The man knew nothing about politics, but he knew electronics. Jude wasn't an alarmist. He wouldn't have sent Sanchez for me in the middle of the night if it hadn't been important.

"Who else is there?" Officially, they all had Memorial Day weekend off, but since terrorism didn't take holidays, neither did they. However, the members of the elite task force did need to sleep. Some, like Jude, spent more time on a cot in the "quiet" room than they did in their own beds. You couldn't buy dedication like that, and Uncle Sam didn't try.

"Just me and Jude. Place is like a tomb."

An involuntary shudder raised tiny bumps on my flesh. I tried not to dwell on the fact my workplace resembled a burial ground. Deep beneath the runways of Dulles International Airport, untold numbers of pale, sometimes zombie-like creatures toiled away in its vault-like rooms. Every federal agency with even a passing need to know had offices in the underground bunker—physically side-by-side, yet worlds apart when it came to sharing information. When President George W. Bush created the Department of Homeland Security, he'd envisioned all the law enforcement and intelligence communities snuggling together under one cozy blanket, whispering secrets to each other in the dark, thereby shedding light on those who would perpetrate evil against Americans. What he'd gotten was a fortified box filled with cracked eggs who trusted no one and believed every shadow contained a monster.

In my experience, they weren't wrong. I possessed a healthy respect for dark corners.

"Rodgers put you in charge this weekend. What do you want me to do?" Sanchez asked.

I'd wondered more than once what Colonel Rodgers had done to get assigned to supervise our project. He had an office near mine he rarely used. I couldn't blame him for preferring the one he had at the Pentagon. It had a window. Given a choice, I might do the same, but then again, windows worked two ways. If I could see out, others could see in. Give me a bunker anytime, thank you very much.

"Let's not bother the colonel...yet." I'd be damned if I'd get the man out of bed until I knew what we were dealing with. He checked on us every day, either by phone or in person, which either meant someone higher up the food chain was keeping tabs on us or he was dotting every I and crossing every T because someone was looking over *his* shoulder. I wasn't paid to speculate as to which it was, but my money was on the latter. "Call everyone else. Tell them vacation is canceled, and if their butt isn't in their seat by 0430, they'll be scooping mashed potatoes in the cafeteria by afternoon."

Kwon Seul-ki
North Pacific Ocean
Monday 07:30 Zulu (Sunday 17:30 ChST)

O ne of the things Seul-ki had learned while attending school in the United States was the concept of a single deity with dominion over all. Many of his fellow students had believed in such a being and spoken of Heaven and Hell as if the places existed outside the realm of their earthly world.

Seul-ki couldn't quite relate to an unseen god directing the daily lives of individuals, yet allowing those same individuals the latitude to choose their own paths leading to either Heaven or Hell depending on the kind of life one led. In his world, the god was visible, a human puppeteer who directed the lives of millions with the promise of misery for those who defied him or lack of misery for those who went along without question. In his world, Heaven was enough food to feed your family and anonymity. Hell was coming to the attention of the Supreme Leader for any reason whatsoever.

By his own definition, he'd been in Hell for most of his life, and all because he'd been a good student. His family had lived a heavenly existence until Seul-ki had come to the attention of Choi Min-ho. Every moment since had been a living hell for him and his family.

He'd considered asking for asylum countless times during the four years he attended the University of Southern California. Only thoughts of his family and the misery he'd already brought upon them kept him from doing so.

Sitting in the midst of his electronic world, feeling the tug of the puppet master's strings, he knew he'd made the wrong decision. He should have escaped while he'd had the chance, for he was now certain, despite Supreme Leader's threats, the plight of his family had already been determined. As had his. If there was a Hell beyond the one here on Earth, he was destined for it.

It was too late for him. Too late for his family. He would do what the puppet master ordered him to do because if he didn't, he was certain there was another puppet to take his place. And another. An endless supply of marionettes with strings tied around their hearts and necks. The only way to stop the madman holding the strings was to lead the world to his doorstep.

Delivering planeloads of innocent people into slavery at the hands of Supreme Leader just so he could expand his inventory of long-range capable aircraft was one thing. Murdering a planeload of people for no apparent reason was another. What would be next? Would he be ordered to turn an airliner into a missile, like the ones used to strike those buildings in New York City? Yes, he'd seen the video footage of the attacks that had never been mentioned on the news in North Korea, though no doubt Supreme Leader had known about them and probably rejoiced. His hatred of the United States was no secret. Any and everything bad that befell his country was blamed on the evil Americans. Earthquakes. Floods. Mudslides. Drought. All the Americans' fault.

He had no illusions. He couldn't stop Choi Min-ho, but the Americans could. All Seul-ki had to do was lead them to his doorstep.

For Seul-ki, there was no night or day. He worked until he couldn't keep his eyes open, then he slept, rising to do it all over again. He knew whether it was day or night by the rhythm of his guards. Most of them slept at night, leaving a single guard posted outside his door. It was the only time he was left alone, and he'd begun to use the time wisely.

Diving past the Deep Web to the darkest recesses of the Dark Web where creatures of the night, like himself lived, he accessed the complex network of satellite hookups he'd cobbled together from bits and pieces of time stolen from legitimate enterprises. The process of altering computer code to create a tiny breach in the system wasn't difficult for him, but it did take precious time that could get him killed if he didn't accomplish his assigned task. It was a risk he had to take. He lived because a madman wanted him to, and he had no doubt he would die when the madman had no more use for him.

Somehow, he knew the end of his usefulness was coming sooner rather than later. How many more chances would he have to alert the Americans?

Working through the night, he managed to create a small crack in the wall of defenses he'd erected to mask his work. Now, all he could do was pray to the all-seeing god the Christians spoke of that someone out there would be watching and listening. Someone capable of tracing the signal. Someone who could sever the strings and let him go on to this other plane of existence they spoke of—Hell. It surely had to be better than the one he existed in now.

Captain Toby Bledsoe
Global Airlines Flight #2455
Monday 07:30 Zulu (Sunday 21:00 HST)

Through the aircraft's windscreen, minuscule given the size of the Boeing 767-300, Captain Toby Bledsoe searched the heavens for a glimmer of something—hope, perhaps, or direction. His gaze slipped toward the horizon, indistinguishable this far out at sea. Nothing but unrelenting blackness—something he knew intimately since his wife and daughter had been taken from him. Snatched from the mortal world by a madman with an assault weapon and a hard-on for celestial virgins.

How easy it would be to ease the plane's nose down—descend rapidly into the darkness instead of inching down one day, one hour at a time as he had been these last few months. He flexed his fingers where they hovered a fraction of an inch above the yoke. So damned easy. It could all be over in a few seconds. No more pain. No more guilt. Peace.

"It should have been me," he whispered to the universe since he'd long-since decided there was no god. No one to hear his prayers, and by God, no one to award the bastard who had killed his family his seventy damned virgins. Or whatever other nonsense the kid had been brainwashed to believe. Heaven? If it existed, Bethany and Mary Beth were there now. They'd never done a thing to another living being. They had been pure of heart and soul.

Hell? He knew for a fact it existed. Right here on earth. He'd been living in it since he'd heard the knock on the front door and opened it to find two police officers standing on his front porch.

Bethany had asked him to run to the store to pick up some frozen bread dough—insurance, she'd said, against the rolls she'd made from scratch for their Christmas dinner the next day turning into unleavened bread. He'd made an excuse—some nonsense about needing to check the electrical circuits to make sure the lights he'd strung outside wouldn't overload the system when they turned on every light in the house, too. He'd only wanted to get her out of the house long enough to bring in the present he'd bought for her so he could wrap it and slip it under the tree.

She'd known, of course. He could lie like a champ to everyone else—the sole reason he was still flying and not locked up in a nut house. He'd convinced everyone he was doing okay. He had his shit together.

Bethany would have known better, just as she'd known what he was up to and had let him get by with the fib. With a knowing smile and a kiss to his cheek, she'd bundled up herself and their three-year-old daughter and driven to the market, promising to take her time. Yeah, she'd known what he was up to. There were times when he thought she'd made up the trip just to allow him the time he needed. He wouldn't have put it past her. She'd been intuitive—always seeming to know what he and their daughter, Mary Beth, needed.

She'd been more than his wife and the mother of his child; she'd been his best friend.

She wouldn't want you to kill yourself, and she sure wouldn't want you to take three hundred innocent souls with you.

He drew his hands back, wiped his sweaty palms on his trousers, and closed his eyes. The shrink he'd seen a few times right after his wife and daughter had been taken from him had suggested breathing exercises to help him through the waves of grief that overtook him at the oddest moments. He'd been stupid to think anything would help in those instances, but modulating his breathing did help him deal with the rage flare-ups and the depression—so maybe the guy hadn't been so dumb after all.

Breathing deep, he counted to ten before forcing the air out through his nose in a burst that flared his nostrils and pancaked his lungs. He repeated the process. On the third exhale, with ample oxygen greasing the wheels of reason, he opened his eyes and instinctively scanned the console for trouble. Finding none, he reached for his portable electronic tablet and brought up the reading app.

His first officer snored loud enough to rattle the fiberglass panels lining the cabin walls. The Air Force Reserve pilot hadn't been in any shape to fly. He'd hidden it well enough to get on board then retreated to the flight crew's quarters below the cockpit to sleep off whatever he'd overindulged in during their layover. Honolulu to Dallas wasn't the best of possible routes for Skip, given the man's lack of restraint and the readily available dens of depravity in Hawaii. As best as Toby could tell, there wasn't a vice on the planet Skip Bernard wouldn't indulge in.

Once upon a time, Toby had been the same—sampling everything in every port of call, but he'd given it all up when he'd met Bethany. She'd given him a reason to take care of himself, so he'd sobered up and walked straight down the aisle with her. From the disapproving way the flight attendant, Monica, looked at him, Toby was pretty sure Skip's days of drinking, whoring, and gambling were numbered, provided the man could focus long enough to see what she was clearly offering. The woman had to be a saint to want a derelict like his first officer—or she was crazy, thinking she could change the man. If waking up every day to a light as bright as Monica's wasn't enough to make Skip change his ways, maybe the flight attendant wasn't the one. Toby well knew, only the right woman could make a man want to walk away from his vices, and do so willingly. All the good intentions in the world, on her part, wouldn't be enough if the sinner in question didn't want the woman more than anything else in the world.

Toby checked the flight data one more time before directing his attention to the eBook he'd started in Hawaii. After nearly a decade as a commercial pilot, tonight was just another boring night babysitting a plane capable of flying itself. Hell, it *was* flying itself. Nothing like the years he'd spend behind the stick of an F-16. The Falcon had demanded his attention every second, not like this bird. He'd lost track of the hours he'd spent in the left seat doing absolutely nothing except giving the required passenger pep talks after takeoff and before landing. Why they needed to know their cruising altitude or the weather conditions at their destination was beyond him. Wasn't like anyone aboard could do a damn thing about either one. Mother Nature alone could change the weather, and a computer would determine everything from their cruising altitude to whether it was safe to remove their seat belts and go take a piss. In the Boeing 767-300, the flight crew basically provided backup for the computer system and reassured the passengers. He didn't think the average traveler was ready for a fully automated cockpit, though, in effect, that was what they had. He and Skip amounted to stage props, there to appease the traveling public.

He checked the flight time—six long hours to DFW. Plenty of time to see if the hero in his book and the world survived this latest threat. Captain Bledsoe flicked his index finger over the touchscreen device in his lap and continued to read. The hero in the thriller series he'd begun a few months ago had a few hours to find the culprit and neutralize him or Western civilization, as we knew it, would cease to exist.

Since the book wasn't the last in the series, he expected a positive outcome. As for his ass, he wasn't so sure. It had gone numb an hour into the flight. He'd give anything to stretch out in the bunk for a little while—and would as soon as his asshole of a first officer woke up.

"Nothing but a babysitter," he mumbled and resumed reading.

Major Megan Sloan
Freedom Center, Herndon, Virginia
Monday 08:00 Zulu (04:00 EDT)

The array of video monitors taking up every available inch of wall space like patches of animated wallpaper held my attention. Every dot, every neon-bright line, represented a commercial plane, passenger or freight, in the air at the given moment. Given the hour, traffic was light in the western hemisphere—mostly air freighters—but in another two hours, the number of planes would double. In three hours, it would triple, and so on, following the time zones across the continents.

"What time did you intercept it?"

Behind me, Jude answered. "About 2:30. Sanchez was sitting right here, keeping me company."

"Have you isolated the plane?"

"Not yet. It could be any one of a dozen, or it could be none of them. It's only a hunch."

A hunch I believed in, yet in the nearly three years we'd been at this, we didn't have a scrap of proof to substantiate my belief. If it turned out we were wrong, the government would have wasted millions of dollars on a wild-goose chase, but if we were right, possibly hundreds of lives could be in danger.

"Sanchez?"

"Boss."

"I want to see a list of every aircraft that could have possibly been the target of the ping you intercepted. I want to know everything about them—where they came from, where they're going, who or what is on board. Passenger and crew lists, cargo manifests. Everything. And I want it ten minutes ago." If Jude was right, and I thought he was, there wasn't a second to waste.

I tore my gaze from the monitors and forced my shoulders to relax. It had been months since the last plane had gone missing. The French airliner with 200 souls on board had left Paris bound for Sydney and vanished without a trace somewhere over the Indian Ocean. Jude had picked up a ping then, but by the time he'd isolated the electronic signal to a specific region, it had been too late to pin it to a specific aircraft, much less the one that had gone missing.

Nevertheless, any signal of unknown origin, anywhere near a plane when it goes missing, was worth another look. Some had pointed out it could be coincidence, but any spy would tell you, there was no such thing. If it walked and quacked like a duck, it was a damn duck. I was far from being an electronics expert, but my gut told me we weren't whistling "Dixie" up the Intelligence community's ass either. Something—no, someone, was behind the plethora of planes that had seemingly vanished into thin air, never to be found—three in the last year alone. Coincidence? Not on your life.

When MH370 had gone down, conspiracy theories had numbered in the thousands. Some had been plausible—pilot suicide being one. Why shoot yourself in the head when you had a big ole plane filled with innocent passengers at your disposal? Unless there had been someone specific aboard the pilot wanted to murder, that theory didn't hold up in my mind. The guy might as well have driven his car over a cliff somewhere. Going with the *if I'm going to go, I'm not going alone* frame of mind, it made more sense to shoot up a mall or nightclub and wait for the cops to kill you. It was possible the pilot didn't have the stomach to actually see the others die. Murder/suicide was a power trip whether the murderer looked his victims in the eyes or not.

Sure, there was at the one documented instance of a suicidal pilot taking a German passenger plane down with him, but as logical as the theory sounded, I had a hard time believing that many suicidal pilots existed at any given time—unless someone was messing with their heads. *That* was another conspiracy theory, one so bizarre and full of pitfalls even the CIA wouldn't touch it, and there wasn't much the American intelligence gathering agency wouldn't do to achieve their goals. Being a pilot myself, I knew my share of flyboys and girls, and though I would categorize them all as thrill seekers, I'd never known one to have a death wish. In fact, every single one I knew thought themselves invincible. Except for me. I'd learned my lesson the hard way.

So, while the powers that be spouted platitudes about rogue suicidal pilots and bombs no one took credit for, my merry band of electronics geeks and I sat in the sub-basement of the basement of a bunker few in the world knew existed and searched the airwaves for a blip or a ping or any goddamn thing to suggest a force or entity outside the metal birds could be responsible for all those deaths.

I didn't know who had decided someone had devised a way to hijack planes from their easy chair, but whoever it was had convinced someone, somewhere, to invest a shit-ton of money and human assets into seeing if it was true. The Drone Theory Task Force had been put in place, under the direct command of Colonel Rodgers. My official title here was advisor, for reasons I didn't want to think about, but, in reality, I rode herd on Jude and a dozen or so other analysts so Colonel Rodgers didn't have to do it.

Before this gig, I'd been twiddling my thumbs, supervising young recruits mining financial data from around the world looking for suspect transactions. Chasing the monkey's tail, Jude called it. If you caught the tail and could hold onto it, you might be able to work your way up to the ass end of the critter. From there, if your luck held, you might be able to crawl up its asshole and sort through the shit to find out where the money had come from. It would take a good proctologist to surgically remove the cancerous source, thus slowing down the spread of Islamic terrorism across the globe. It was a good theory and tedious work. It took more patience than I possessed, but, thankfully, the people who did the actual work were good at it.

Seemed I had yet to pay my dues for screwing up in the field, but at least The Drone Theory Task Force was a step closer to my old life. We hadn't caught any monkeys by the tail yet, but if we did, I hoped my handlers would let me out of my cage. I'd sat on my ass long enough. It was time to climb the monkey's tail again and do some serious surgery.

"There it is again." The excitement in Jude's voice had me scrambling around the end of the row of workstations to stand behind the analyst.

One hand braced on the desk, the other gripping the back of Jude's chair, I leaned down to his level. "Can you tell which plane it's directed at?"

"Hold on a minute." He typed rapidly, the keys sounding like plastic teeth chattering. "I've got it!"

"Are you sure? I mean, absolutely certain?"

"As sure as I can be. The signal bounced all over the place, but I knew what to look for this time."

It had been a long time since I'd felt the rush of adrenaline, but I recognized it. I sucked in a breath and held it until my lungs burned before letting it out. "Sanchez!"

"Right here, boss." I nearly jumped out of my skin—a testament to how rusty my nerves had become since my last field deployment—as his voice sounded behind me.

"Get Director Lowell at the Federal Aviation Administration on the line. And call Colonel Rodgers."

Major Megan Sloan
Freedom Center, Herndon, Virginia
Monday 08:32 Zulu (04:32 EDT)

"Talk to me, Jude."

"It was sheer luck, ma'am. I could be wrong."

"But you don't think you are."

"No, ma'am. It's the same ping as before, only this time the intercept program we added recognized it and began the trace immediately. Not like the other times when all we could do was sit here with our thumbs up our asses."

Jude's phone chirped. He picked up the receiver and handed it to me. "Hello. Director Lowell?"

A less than friendly voice came over the line. "Do you have any idea what time it is?"

I refused to flinch at the gruff remark. I'd roust the president and his entire cabinet out of bed if it meant preventing another plane from going down. "Sorry to bother you, Director Lowell, but we've got a situation here."

"What kind of situation, and where is *here*?"

"You've been read in on The Drone Theory?"

There was a pause on the line. I imagined the man mentally sorting through his intelligence briefings for the appropriate reference. "That's rubbish. An impossible scenario."

"Not impossible, and we're about to prove it."

"Who did you say you are?"

"Major Megan Sloan—Air Force Intelligence. I'll have someone from the Pentagon call you to confirm." I glanced up at Sanchez who stood sentry. He nodded and picked up the nearest secure line. Lots of people were going to lose sleep tonight. "When they do, I need your full cooperation. We have reason to believe another plane is about to go missing, only this time, we know which one it is." I heard another phone ring in the background.

"I'll hold while you answer your other line." I nodded my thanks to Sanchez who stood with a phone receiver pressed to his ear. Sanchez smiled at me. After speaking to the person at the end of the line, he hung up. While I waited for Lowell to get his ass chewed on his other line, I waved Sanchez over.

"Get me the info on the flight." Other members of the task force were filing in now, looking sleepy, tired, and pissed off. "Grab as many people as you need. I want everything."

"Aren't you jumping the gun?" Jude asked. "We aren't even sure the plane is in trouble."

"Do you really believe everything is fine?"

Jude shook his head. "No."

"I didn't think so."

The director clicked back on the line. "What do you need, Major Sloan?"

Amazing what a phone call from the right person could accomplish. "Global 2455. Somebody needs to make contact with the flight deck. Try the radio first. If it doesn't work, try the secondary system." Every airliner came equipped with the text-based Aircraft Communications and Reporting System (ACARS). While radio communications were mostly restricted to talking with air traffic controllers, ACARS allowed ground-to-aircraft communications regarding weather, routing, and gate assignments, as well as functioning as a backup system if radio communications were lost. "We need every commercial aircraft within five hundred miles of Hawaii to try to contact Global 2455 on Guard Frequency. That's 121.5 if you don't know."

"I know what it is, damn it," the director grumbled. "I'll get right back to you." He clicked off.

I passed the handset to Jude. "Sanchez! What have you got?"

More office manager than analyst, Sanchez hustled over with his familiar yellow pad.

"Shit."

When Jude swore, it almost never meant anything good. "What?"

"It's gone. Disappeared."

I searched the wall of monitors for the tiny pinpoint representing Global flight 2455. "Just like that? It's gone?"

"Just like that," Jude confirmed. "Just like the others. Here one second, gone the next."

Except we hadn't been watching the others when they disappeared. We'd found out after the fact on the others. This was different. Because we'd been watching this particular radar blip, we might have a chance of locating the plane in a timely manner. And, if our operating theory proved correct, we might find the person or persons behind the missing planes.

"Last known position?" I signaled Sanchez to write it down. With no radar image to draw from, Jude rattled off the coordinates. "We need eyes on this plane, or what's left of it, right now. Sanchez, get Rodgers on the horn again."

Ordering fighter jets into the air to search for a missing plane was way above my pay grade, and if there was one thing I'd learned from my time in the field, it was to let each member of your team do what they did best.

Colonel Clint Rodgers
Bethesda, Maryland
Monday 08:35 Zulu (03:35 EDT)

Colonel Clint Rodgers wouldn't be getting any more sleep tonight. The first phone call from Sanchez had ended any hope of returning to bed. After securing the help requested, he fixed a cup of coffee—knowing the middle-of-the-night phone call wouldn't be the last.

A former Army Ranger with enough commendations and campaign ribbons to open his own museum, Colonel Clint Rodgers had been tapped to lead their merry band of troll-like warriors. Which meant he rode herd over two distinctive groups. The larger group spoke geek, a language he had no hope of mastering, and were happiest bent over computer keyboards while the smaller group lived on adrenaline and spoke in monosyllables. In many ways, it was the command from Hell, and he'd been compared to Satan more than once, but they all knew they could count on him to have their backs—especially the lead agent on the task force, Megan Sloan.

Smart, dedicated, and fearless, she was a lethal weapon wrapped up in a deceptively beautiful package. Under his direct command, she was strictly off-limits. He adhered to the restraints during the day, but at night, his subconscious had no such restrictions.

He sat up and pressed the phone to his ear. "Rodgers."

"How long will it take to scramble a couple of fighters and a Hawk out of Guam?"

Breathless, the Air Force intelligence officer didn't waste time with apologies for waking him in the middle of the night. Major Sloan had earned her stripes in the sandbox and understood inconvenience came with the job. If you expected regular hours and sympathy for lost sleep, you were in the wrong business. Because he knew the sacrifices she'd made for her country, he didn't dare question her request. If she said she needed fighter jets and an ISR (Intelligence, Surveillance, and Reconnaissance) plane, she goddamn needed them. His feet hit the floor as his brain calculated the logistics involved. "What's going on?"

Wearing nothing but army-green boxers, he headed to his home office as she briefed him on the Global Airways airliner that had disappeared from radar. He clicked on the banker's style lamp he'd taken with him from post to post ever since his first wife found it, and the desk it sat on, in an antique store in Alabama while he'd been stationed at Maxwell. At the time, he'd thought their marriage would outlast the bargain finds, but he'd been wrong. Turned out the woman had known class but hadn't possessed any.

He tore the top square off a cube emblazoned with the Air Force insignia and jotted down the airliner's last known location. "Let me make some calls. I'll get back to you."

He clicked off and brought up his contact list. His call was answered on the second ring.

"I need planes in the air in the next half hour."

The man on the other end had been given a head's up to expect such a call, but like most everyone who'd been read-in on The Drone Theory, he'd probably assumed he'd never receive one. "No shit?"

"No shit," Rodgers said. "Got something to write on?" He waited while the Chairman of the Joint Chiefs found a pen and paper before he read off the coordinates.

"What are they supposed to look for?"

This was where it became dicey. "Anything. Everything." He explained how the Global Airlines plane had disappeared from radar while his team had been watching. It was the first break they'd had, and there wasn't a second to lose. "Logic says the plane is in the drink, but my people think otherwise. We need confirmation, one way or the other—and we need it ten minutes ago."

"I'll call you with an ETA to last known location in a few."

Rodgers hit redial on the call from Major Sloan. He put the phone on speaker and headed to his bedroom. Sloan answered, and Rodgers passed on the information while he dressed in his walk-in closet. Like everything in his life, the space was spartan and organized. One side held a small assortment of civilian clothes. The rest was devoted to work clothes. The toughest NCO in the Air Force wouldn't find fault with his locker. He conceded his adherence to regimentation at home had been one of the things his wife had never warmed up to. On the other hand, he'd never understood why her side of the closet had always looked as if it had taken a mortar round. Just one reason among many the marriage failed—his job being the number one reason.

Ten minutes later, Colonel Rodgers pointed his car toward Virginia and the Freedom Center at Dulles International Airport. Three years with little more than a theory to go on. Could they finally have found a way to identify a plane in distress? His heart rate accelerated. The concept of any group or nation, much less one with hostile intentions toward the United States, with the capability to control an airplane in flight from a base station, was enough to scare the bejesus out of the most badass soldier on the planet. But it was the exact premise his task force operated on.

The idea wasn't without merit. The United States had hundreds, if not thousands, of unmanned aerial vehicles (UAVs), both armed and unarmed, in the skies every single day—all controlled by humans on the ground, sometimes thousands of miles away. Drone technology was a closely guarded secret, but like all technology, it could be replicated—especially if the person building the clone had a template to go on.

Someone did.

In December of 2011, an American RQ-170 Sentinel fell into the hands of the Iranian government. The UAV belonging to the CIA had been collecting data on Iranian nuclear facilities when it fell from the sky, landing mostly intact on the wrong side of the Iran – Afghanistan border. The Iranian government claimed their cyber warfare unit had hacked the flight control system of the unmanned aircraft and instructed it to land at a place of their choosing. If that had been the case, why did it land in the desert rather than at an airstrip?

A war of words erupted between the United States and the Iranians. The American president maintained innocence and politely requested the UAV be returned while Iran protested through diplomatic channels and proceeded to dismantle the captured drone. Privately, the CIA had taken responsibility for the loss of Top Secret technology and, with the help of Air Force sources already on the ground, covertly sent agents to find and destroy the hardware before it could be sold to a more technologically savvy country.

Rodgers had seen the file on the failed mission. A shit-show from beginning to end, it was a minor miracle anyone survived. Major Sloan almost hadn't. The agents had arrived too late to prevent the sale but were able to confront the band of mercenaries sent to pick up the drone for the unknown purchaser. In the subsequent gun battle, Sloan sustained life-threatening injuries and within the parameters of the clandestine operation—meaning the United States government would deny it ever happened—was left for dead. The classified report was less than clear on how she'd managed to get across the border, but she had. She claimed she wasn't even sure how she'd done it. The doctors who had treated her chalked it up to her will to live, but Rodgers suspected there might be more to it. Given the right provocation, otherwise average people could do extraordinary things. He often wondered what had provoked Megan Sloan to keep moving when the odds were stacked against her. At times, he thought he could see it in her eyes—a secret pain that, like a nuclear reactor, fueled her.

The mission had failed to accomplish its only objective—to retrieve the classified technology—and, according to her psych eval, Sloan blamed herself.

Rodgers reported directly to the Chairman of the Joint Chiefs, which told him everyone at the Pentagon believed The Drone Theory was more than science fiction. He'd never voice his suspicions out loud but he figured they were so worried about taking this scenario seriously because we were working on, or already possessed the technology ourselves.

The people under the colonel's command were competent, and most importantly, they were dedicated to what seemed like an impossible mission. They'd been pulled from every corner of the clandestine world. If the agency's initials included an I or an S, they had assigned a person to the task force. Sloan was AFISR (Air Force Intelligence, Surveillance, and Reconnaissance). Jefferson and his crew were National Security Agency (NSA). Kern came from the Defense Intelligence Agency (DIA), the DOD's version of the CIA. There were a couple of CIA agents whose names might or might not be their real names, so he hadn't bothered to get to know them. The TSA, in an effort to protect the interests of commercial aviation, had loaned personnel to the task. Engineers from Lockheed Martin's Skunk Works division, the manufacturer of the RQ-170, were on call, as were some of the finest minds in weapons engineering in the world. And if the theory proved to be true, they were going to need every one of them to track down and destroy this enemy.

First Officer Skip Bernard
Global Airlines Flight #2455
Monday 09:00 Zulu (Sunday 23:00 HST)

Skip Bernard woke with a start. He'd been dreaming of white sand beaches dotted with scantily clad women. He'd spent a week in Honolulu, not nearly long enough in his opinion, but it had been all the vacation time he could spare. He'd promised his parents he'd spend a week with them at their lake house in upstate New York this fall. Add in a few days around the holidays, and he'd be tapped out on paid days off. Anything else he wanted to do, he'd have to squeeze in between days in the saddle.

Reaching up, he flicked on the reading lamp and groaned as the harsh light flooded the small sleeping compartment. He wiped drool from his chin and blinked to clear the sleep from his eyes. A glance at his watch confirmed he'd been out longer than he'd planned. Toby was going to be pissed. Speaking of...he needed to piss before he took his turn babysitting the controls. Though the state-of-the-art 767-300 could practically fly itself, it was still a piece of machinery put together by human beings—meaning things could and did go wrong on occasion.

Stretching his six-foot frame as much as the cramped quarters allowed, he rolled from his bunk and made his way down the short ladder to the flight deck. He rubbed his eye sockets with the heels of his hands, blinking to adjust to the lower light level in the cockpit. A quick glance told him nothing was amiss. He would have heard the beeps and tones if something had gone wrong. Years of flying had conditioned his body to listen for the warning sounds even in his sleep.

"Hey," he said, leaning against the bulkhead. "I'm going to go take a piss. You need anything?"

Without looking up from the tablet in his lap, Captain Bledsoe called over his shoulder. "Diet Coke?"

The first officer lifted the handset that would connect him to the flight attendants in the passenger cabin. "Roger that," he said. When Monica came online, he relayed the order, diet soda for the captain, coffee for himself. "We got any of those cookies with the chocolate in the middle on this trip?" Most of the stuff they served the passengers was shit—those cookies being the exception. A delicacy reserved for the first-class travelers, they were a cut above, and he looked forward to a pack or two when they were on the menu.

"Shit," he said, hanging up the phone.

"I think they discontinued those," the captain said without looking up from his tablet. "Got a bid for a cheaper alternative, I suspect."

Focusing on the dark sky beyond the windscreen, he rested his hands on his hips and sighed. "Goddamn it. I liked those."

"Therein lies the problem. Everyone else did, too. If there aren't any left to take off the plane at the end of the day, they have to go. Can't go serving something people actually ask for. Costs too much."

As far as he knew the airline didn't have any such policy, but it sure seemed to at times. The good things didn't last long before the bean counters found a less costly alternative. "Damn bean counters."

"You could bring your own."

Wisdom he didn't need. "Why should I spend my money on something I can get for free? We should talk to our union rep. Cookies should be part of our compensation package, don't you think?"

"Sounds good to me," Toby said. "But I wouldn't hold my breath waiting to see it in our contract."

Skip chuckled. "Tightwad airline. Next thing you know they'll be charging the flight crew for coffee." He studied his toes as he waited to open the cockpit door for the flight attendant. After 9/11 and the installation of new, more secure cockpit doors that could only be unlocked from within, federal regulations required two people in the cockpit at all times, so Skip waited for a flight attendant to take his place while he visited the john. German airlines didn't have the same regs, and they'd paid the price for it when a suicidal pilot had locked his first officer out of the cockpit and crashed the plane while the remaining crew member used everything, including a fire extinguisher, to try to defeat the lock mechanism and gain entry.

A knock sounded on the door. He checked the peephole, ascertaining Monica was alone and had blocked the passageway with a food cart to prevent some deranged passenger from bum-rushing the cockpit the instant he opened the door.

It's a crazy world we live in. He disengaged the lock and swung the door inward. The scent of hot coffee preceded the smartly dressed flight attendant. As much as he enjoyed a good cup of coffee, flirting with the newer crew members was like air to him. With a wink and a grin, Skip scooted past, closing the door behind him. A quick glance told him the forward restrooms were both occupied. Stepping into the galley to wait his turn, he weaved his fingers together behind his head and arched his back.

God, it felt good to stretch. He smiled at the other attendant assigned to the first-class cabin. "How's it going?" Jeff had been a senior flight attendant as long as Skip had been a pilot.

"Pretty quiet. Even the folks in the economy section are behaving themselves."

"That can't last."

"Tell me about it." Jeff shook his head. "You can't pack people in like sardines and not expect problems. If they ever try to put me back in coach, I'll quit."

At the familiar *snick* of a bathroom lock sliding free, Skip said goodbye and hustled to snag the opening before someone else got to it. He completed his business and washed his hands in the tiny sink then opened the door. Turning sideways, he stepped through the narrow passage and made his way to the cockpit door. He knocked then grinned at the peephole. Moments later, the door swung open and he stepped inside. Monica took her time, making full-body contact as she brushed past him. Lord, she was something. He'd like nothing more than to show her how to fly, but despite the way she went out of her way to make physical contact every time he got close, she didn't seem like the no-strings-attached type. A woman like her was looking for permanent. Flirt? Hell, yeah. No harm done, but he'd be crazy to do more.

Too bad, he thought as he double checked the lock and prepared to take over the pilot's duties.

Skip settled into his seat before picking up his coffee and taking a sip. He automatically scanned the various switches, status lights, and screens. At first glance, everything seemed fine, but his gaze returned to the compass reading.

"Where're we going?" He'd made this trip almost as many times as Captain Bledsoe. Once the autopilot was set, unless there was weather to avoid, the flight path to Dallas was straight as an arrow.

Toby looked up from his iPad, blinked a few times. "What do you mean? We're going to DFW." He seemed genuinely confused by the question.

Skip studied the instrument panel. "Not now. Did you change the flight plan?" How long had he been asleep? He checked his watch. They'd been in the air just over three hours, and he'd been asleep for almost as long. Crap. He'd heard the stories about suicidal pilots changing course and all manner of other shit. He didn't think Toby was that kind of crazy, but who knew?

"What the hell?" Bledsoe tapped the glass covering the magnetic whiskey compass—a relic from days gone by and only used if there was a total loss of power to the instrument panel. "We're flying due west!"

Nothing would be gained by panicking. As long as they were still in the air, he told himself, everything else could be fixed. "How long have we been on this heading?"

Captain Toby Bledsoe
Global Airlines Flight #2455
Monday 09:15 Zulu (Sunday 23:15 HST)

"What the hell?" Toby Bledsoe glared at the course displayed on the screen. How had he missed the change? His fingers clenched on his tablet that still displayed the thriller he'd been reading for the last couple of hours.

"How long have we been on this course?" his first officer asked.

Toby shook his head. "I don't know." He set his tablet aside. "I haven't touched a thing since we set the autopilot." His mind raced, frantically retracing the steps they'd taken to engage the automated flight system. "You verified the flight plan, right?"

"I always do." Skip's non-answer wasn't lost on Toby, but it didn't matter. He'd programmed the correct flight plan. Somehow, it had been changed.

"Did Monica touch anything?" Skip asked.

Toby tried to recall if he'd known where her hands were every second she'd occupied Skip's seat while his second-in-command had gone to the head. "I can't be 100 percent certain, but no, I don't see how she could have."

"Then we've got a problem."

"Maybe the autopilot went on the blink. Damned computers. Put the flight plan in the box." He glanced at the fuel gauges. "Better recalculate the fuel, too. Make sure we have enough to make Dallas; otherwise, we're diverting to LAX." Toby's brain raced along with his heart rate as he grasped the yoke to hold the plane steady while he reached up to disengage the autopilot switch. He pushed it once. The red light came on indicating the system had been turned off. Anticipating the telltale change in the yoke when the automated system

35

gave way to manual control, he gripped the yoke even tighter. "What the hell?"

"What?" Skip looked up from the electronic tablet where he'd been running fuel calculations.

"I've got nothing. Autopilot switch says it's off, but it's still flying the plane."

Both pilots' gazes landed on the switch in question. The status light glowed red in the darkened cockpit.

"What the hell?" Skip put one hand on the yoke in front of him and pushed the button again. The lamp turned green. He pushed it one more time, and the red light illuminated. With both hands on the yoke, he steered into a gentle turn. The plane continued on its course to God only knew where. He tried the autopilot switch on the yoke, swearing when it too failed to disengage the system. "Nothing. I've got nothing."

"Same here. What's wrong with this thing?"

"Try your switch," he said, referring to the autopilot switch on the pilot's yoke.

Toby went through the same routine, getting the same negative response.

Skip ran his fingers along the rows of switches on his side of the cockpit. "How the hell could all the autopilot switches fail at the same time? Check everything on your side. Something's clearly out of whack."

A minute later, the two men looked at each other over the console.

"Anything?" Toby asked.

"Nothing." Skip reached for the clipboard containing the Quick Reaction checklist they'd gone over twice since they'd discovered the problem. "Let's go over this again. One step at a time."

"Can't hurt," Toby said.

"Well, that's it." Skip slammed his fist down on the clipboard. "Everything checks out fine. Except for the damned autopilot. It makes no sense."

"We've got to be missing something." Toby scanned the wall of darkness outside. He pointed toward the readout indicating their compass heading. "If we stay on this course, where will it take us?"

"Hell if I know." Skip tapped the screen on his tablet. Seconds later, he dropped the device in his lap and closed his eyes.

"What?"

Skip held up the tablet so Toby could see the screen. "Nowhere. We're going nowhere."

Toby stared at the display. Nothing but ocean for a few thousand miles. Unless they found a way to put the plane on a different heading, they would run out of fuel before reaching land. "God Almighty."

"God hasn't got anything to do with it," Skip said as he adjusted his tall frame in the seat. "Some lazy-ass maintenance worker is behind this." He scrubbed his hands over his face. "Jesus, we've got to find a way to override the system—and fast."

"How's the fuel?"

"If we got back on course now, we'd be lucky to make it to LAX. I say we figure out how to reestablish control for now. Once we do that, we can figure out where we're going to set this can down."

Toby had been in tight situations during his fighter jet days. He'd always had a way out, but ejecting wasn't an option on a commercial jetliner filled with passengers. If this plane went down, he'd have no choice but to go with it. "Then let's find a way. Where's the manual on this thing?"

On any aircraft, every ounce of weight counted, whether it was luggage or passengers or components used to construct the airframe. It all added to the sustainability of flight. Technology had vastly improved since the Wright brothers had built the first flying machine in

1903. Wood and canvas frames controlled manually had given way to aluminum and plastic controlled by miles of cables and wires that operated physical switches. Now, new composite materials made the ships lighter and stronger while wireless communication and computers had not only eliminated thousands of pounds of equipment but had added greater safety and stability to the aircraft. The invention of electronic books had allowed airlines to remove the cumbersome flight manuals from the cockpit, reducing weight and allowing more room in the cockpit for the flight crew.

Skip consulted his tablet while Toby racked his brain for anything that might explain what was happening. He hadn't touched a single thing other than his eReader since they'd cleared Hawaii Center shortly after takeoff. By then, Skip had already been snoring in the crew bunk. Other than the short time Monica had joined him so Skip could take a leak, there had been no one in the cockpit but him, and he sure as hell hadn't changed the heading.

It had to be a computer glitch. Unfortunately, the Northern Pacific Ocean was a virtual no-man's-land. There was no one they could contact to request assistance. Nowhere to land, even if they could find a way to override the system now in control of the plane. Yet, they had to find a way or everyone on board was going to die. "Got anything?"

Major Megan Sloan
Freedom Center, Herndon, Virginia
Monday 09:15 Zulu (05:15 EDT)

The hodgepodge group gathered around the oval conference table represented every investigative and intelligence-gathering organization in Washington. Despite their combined decades of experience, they'd yet to come up with a single thread to pull on this investigation, and that wasn't acceptable. Someone needed to rip them a new one, and I was dedicated to the job.

"I know you're all wondering why you've been called in this morning." A chorus of grumbles went around the conference table. To be expected, but I was in no mood to tolerate it. "This is it, folks." I let my gaze touch on every face, making sure I had their undivided attention. "We started out with nothing but the theory that someone on the ground has the capability to take control of an airplane in flight. As of this morning, this is no longer a theory."

The expected questions flew from those who'd consumed enough coffee to process my words. The rest squirmed in their seats while their brains scrambled to catch up. The waiting and watching had been slowly killing me. Since we finally had something to go on, I was itching for action. I signaled for quiet.

"Jude was on the wall this morning when it happened. You can thank him later for having your weekend plans canceled." All eyes turned to the analyst. "Fill them in, Jude."

I didn't pretend to understand half of what Jude said. Everyone here knew I didn't speak computer, but I did speak details. I let Jude fill them in on what we knew of the plane's original flight plan, emphasizing that they'd checked in with San Francisco radio after leaving Hawaiian airspace before jumping in. "We had eyes on them up until that point. Then they disappeared. We've tried contacting the aircraft via all the usual channels—radio, ACARS, other aircraft—with no response. From now on, we'll assume The Drone Theory is fact."

Waving them to silence again, I stood and placed my hands flat on the table, staring them down. "What I want to know from each of you is, what are we going to do about it? I want answers. Let's start with finding Global 2455." Straightening, I rolled my shoulders to ease the tension that had been building for the last few hours and locked gazes with Clint Rodgers at the opposite end of the table. "What's the status on the search?"

I'd half expected him to argue with my early morning request for military assistance, but he'd done exactly as I asked, then—to my surprise—he'd shown up here less than an hour later. It was good to know someone else believed in the theory besides me.

"As you know, we scrambled fighters and a Global Hawk IRS aircraft as soon as we were notified this morning. In addition to eyes in the sky, we've got every ship and military radar installation in the Pacific on the lookout for an unidentified aircraft in their airspace."

Sighing, I rubbed my temples. The probability of finding a single aircraft—even one as large as a 767 over the vast Pacific—without a single clue as to its location was roughly equivalent of a blind man locating a specific grain of sand on Waikiki Beach. There wasn't a gambler in Vegas who would take those odds, but, in reality, it was the only chance we had of locating the plane.

"Anyone have anything to add?"

Terence Jefferson from the NSA sat forward. "I've got a team monitoring the airwaves for any unusual communication in that part of the world. If the flight crew is able to get out a message of any kind, we'll pick it up."

I nodded. The NSA had the biggest ears on the planet. If they couldn't pick it up, no one could. I asked, "What about ground-to-air communication with the plane? Any chance of tracing the ping?"

"Thanks to Jude picking up the signal this morning, we know what to listen for and have an area to focus on. We could get lucky." He shrugged. "It could happen. If it does, we'll do our best to track the signal to its origin."

"I want to know the second you have something."

"Yes, ma'am. You'll be the first to know."

I found the next person on my list halfway down on the opposite side of the table. Special Agent Reed Wilson had been with the FBI for nearly two decades and was looking retirement in the eye. He'd been put in charge of a group of cyber-snoops whose sole focus was to ascertain who, within our own borders, might be capable of turning a jetliner into a drone. They'd begun with a long list of hackers. So far, they'd nailed an eight-year-old in Denver who'd cracked the code on his favorite video game and a group of teenagers in New York who'd infiltrated the automated toll plaza system up and down the Eastern Seaboard, giving commuters a free ride for twenty-four hours before the FBI closed in on them.

"Wilson?" He looked up from the notepad where he'd either been doodling or taking notes. "Caught any more toll runners lately?"

Reed sat up, squaring his shoulders. He'd taken a lot of shit about the toll hackers but hadn't let it get to him. "No more toll runners, but we found a guy in California who was siphoning a few dollars here and there from accounts at his local bank, stashing them in an offshore account." Reed chuckled, "Said he was saving for his retirement."

Everyone seemed to think the comment was funny except me. "Tell me you have something besides a guy whose retirement plan is a room at Leavenworth."

"As a matter of fact, thanks to him, we've narrowed our search."

"How?"

"During his college days at MIT, he was part of an online group of hackers—sort of a private club that only admitted the best of the best. The group has since disbanded, but in exchange for a job that will provide a decent, legal retirement, he provided us with a list of names. According to him, a few of the members were capable of what we were asking about. We're in the process of running the leads down now."

"Time isn't our friend, Special Agent Wilson," I said. "Go straight to the top if you have to. I want agents knocking on every door on his list within the hour."

Next, I sought out Rick Sanderson, an analyst in the cyberterrorism section of the CIA who had been assigned as a liaison to the task force. "What about the agency? Any progress on the international front?"

"As you know, we've been trying to track the pieces of the drone we lost in Iran back in 2010."

I could feel Colonel Rodgers' gaze on me. I'd wondered how much he knew about my involvement in that debacle. Now I knew. Of all the people in the room, he was the only one with a high enough security clearance to have read the reports. Was he wondering if I was up to this mission, given what I'd been through? I fought the urge to touch my hip and, instead, forced the memories of a mission gone wrong out of my head. *Focus on today. On finding this plane before it's too late.*

"We believe the Iranians reverse engineered the flight system and may have sold the technology to other countries including Libya, Yemen, Syria, and/or North Korea. We've got feet on the ground in all of those places, trying to ascertain if they purchased the technology, and if so, what they did with it. Could be nothing. Could be they're using the knowledge against us."

Colonel Rodgers sat forward, hands clasped in front of him on the polished wood surface. "If you had to guess, based on what you know, which one of those is most likely to be involved?"

"Hands down, North Korea. Not only do they have the capability, but Choi Min-ho is batshit crazy."

Captain Toby Bledsoe
Global Airlines Flight #2455
Monday 09:20 Zulu (Sunday 23:20 HST)

He'd felt this sick feeling in his stomach once before in his life. He knew what it was—fear. Stark, cold fear. He hadn't let it get the best of him then and had lived to fly another day. Toby Bledsoe damn sure wasn't going to let it overtake his ability to reason now. He thought about all the innocent souls on board. They'd put their trust in him, and he had no intention of letting them down. Whatever the hell was wrong with this aircraft he would find and fix, or die trying.

"Transmit a Mayday on 121.5. Hell, get anyone you can on the horn and get us some help. We've got to find a way to override the autopilot and find a place to land this bird before it runs out of fuel."

"I'm on it." Skip's voice trembled, but his hands appeared steady enough as he operated the radio equipment. Toby didn't agree with the younger man's lifestyle, but he was a good pilot. He'd come up through the ranks fast due to his skill in the cockpit. Between the two of them, they'd find a way to land the plane. He was sure of it.

Skip's shoulders slumped, and he dropped his hands into his lap. "Damn."

"What now?"

"HF radio's out. So is Com 1 and Com 2."

"How can that be?" Ignoring the knot steadily growing in his gut, Toby tried the radio controls on his side of the cabin on the off chance the outage only affected the right side controls. Met with only silence, he resisted the urge to hit something. Instead, he took a deep breath, giving himself an extra heartbeat or two to master his fear. "Nothing. How is that possible?"

"Even the Wi-Fi is down."

Toby pulled his personal cell phone from his pocket. A quick glance at the screen made him want to puke. Two tiny words across the top caught his attention. "No Service." Where were they? "Shit." He glanced at his first officer who also had his phone out. "You got anything?"

"Not a thing. I even turned on my personal hotspot. Still no Wi-Fi, no service. Thing might as well be a brick."

"Try the ACARS," Toby said, referring to the Aircraft Communications and Reporting System, a digital data link that communicated vital information, like when the plane left the ground or touched down on the runway, via sensors, sending the data to the airline through a satellite hookup. "Tell those bastards on the ground to find a way to override the computer before we end up at the bottom of the ocean."

"On it."

While Skip typed the distress message, Toby glanced over the panels of switches as his brain dutifully ticked off the position each should be in. As confident as he could be every switch was in the correct position, he turned his attention to the fancy multi-function display that had replaced the old gauges every pilot relied on. At least the computer was still working—albeit on its own. Though they were hundreds of miles off course and headed in the wrong direction, they were still in the air. For now.

"Message sent," Skip said. "At least I think it sent. If no one answers, we'll know it didn't go anywhere."

Toby nodded. Let's give it a few minutes. In the meantime, let's recalc the fuel. I want to know exactly what our chances are of making landfall, and I don't trust what the onboard computers are telling us."

"I'm on it. Give me a few minutes."

Neither one mentioned the readouts they were seeing could all be wrong. All it took was for one to be off to make their calculations worthless. But what the hell else did they have to do?

"Based on what I'm seeing, which seems accurate given our rate of climb out of Honolulu, the distance we've traveled, and our altitude, we're screwed."

"Can't make landfall anywhere?"

"Not unless there's a new island with an airstrip out there I don't know about."

"Shit." Toby checked the instrument panel once again. "And still no response from Global."

"Not a peep," Skip confirmed.

"Let's squawk 7700 then go through everything one more time. We had to have missed something."

"Roger that." Skip reset the transponder with the emergency code, 7700. If the transponder was working, any air traffic controller within range would pick up the emergency code.

First Officer Skip Bernard
Global Airlines Flight #2455
Monday 09:25 Zulu (Sunday 23:25 HST)

"We've been over and over the panel," Skip said. "Everything checks out."

"Maybe we popped a breaker, or a rat ate a wire or something. Go down in the avionics bay and take a look."

They were grasping at straws, hunting for anything to explain the inexplicable.

Skip pulled up the access panel built into the floor behind Toby's seat. A blast of cold air emitted from the small compartment carved off the front of the forward cargo hold to house the avionics and computer equipment as well as the emergency oxygen system for the cockpit. "Shit, it's cold down there."

"At least we know the computers aren't overheating."

The thought had crossed his mind, too. Though the pilot couldn't see him, he shrugged and said, "One more thing to cross off our list."

After descending the short ladder, he used the flashlight app on his cell phone to find the light switch and turned it on. Racks of computer equipment, the brains of the aircraft, lined the interior wall. Despite the air conditioning, he could feel the heat generated by the thousands of electrical components which, as far as he could tell, were all functioning. Without a manual to determine what was what—hell, even with a manual—he'd do more damage than good if he started poking around, so he kept his hands to himself as his gaze swept over the racked computer equipment.

"Not a red light in sight," he called through the access hole. "Everything looks fine." He wiped a bead of nervous sweat from his

47

forehead and fought the nausea building in his gut. He'd give any-thing right this minute for an old-fashioned plane—one with gauges and meters—something a guy could trust. If a fuel gauge said the tanks were empty, they were empty. What you saw was what you got. Not like this thing where even the fail-safe computer systems had re-dundant systems—just in case.

"In case it goes crazy on you," he mumbled to himself. "Then you're screwed."

"You say something?" Toby yelled down through the hole.

"No." He spoke louder this time to be heard over the roar of the engines. "I'm going to try resetting the circuit breakers. Let me know if anything changes."

He flipped the breakers off and then on, one at a time, listening for any response from Toby. When he'd been through them all, he grabbed the ladder, preparing to exit, when his gaze landed on the cockpit emergency oxygen system. It wouldn't hurt to check it out while he was down here, just in case.

A quick look told him the system was good to go. He'd never had to use the emergency oxygen system in a commercial aircraft, and he prayed he never would, but if there was a problem with pressuriza-tion, and they couldn't get the aircraft down below eighteen-thou-sand feet, the system would buy them a minimum of ten minutes to try and save their asses.

Everything appeared to be in working order, but looks could be deceiving. Everything about this plane looked fine, but something had gone seriously wrong, and he didn't have a clue what it was or how to fix it. One thing was clear, if they didn't do something soon and the plane continued on its present course, they'd run out of fu-el somewhere over the Pacific Ocean. Then they'd fall from the sky like a rock. MH370 came to mind. Had the same thing happened to them?

Skip clenched his eyes shut, willing the panic to subside. He took a deep breath, held it in his lungs until they burned before letting it out. The thought crossed his mind it might be the last good breath he took.

"What if it's someone on board?" Toby's fingers stilled over the now useless keypad. He'd been going through the checklist again, pushing buttons, trying to find a way to reboot the damned computers—or something. Anything. "One of the passengers?"

Skip nodded, his eyes bright with enthusiasm for his theory. "Maybe the interference is coming from right here on the plane." Hand curled into a fist, he pointed a thumb over his shoulder toward the passenger cabin. "Could be some terrorist asshole with a computer. Hell, it could be a cell phone or a tablet."

It sounded like sci-fi, but technology evolved so fast these days, anything seemed possible. "We can't confiscate every electronic device on board. There'd be a riot."

"The hell we can't." Skip raised his right leg so his heel rested on the edge of his seat giving him access to the 9 mm Glock he kept in an ankle holster. He removed the weapon, released the fully loaded clip, and reinserted it before pulling back the slide to verify the chambered round. "They'll turn them over or end up in federal prison for interfering with a federal flight deck officer."

"Don't do anything stupid."

Skip slid the weapon into the holster and adjusted his trouser leg then climbed over the console. "I have no plans to shoot anyone, but I won't hesitate if I find the bastard who's doing this. I'll be damned if I'm going to sit here and let some jihadist claim his virgin reward for killing innocent people."

Toby winced as Skip's words hit home. He sighed. "We have to be careful how we handle this, that's all I'm saying."

"Unless you have a better idea, I'm going out there."

"Wait just a damn second, okay? Let's think this through."

Skip returned the intercom handset to its cradle. "Shit, Toby. What's to think about? One of those people back there could be a terrorist. Are we going to just sit here and let him bring down our plane?"

Skip was right. Toby recalled how helpless he'd felt when he'd learned the identity of the person who'd massacred his family. If those same religious extremist ideals were at work here, he had no intention of letting them win. "No, we aren't. But you can't go out there and go cowboy on their asses either. Let's call the crew, give them some bullshit about interference with radio communications. Ask them to make a general announcement to turn off every electronic device. We'll have them go row by row to verify. Even have them inspect luggage in the overheads and the shit they have stashed under their seats. If anyone refuses, you can go out there and persuade them."

"The crew will know something is up. They've known the crap about interference from personal electronics was bullshit from the beginning."

"Then we tell them something else. Tell them we've had a bomb threat and have been ordered to inspect the entire plane. That'll motivate them."

"Yeah. It could work." He returned to his seat to make the call.

"Get Monica on the horn. We'll let her tell the others," Toby said.

"What's up?" Monica asked.

"We've got a situation," Skip said. "According to the folks at corporate, someone has made a threat against the airline. They want us to confiscate every electronic device the passengers brought on board."

"What? We can't do that!"

"You sure as shit will," Skip said. "Empty the food and beverage carts. Go row by row. Tell them we'll return their belongings when we land this thing safely and not a minute before. If anyone gives you any shit, call me. I'll persuade them to cooperate."

Her voice lowered to almost a whisper. "You're serious. You really think there's a bomb on the plane, don't you?"

"We don't know anything for sure, but we aren't leaving anything to chance. Our job is to get all these people to Dallas in one piece, and if we have to tear this plane apart to do it, we will." He didn't want to start a panic among the flight attendants, but he needed their cooperation. "Make sure every device you confiscate is turned off. I mean really off, not just in sleep mode. Don't take any shit from anybody."

Voice trembling, the senior flight attendant said, "Okay, but can't we just verify it's off? Do we have to confiscate everything?"

"What's to keep them from turning them on again as soon as your back is turned?"

"Nothing, I guess."

"Inspect every piece of carry-on, and I mean every piece. Pretend you're TSA. Dig around in every bag, box, or whatever. Don't just peek inside and move on. Take a moment to get yourself together then go tell your crew to get a move on. The sooner we verify the threat is bogus, the sooner we can all relax."

"I can't believe this is happening."

"I know this goes above and beyond, but our job is to protect the passengers, and that's what we're going to do, even if they don't want us to."

"Oh, they aren't going to want us to take their possessions away from them. I can assure you we're going to have a fight on our hands."

"Get your crew in order and be ready to move. Call the flight deck, and we'll make an announcement, so the order will be coming from us, not you. That should help some. There are going to be assholes who think they're special, but they're not. Not on this flight. If anyone refuses to hand over their devices, let us know. Believe me, they'll comply or else," Skip said.

He hung up the phone. "You think she's up to this?"

"She has to be, and I think she knows it."

The intercom buzzed ten minutes later. Skip picked it up. "Everything set?"

"The crew isn't happy about this, but they're ready to go."

"Stand by. We'll make the announcement."

Major Megan Sloan
Freedom Center, Herndon, Virginia
Monday 09:35 Zulu (05:35 EDT)

"Who's on the plane? Anybody we know?" I asked.

"We ran all the names through the database. Came up with a few notables." The hesitation in Sanchez's voice made the hackles rise on the nape of my neck.

"Put the list up on the screen."

I focused on the bright background dotted with black lines of type. The black lines coalesced into names. Sanchez had made notes next to a few of them. I skipped over the ones with no notations.

A misfit wanted for drug dealing in Chicago. A convicted felon who had served his time and had, apparently, been clean for a decade. Half a dozen others had served their country in the Armed Services. Two Navy, one Marine, and three regular Army types. All discharged honorably after completing their enlistment. A rapper known for his attitude. A Texas Ranger had filled out the necessary paperwork to carry a weapon aboard.

"What's the deal with the Ranger?"

"Nothing unusual. He filled out the required paperwork. He's part of a multi-agency drug enforcement task force. Looks like he flies between Dallas and Honolulu on a regular basis."

"See if you can get a look at his file, just in case."

"Will do. Anything else?"

I stopped on the next-to-the-last name on the list. Sanchez had put an asterisk beside the name but no notation. "What's the asterisk for?"

"He was traveling on a Japanese diplomatic passport. I didn't know if you wanted me to contact their embassy and inquire or wait until we know more."

"Ask Sanderson to run the name through the agency's database. They should have something on him. Anyone else I should know about?"

"The first officer—Skip Bernard—is an FFDO." A federal flight deck officer. A member of the flight crew, trained and legally deputized as a federal law enforcement officer. Licensed to carry a firearm aboard.

"Background."

"He's a captain in the Air Force Reserves. When he isn't flying for Uncle Sam, he makes extra money in the private sector. Single—never married."

"Is that it?"

"That's all we came up with. I can dig deeper if you want."

"We can't afford to leave any stone unturned."

"Under the microscope he goes, then," Sanchez said.

I massaged my right temple where a headache was brewing. "Who's in the left seat?"

"Toby Bledsoe. Fifty-five years old. Widowed. Nearly five thousand hours in the left seat—most of those in the seven-six-seven."

I listened while I scanned the wall-mounted monitors for inspiration. Sanchez read off a list of stats not uncommon for a veteran airline pilot.

"Wait." I grabbed his forearm. "What happened to his wife? Does he have kids?"

Sanchez flipped pages until he came up with the information. "Wife Bethany and daughter Mary Beth were killed by a lone gunman on Christmas Eve several years ago."

"Where?"

"Grocery store near their house."

"I remember hearing the story. A lone-wolf attack. Half a dozen casualties. The guy spouted jihadist rhetoric before he opened fire. An off-duty detective was in the store. Shot him dead in the bakery section, as I recall."

"Yep. That's the gist of it."

I let the information sink in. Had Toby Bledsoe decided to put an end to his misery and ditch the plane? There'd be no line of sight from beneath the ocean. That would explain it dropping off the satellite feed, but not the mysterious ping. In my world, there were no such things as coincidences. Still, I had to consider the possibility the pilot had ditched the plane in the ocean. "Show the intel on Bledsoe to Colonel Rodgers. Tell him I want a search within a fifty-mile radius of the last known coordinates of Global 2455. Given this information, we can't ignore the possibility he simply took the entire plane for a swim."

"How far can this thing fly before it runs out of fuel?" I threw the question out there, knowing if someone hadn't already come up with the answer, I'd have it in a matter of minutes.

"Patrick's on it, boss."

I nodded toward Sanchez and continued pacing. Patrick O'Donnell, late of Boston, Massachusetts, came from good Irish stock. Standing six feet one, with dark hair, green eyes, and the face of an angel, he was easy to look at. Factor in a graduate degree in aeronautical engineering, a healthy libido, and a way with the blarney, and you had the whole package—a cocky son of a bitch with a brain. He was also one of two liaisons on loan to the task force from Boeing. He reminded me of someone else I'd once known, and I was constantly reminding myself he wasn't Liam Donovan.

For the last few years, Patrick had spent most of his time at the Freedom Center, wandering the hallways, looking for his next female conquest. Last I'd heard, he'd planned to spend the long holiday weekend at the beach with one of the clerks from DHS. Apparently, he'd been trying since his first day in the building to get her to go out with him, and this weekend had been a major score for him.

If he'd been anyone else, I would have felt sorry for ruining his plans, but his resemblance to Liam, unfortunately, colored my judgment where he was concerned. "I want the answer now, not tomorrow when he pulls his head out of the sand and decides to answer his phone."

"No problem." Patrick's deep Boston accent startled me.

I turned to see the man, dressed in a white button-down shirt, sans tie. He'd left the top two buttons undone and rolled up his sleeves to reveal toned and tanned skin. His slightly longer than acceptable hair looked as if he'd just crawled out of bed.

"Got it right here." He held a notepad in the air as he made his way across the room.

"I did the initial calculation based on Boeing's official numbers, but once Sanchez was able to give me more information, I was able to come up with a better estimate." He walked right past me to the electronic map littered with "pins" representing the last known location of every plane, commercial or otherwise, that had gone missing in the last decade. When all the "pins" were lit up, it looked like the White House Christmas tree.

Stopping in front of the vertical screen, he touched the glass, bringing the image to life. I noted the addition of a new pin representing Global 2455. My team was nothing, if not efficient.

Patrick looked around for a moment. Seeing what he wanted, he grabbed a dry-erase marker off the top of the adjacent file cabinet and snapped the cap off.

"This is the last known for Global 2455?" He circled the newly added pin.

"Yeah." Jude came to stand behind O'Donnell. "I noted the coordinates as soon as the plane disappeared from radar."

"That's good." Patrick shook his head. "Not good good, but good for our purposes, if you know what I mean?"

"We know." My patience was nothing more than a line, thinner than the one he'd drawn around Global 2455. "Just get on with it. What's our best-case scenario if this thing's still in the air?"

"There is no best-case scenario." He tapped the screen, and the latitudes and longitudes appeared as faint lines in the background. "Given the information we have regarding the fuel load and fuel burn, figuring in the wait on the tarmac, weather conditions, added weight and balance and rate of climb upon takeoff, and"—he drew the last word out—"assuming they maintained altitude above thirty-six-thousand feet and a reasonable airspeed of Mach 78, tracking from the last-known position..." Patrick consulted his notepad then walked his fingers across the glass toward the nearest landmass, stopping short of Guam by the width of a finger. He pressed the tip of the marker onto the glass, creating a blood-red blob.

"This is the best-case scenario."

I tasted bile and mentally reminded myself to breathe.

Jude pointed to the splotch of red. "How far from Guam?"

"Too far," Colonel Rodgers said from the rear of the small crowd now gathered to watch O'Donnell. "Even if they were to keep the thing in the air for as long as possible after the tanks ran dry, they won't be able to make landfall."

Patrick nodded. "That's my assessment, sir. He turned toward the board and drew a circular dotted line. "No matter which way they turned from their last-known, they'd end up in the water."

Patrick's words were met with silence as we collectively acknowledged there was nothing we could do to save the passengers and crew of the missing aircraft. We could only hope the pilots could somehow manage a controlled water landing—a la Captain Sullenberger and the so-called Miracle on the Hudson. Never mind there was a big difference in ditching a plane on the glassy surface of a river and setting one down in the middle of the Pacific Ocean.

I let my shoulders fall. Closing my eyes against the brightly lit panel, I pinched the bridge of my nose. "We need eyes on that plane. Now."

Flight Crew
Global Airlines Flight # 2455
Monday 09:45 Zulu (Sunday 23:45 HDT)

"Ladies and Gentlemen. Can I have your attention, please?

"This is your captain speaking. As a safety measure, your flight crew will be coming down the aisles momentarily to collect all your electronic devices. Please make sure they are completely powered down before handing them over. Rest assured, your belongings will be returned to you when we land in Dallas. Until we're safely on the ground, I must ask you to cooperate fully with the crew. They have been instructed to inspect all carry-on luggage—that means everything from your diaper bag to the bag of souvenirs you picked up at the airport. We understand everything brought on board has already been inspected by TSA agents at the security checkpoints, but we've been instructed to take these extra precautions to ensure your safety on this flight.

"Your flight deck crew appreciates your cooperation with the cabin crew. We are all here for one reason, and one reason only...to get you safely to your destination. Please be patient as we do everything we can to ensure your safety.

"Flight attendants, you may begin."

Monica and Jeff stood at the head of the aisles in first-class. Half the passengers hadn't heard a word of the captain's speech after the part about collecting their electronic devices. They'd been too busy shouting their outrage for any and all to hear. Her heart went out to the less experienced attendants working the economy cabin where most of the shouting originated. Already crammed together like sardines, they were a difficult group to handle on the best of days. This was far from the best of days.

Ignoring the raised voices directed at her, she locked gazes with Jeff before nodding—a signal to get on with it. If there was a bomb on board, there was no time to waste. She'd flown this route enough to know they'd passed the Equal Time Point. They didn't have enough fuel to make it back to Hawaii, and it would be hours before they reached the West Coast of the United States. They were on their own. She'd do whatever it took to keep the plane in the air, including telling the obnoxious rap star sitting against the bulkhead where he could put his indignation.

The passengers in the first few rows vocalized their displeasure with the search and seizure of their property, but, in the end, they reluctantly complied, "for everyone's safety." She recognized the rap star the moment he'd stepped foot on the aircraft. Known for his lewd lyrics and gangster persona, he had been a pain in the ass from the get-go, treating her and Jeff as if they were his personal servants rather than the people tasked with saving his ass if the flight ran into trouble. He'd been on a tirade ever since the captain made his announcement, spewing his defiant words to anyone who would listen and, from the looks of the other passengers, even the ones who didn't want to hear it. She didn't know how long he'd been at it, but he, along with several others in the coach section, held cell phones up, no doubt recording everything. If they managed to land this thing on firm ground, those videos would go viral faster than the latest flu bug.

As she advanced toward the rapper's row, she dreaded the confrontation awaiting her. She'd try to handle it on her own, but she had a feeling she'd end up calling for reinforcements. There was a LEO in coach, but she couldn't recall his seat number. Because the law enforcement officer was armed, they'd been informed of his seat number before boarding. If things got out of hand, she hoped she could count on the off-duty officer to help out.

Skip Bernard, the second-in-command pilot, was also a federal flight deck officer, meaning he'd undergone rigorous training to prepare him to defend the flight deck against a takeover and was licensed to carry a weapon within the confines of the flight deck. It wasn't unusual to have an FFDO on board, as most commercial pilots were military before jumping to the civilian side, but they weren't supposed to leave the flight deck if there was a threat. They were armed in order to protect the cockpit from a takeover, nothing more. The last thing she wanted to see were bullets flying. Innocent people could be injured or killed, and a stray bullet through the fuselage could endanger everyone on board.

After listening with a deaf ear to the passenger's profanity-laced rant, she tried her best to put on a pleasant air. "I'm sorry, sir, but captain's orders. Please hand over your phone, your laptop, and any other electronic devices you might have."

"Screw you. I don't have to give you nothin'."

"Sir, please hand over your phone and your laptop."

"Ain't no terrorist, but I'm about to go postal on your ass. Smile for the camera and move your sorry ass on down the aisle." Multiple gold rings flashed as he waved his hand in the air.

She cut a glance at Jeff. While showing the older lady in the aisle seat how to power off her phone, he shook his head in sympathy for her plight. He'd had a few arguments of his own, but nothing like this.

She tried one last time to reason with the man. "No one is accusing you of anything, sir. This is only a precautionary action to ensure you and everyone else on board makes it to Dallas safely."

"I said, screw you, woman. Now leave me the hell alone."

"Sir, I insist."

He grabbed the headrest of the seat in front of him and stood. At well over six-feet and weighing a good two-hundred and fifty pounds, he filled the small space. Monica was glad for the heavy metal cart between them.

He pointed one thick finger at her. "I said to back off, woman."

Monica risked another quick glance at Jeff. "There's a LEO in coach. Find him."

With a nod, he stuffed the phone he'd just confiscated into the top drawer of his cart and headed down the aisle. Expecting trouble, they'd agreed to go for help if the situation turned ugly, and this had decidedly turned ugly. Taking a step back, hopefully out of the man's reach, Monica tried to reason with him one more time. "Sir, there's no need to threaten me. I'm only doing my job, which is to protect the passengers on this plane—all of them."

"I can protect myself, cunt, so take your little cart and get out of my face."

"There's no need to be rude to the lady." A shiver raced down Monica's spine at the authoritative masculine voice. She glanced across the heads of the passengers in the center section to see a tall gentleman standing next to Jeff. Fair skinned and wearing a suit, he looked out of place among the vacationers returning home. He sported a mild sunburn, short hair, and a frown that no doubt made run-of-the-mill criminals cower. There was a badge pinned to his lapel—a circle with a Texas star inside.

"And who do you think you are?" the rapper asked.

"I'm the man with the gun."

Cabin Crew
Global Airlines Flight # 2455
Monday 09:50 Zulu (Sunday 23:50 HST)

A gasp rose from the startled passengers occupying the nearby seats.

"Captain Lamar Hayes," the man said. "Texas Rangers." He smiled at Monica as he shifted, his right hand, pushing his jacket open to reveal his holstered weapon. "I'm sure all these passengers appreciate all ya'll are doing to keep them safe, ma'am. I sure do."

Monica opened her mouth to thank him, but the belligerent passenger interrupted before she got the words out. "She ain't doing nothin' to keep us safe, just stickin' her pointy nose where it don't belong."

"She's just following the captain's orders. So why don't you do as she asked?" He gestured with his left hand to the phone the man held. "Shut your phone off and hand it to the lady."

The rapper spoke to no one in particular, making sure he had the last word. "You all seein' this, right? De man pulled a gun on me. Ain't right. This video better still be here when we land, too." That said, he tapped the screen a few times to log out of the camera app. He powered the device down and handed it over.

"I haven't drawn my weapon, and I won't as long as you continue to cooperate." Capt. Hayes nodded toward the floor. "Pull your bag out. Let's see what's in it."

"You got no right."

"Maybe. Maybe not, but I need to get home to Dallas, so pull your bag out and let the lady take a look."

He complied, cursing and threatening legal action with every breath. The Texas Ranger didn't seem fazed by the tirade. He'd probably seen much worse, but Monica was grateful for his help anyway.

The remaining first-class passengers had fallen silent, the ones not yet approached hurried to collect their devices so they could hand them over when asked. As word spread from the front to the rear of the plane, the noise level dropped considerably as everyone waited to see what would happen.

Monica took a tablet from the rapper's carry-on. "Turn it off," she said. If looks could kill, Monica would be dead, but the man did as she said before handing her the device.

"This is a violation of my civil rights. I'll own this airline and both of you will be my bitches for life before this is over."

Good luck with that buddy. I sure as hell hope you have the chance to try. Monica checked to make sure the device was off before stowing it inside the drink cart.

The rapper sat, his legs doing a nervous dance as his gaze jumped between her and Capt. Hayes.

The unfortunate passenger seated between the rapper and the window reached across the man's seat, a small laptop and cell phone in her outstretched arm. Taking the freely offered devices, Monica ascertained they were turned off before stashing them in the bin with the rapper's possessions. She issued a polite, "Thank you," to the passenger before glancing over her shoulder to the Ranger, who dipped his chin, acknowledging the silent *thank you* she sent him. With one last warning look at the rapper, Capt. Hayes returned to his seat.

"That's it for first-class, she said to the other flight attendant.

Jeff nodded. In unison, they crossed the line into the coach cabin and continued to collect electronic devices.

No one objected, though a few made their displeasure known with their facial expressions.

Monica stowed her cart in its proper place. Leaning against the tiny counter, she took a moment to breathe. She'd been in stressful situations before but never anything like this. She couldn't imagine what the less experienced crew members were thinking.

With a forced calm, she called the attendants in the rear galley to give them further instructions. "I know that couldn't have been easy, and this next part isn't going to be any easier," she said. "I can't stress to you enough how important it is for us to take this threat seriously. As soon as Captain Bledsoe makes the announcement, I want everyone moving. Open one overhead bin at a time and take everything out. Search every bag and the compartment itself for electronic devices or anything unusual. Leave the bin open when you're through with it and move on to the next. When they've all been searched you can go back and close them. Don't take any crap from anyone. If you find anything unusual, let me know immediately."

She hung up and immediately placed a call to the flight deck. Moments later, Captain Bledsoe announced the new round of searches. She exchanged a resigned look with Jeff before the two of them began to search the overhead bins in first-class.

Major Megan Sloan
Freedom Center, Herndon, Virginia
Monday 10:00 Zulu (06:00 EDT)

"**E**very available asset in the region is on the lookout for it. If it's there, we'll find it." Col. Rodgers sounded convincing, but I had my doubts. They were talking about millions of square miles of water. At night. Even if the crew were to somehow do a controlled ditch, without communication equipment to send out a Mayday, help couldn't possibly arrive in time to save the survivors. I grudgingly acknowledged that *even if* the flight crew managed to issue a Mayday, help would still likely arrive too late.

The group began to talk among themselves in subdued tones. Patrick's news had torpedoed the optimism and enthusiasm from their earlier discovery of the ping. They'd continue to do their work, but the fate of the passengers and crew of the missing airliner weighed heavy on all of them. I watched them return to their workstations before turning to Patrick. "It's not your fault."

O'Donnell shrugged. "I know, but that doesn't make this any easier."

"We'll find out who's doing this, I promise."

"I know every inch of that airframe as well as I know my own skin. If there was anything we could have done to prevent this from happening, I'll never forgive myself."

I appreciated Patrick's dedication to his job, but none of this was his fault. "You didn't have anything to do with the avionics, and that's what this is all about. Someone has found a way to hack into the onboard computers. It's the only explanation."

"When I was assigned to this task force, I thought it was a joke," he said. "Hell, even a few weeks ago, I would have told you it was impossible to do what you're talking about."

"You aren't the only one, so don't let it bother you. You came through when we needed you, and that's what matters."

"Yeah, well...tell that to the families of all those people. I'm sure it will make them feel better." Shoulders hunched, he took one last look at the circle of doom he'd drawn on the board then tucked his notepad under his arm and shuffled off. I almost felt sorry for him. Would have if my own culpability in this fiasco didn't exponentially outweigh his.

"What was that all about?" Rodgers rose from the desk he'd been leaning on during the briefing and approached.

"Nothing. He's feeling guilty for not taking the theory seriously until now."

"Few did, so he's in good company."

"It still could be an inside job. One of those names on the passenger list could be a plant."

We'd been over the passenger and crew lists of every plane that had gone missing since MH370 and come up with nothing. No one with the knowledge or motivation to bring an airliner down. "Speaking of, I need to go over this list again." I held up the manifest Sanchez had printed out for me earlier. "Just in case."

Rodgers fell into step as I headed toward my office. We'd just been informed of the Japanese diplomat's identity. "The agency come up with anything on the Japanese prime minister's nephew?"

"Not that I know of. You think him being on the flight has anything to do with why this plane was singled out instead of one of the dozens of others that left Honolulu last night?" I scanned my ID card and pressed my right index finger to the glass. There was a soft click as the electronic locking mechanism released, allowing us to enter. Rodgers closed the door behind him.

"We can't rule anything out at this point."

I dropped into my chair. The colonel took the only other seat in the room, a molded plastic number that looked like someone had hijacked it from the cafeteria. In fact, that was exactly where it had come from. Everything was standard government issue except for one lone desk ornament I set in motion the moment my butt hit the chair. The rhythmic clack of stainless-steel balls tapping together, first one end then the other, echoed off the empty walls.

"What's with that thing?" Rodgers pointed to the toy.

"It's annoying," I said by way of explanation.

Rodgers laughed. "That it is. I won't keep you long. Just wanted to let you know you're out of here the second we have confirmation of a sighting. I need you, boots on the ground, or in the water, as the case may be. We need the data recorders from this plane. Do what you have to in order to recover them. Every asset we have will be at your disposal."

There weren't enough SOFs, special operations force soldiers, on the planet to keep me from the front lines on this investigation, but I asked the expected question anyway. "Why me?"

"Because you, more than anyone here, should be first on the scene. This is your mission, always has been."

I nodded. Rodgers stood and headed for the door. Only a handful of people knew what had happened to me. Apparently, Rodgers was one of them. That he still trusted me to see the job to completion made him either a fool or an upstanding guy. I didn't know which.

He paused with his hand on the door handle. "Everything you need will be on a plane waiting for you at our hanger."

Any hacker with decent skills could get into the Global Airlines system with a few keystrokes and mine the data necessary to select a single flight out of many. From there, it was another step, not as easy as the first, to gain access to the flight's computer system. Seul-ki thought there were few people in the world like him who'd get this far, and fewer still who could work their way through the lines of code to disable all means of communication. His predecessor had succeeded on all counts except the last one. He'd overcome the communications systems on Malaysia Airlines flight 370, had gained complete control of the aircraft, taking it on what the Americans would call a joy ride. His failure to land the plane at the designated airstrip, and his failure to disable the satellite communications between the engines and the Rolls-Royce manufacturing plant had cost him his life. Seul-ki would not make the same mistake.

No one would trace Global 2455 all over the ocean like they had the Malaysia flight. However, if he succeeded, and the Americans got lucky, they might find pieces of the plane. He was going to do everything he could to make sure they did. Since taking over from his predecessor, he'd made no mistakes. Every plane he'd intercepted had made it to its destination unharmed and undetected. He knew the exact number of people he had delivered into Supreme Leader's hands. So many, the camps were surely overflowing by now. He had no guarantee the passengers were still alive, but he also knew Choi Min-ho would not turn down fresh bodies to work in the mines, fields, and munitions factories even if it meant weaker, older prisoners would starve. Like machinery, humans wore out, and if you belonged to Choi Min-ho, you could be turned off just as easily.

Seul-ki's fingers flew over the keyboard. He'd already isolated the plane carrying the Japanese prime minister's son to Washington D.C. A few more keystrokes and the plane would cease to communicate with ground control. A few more minutes, and the plane would be nothing more than a drone.

For the first time, his orders were to drop the plane into the ocean rather than direct it to an airstrip under the control of North Korea's allies. He'd become quite good at landing planes on runways cut out of jungles and hard-packed sand roads. After refueling, the plane with all its imprisoned passengers would lift off again. Next stop, North Korea.

Today would be different, though. These imprisoned passengers had been sentenced to death—not in Choi Min-ho's work camps, but in a watery grave of Seul-ki's choosing.

He'd picked out a spot. The Challenger Deep, the deepest hole on the planet, some two-hundred miles southeast of the American territory of Guam, would do just fine. Once the wreckage sank below the surface, it would keep going, and going, and going, until the pressure crumpled the steel and aluminum frame to dust.

Seul-ki's fingers froze over the keyboard. He was about to murder nearly three-hundred people. Some of them were probably children. Whole families, perhaps. His stomach cramped, and sweat beaded on his forehead as he imagined the horror they would experience as the plane plunged toward the ocean. He'd never harmed a single person in all his life. Even when he'd been a child and the other kids had picked on him for wearing glasses and always knowing the answers in class, he hadn't lifted a finger or fist to defend himself. The idea of murdering this plane full of innocent people made him sick. Yet, he would do what he must.

As he reprogramed the flight's computer system, directing the airplane west instead of east, he couldn't get the image of the horrific death awaiting the passengers out of his mind. He had no choice. It was them or him. He knew it was true as surely as he knew the sky was blue. Today, they would die, but he alone could spare them the horror of witnessing their plunge into the sea.

The hours wore on. Seul-ki couldn't get the imagined terror out of his head. There were less violent ways to die than falling from the sky. In the end, the result would be the same. Everyone would be dead, as Supreme Leader commanded, but at least Seul-ki would spare them those last few moments of comprehension.

It took him longer than expected to gain access to the engine bleed system—the means by which fresh air was brought into the plane—and cut it off. A few minutes more and he'd disabled the emergency oxygen systems. He knew nothing about death by asphyxiation, but he imagined it would be preferable to the terror of being aboard an aircraft plunging into the unforgiving sea.

He'd done what he could for the passengers. Several hours passed before he took control of Global 2455's flight system once again. This time, he programmed in a landing sequence designed to set the giant airliner down to the surface of the ocean as gently as possible. The waves and the weight of the plane would do the rest. When the supreme commander asked, Seul-ki would not have to lie. He would have brought the plane down in the ocean. There would be no survivors. But, with a little luck, portions of the fuselage would remain afloat long enough to be spotted by one of the planes probably already searching for the aircraft that, hours ago, had ceased to communicate its whereabouts to the agencies charged with tracking flights over the Pacific.

This modification in his directive wasn't much. Maybe it wasn't enough, but it was all he dared. For when Choi Min-ho decided he no longer needed Seul-ki's services, the computer programmer would be as dead as the people aboard Global 2455, only Supreme Leader would show no mercy. He'd rather risk capture and torture at the hands of the Americans.

"**M**onica said they're almost done. They haven't found anything suspicious." Skip hung up the phone. "They've gone through everything except the lavatory trash bins, and they're going through those now. Nothing blew up except a few tempers."

They'd considered the possibility the controlling device could have a suicide switch, meaning simply turning it off would trigger whatever end-result the programmer had wanted.

"That's something, I guess." Captain Bledsoe ran a hand over his face. "Not a damned thing has changed here. If we stay on this course..." He mercifully left the sentence unfinished. They both knew what would happen, no use putting voice to it.

"I had a thought."

"I'm all ears."

Skip pulled his personal cell phone from the pocket molded into the plastic panel beside his seat. "I think we should document this. Photos, a video message, whatever, just in case the data recorders have been compromised. When we're done, we seal our phones up in a plastic bag or something. We can use your lunch box. We put everything in there and hope to God it survives. If they ever find us, maybe they'll find the cooler, too."

Toby gazed straight ahead at the dark sky dotted with tiny white lights. Skip checked his connectivity again. Two words he hated, "No Service," lit the status band across the top of the screen. Opening the phone had become second nature to him. He flipped through screens until he found the messaging app. His fingers hovered over the icon. If these were his last minutes on earth, who would he message, and what would he say?

Faces flashed in his mind. His mother. His father. How do you go about saying goodbye to your parents? Would reading his final words be too much for them? Or would they wonder why he'd text-messaged his sister instead of them? And what would he say that would make it easier for them?

"I think you've got a good idea." The pilot's voice broke the silence, jostling Skip from his thoughts. "Unless we come up with something fast, I don't see any way we aren't going down. Stands to reason the bastards behind this wouldn't want a record of it, so we make one of our own and pray it survives long enough for someone to find it."

Still staring at his home screen, Skip nodded. "If we can't help ourselves, maybe we can help someone else. I can't believe this is a one-time thing."

"Me either. I've been giving it some thought. Remember MH370?"

A cold shiver raced down his spine. "They never found the plane."

"Just a few pieces that washed up on shore. No way to tell how far they'd come."

"They tried to blamed it on the pilot."

"With nothing else to go on, it was the only thing they could do."

"I sure as shit don't want this pinned on me." Images of his mom and dad flashed through his mind again. "Something like that would kill my parents."

"Let's do it, then. Record everything we can think of...statements, too. Document everything we've done to try to regain control of the plane. When we're done, we'll do what we can to secure the phone. If there's a god up there"—he pointed at the sky through the windshield—"someone will find it and know we tried everything we could to save the lives entrusted to us."

With the flight attendants busy with what he and Toby both suspected to be a fruitless search, they got down to the business of documenting every gauge and switch in the cockpit. Rigging a makeshift tripod from a clipboard, they positioned the camera phone where it captured both of them in the image, turned on the video feature, and related every detail of their thoughts and actions, down to the various theories they'd managed to come up with as to how someone could have managed to hijack a plane without showing their face, as well as estimates based on their current course and the remaining fuel on board, as to where they expected the plane to go down.

When they were satisfied they'd done all they could to assist the investigators from the NTSB, they took turns recording personal messages to family and friends. Toby emptied the small insulated container he carried snacks and a bottled water in so he wouldn't have to go out once he was in his hotel room. Skip emptied the contents of a zippered sandwich bag into a cup holder in the console then sealed his and Toby's cellphones inside.

"Carrot sticks?" he asked.

Toby shrugged. "I try to eat healthy. Fat lot of good it did me."

"We're not out of this yet, old man." He handed the airtight bag over.

Toby placed the bag in the bottom of the cooler. "We need something to cushion it with. Something light and waterproof in case the outer layer gets torn and lets water in."

"**G**rab your PBE." Skip reached behind Toby's seat and, in one practiced move, unlatched the hinged lid on the plastic container containing his protective breathing equipment. The silver hood with the see-through amber panel resembled something you'd see in a bad sci-fi movie. Designed to protect the wearer from toxic gasses, it had its own ten-to-fifteen-minute oxygen supply.

Toby grabbed his from behind Skip's seat. "What are you going to do with these?"

Skip had already pulled his from the sealed bag and was unfolding the lightweight hood across his lap. "These things are supposed to be waterproof, right?"

"So they say." Toby gave the top of his bag a yank and pulled out the folded-up device.

"We'll attach the lunch box to my seat cushion. If we seal the neck opening of both PBEs with something—a shoestring, maybe—then we can activate the oxygen canister to create a couple of inflatable buoys and secure them to the cushion, too." They'd already dug the stuffing out of the back of Toby's seat to cushion the cellphones inside the lunch box. "If nothing else, the silver Mylar will help get the thing noticed if it makes it to the surface."

The senior officer smoothed his PBE across his lap. "It's not like we'll be needing them."

Skip made no comment. What was the point? Even if they gained control of the plane, they were going down in the ocean. No two ways about it. They didn't have enough fuel to make land anywhere, and the chances of anyone surviving a dive into the North Pacific from thirty-seven-thousand feet was zero. "It's going to be tricky tying them off without activating the oxygen." Ideally, the wearer would activate the oxygen container first before slipping their head through the opening. "We need to wait until we get them sealed up before we fill them with air."

Together, they managed to attach the lunch box to the cushion using their neckties. They tied shoestrings around the necks of the PBEs. Skip used their remaining shoestrings to secure both inflatable hoods to the straps on the underside of his seat's cushion which, like the passengers' seats, doubled as a flotation device. All they had to do was pull the cords on the oxygen canisters to inflate the PBEs.

"There," he said. "If the ties hold, the cushion should keep the lunch box from sinking, and if nothing else, the Mylar might get someone's attention, even if the hoods deflate."

The empty hood lay across the console, spilling over onto Toby's lap. He placed a hand on the thin material. "Ironic, isn't it? This can't save our lives, but maybe it'll save others. You had a good idea."

"I'd rather have found a way to get control back." Happy-go-lucky Skip was gone, replaced by the warrior the Air Force had seen and cultivated. "We should tell the cabin crew."

"Maybe."

"You don't think they deserve to know?"

"It's not a matter of deserving," Toby said. "Think about it. If there was nothing you could do to change the outcome, would you want to know?"

"There *isn't* anything I can do." Instantly regretting having snapped at Toby, he closed his eyes, swallowing the frustration eating at his gut. "Sorry. This isn't your fault."

"I'm as frustrated as you are, Skip. I can't tell you how many times since I lost my wife and daughter I've thought about joining them, but now that it's going to happen, I find I'm not ready to go. Not like this, anyway. Not on someone else's terms. Given the choice,

I'd rather not know. Knowing there's no way to stop it is worse than knowing your ugly mug is the last one I'll ever see."

Skip snorted. "Okay, okay. I get it." He scrubbed his palms over his face.

The intercom buzzed. Their gazes locked for a second before they both cut their eyes to the handset.

"What's up, Monica?"

"Captain, we've completed the cabin search. We didn't find anything unusual, but we've got another problem."

"What kind of problem?" Toby cut his gaze to Skip, who raised an eyebrow in question.

"People are getting sick back here. Dozens of them—both cabins. They're complaining of dizziness, headaches, and shortness of breath. Is there something wrong with the ventilation system?"

He barely heard her question as she'd lowered her voice—probably to keep the passengers from hearing. He appreciated her professionalism. They'd already had enough drama, causing a mass panic in the tight quarters wouldn't do anyone any good. Part of his training to be an Air Force pilot had included high altitude physiology and time in an altitude chamber where he'd experienced firsthand the effects of oxygen deprivation on the body. The symptoms the head flight attendant had just named were the first of a laundry list of things leading up to brain damage and death if the body didn't receive enough oxygen. There was no use in alarming the cabin crew, either—not until they knew what the hell was going on, so he said, "Everything shows to be fine, but we'd better go on O2 up here, to be on the safe side. Tell all the flight attendants to do the same, and try to keep everyone as calm as possible."

He replaced the handset in its cradle. Skip had heard what he'd said to the flight attendant and was already scanning the appropriate gauges, searching for abnormalities. Toby manually activated the oxygen flow on their flight deck emergency systems. Skip hesitated to put his mask on. Toby knew where his partner was coming from and had considered not using their oxygen himself. He didn't want to be alert when they hit the water any more than Skip did, but they didn't have a choice. If there was any chance they could regain control of the plane, even at the last minute, they had to be alive to grab it.

"We have to," Toby said. "We've got to ride this thing out...just in case."

Skip held his mask for a few seconds as he stared straight ahead. Eventually, he put it on and returned to checking the systems breathable air systems. "Cabin pressure and oxygen are showing normal levels. Ventilation system shows to be functioning properly. What the hell is going on?"

"I don't know. Sure sounds like hypoxia, oxygen deprivation. Turn on the backup oxygen system, just in case, but with everything else going on, it wouldn't surprise me to find out the oxygen system has been compromised, too."

Skip flipped the manual switch to activate the redundant system that would flood the passenger cabin with pure oxygen. "O_2 on."

"You think this is the way it's going to end?"

The first officer nodded. "Yeah. Why not? Maybe whoever's doing this has a conscience after all. Without oxygen, they'll all pass out and die in their sleep. They'll never know when the plane hits the water."

Toby nodded as he gazed at the unrelenting black dotted with tiny pinpricks of light surrounding them like a shroud. "I just want to land this goddamn plane and watch all those people walk off—safe and sound—to live their lives. I want to quit feeling sorry for myself and see what else life has to offer. You know what I mean?"

Skip adjusted his tall frame as best he could in his now cushionless seat and stared straight ahead. "I know. I always thought I had plenty of time. Figured I could see the world, have some fun. One day, I'd find the right woman and settle down. Have a couple of kids. My motto has always been, there's always tomorrow."

The crew intercom buzzed again. Neither man moved to answer it.

Choi Min-ho
Pyongyang, North Korea
Monday 14:00 Zulu (23:00 KST)

Min-ho stood off to the side, watching the video monitor. The young computer hacker's hand shook as he wiped a bead of sweat from his forehead. Scared—as he should be. His life and the future of his family members were at stake—traitors all if he could not complete the task assigned to him. Others had tried and failed and paid the price—like the idiot who had dropped MH370 into the ocean. The only thing he'd done right was sink it deep enough the pressure on the outside of the fuselage had crushed it into oblivion. Min-ho had enjoyed watching the search efforts, knowing they would find nothing. Idiots, the lot of them.

The hacker had failed to land the jet unharmed and paid the price. This new hacker had been forced to watch his predecessor die and witnessed soldiers ripping the man's family from their comfortable home to be driven off to work in a prison camp for the rest of their lives. This one would die, too, if Min-ho did not like what he had to say today. There were others where Seul-ki had come from.

Even before Min-ho had taken his father's place as Supreme Leader, he'd had thousands of boys tested for computer aptitude. The best had been sent to schools all over the world to complete their education with one goal in mind—to become the best computer hacker on the planet. He had to admit, so far, this one had done well.

Min-ho could feel it. Success would be his, soon, and the cowardly leaders who thought him an imbecile would know differently. His whole life had been lived for the moment the world would recognize Choi Min-ho as the greatest leader to have ever lived. The world would bow to his superiority and call him Supreme Leader of All the World.

He hadn't always agreed with his father's plan, but now that he could see it coming to fruition, he didn't regret the years the world had laughed at his expense. Under an assumed name, he'd attended the best Swiss boarding schools where he'd been at the top of his class in every subject, yet his report cards had always shown him to be an average if not less than a satisfactory, student. His father had insisted on the subterfuge, saying a time would come when someone would see through the masquerade and know it was Choi Min-jae's son, not the ambassador's son who had studied there. Let them think he'd been a poor student, and thus would make an inferior leader. One they could manipulate.

Let them underestimate. The victory would be that much sweeter when the world saw him as the brilliant man he really was.

It was a good plan, but it all hinged on the hacking skills of one skinny kid with thick glasses and shaking fingers.

The technician finalized the setup of the video equipment and stood, hands clasped in front, his head bowed in deference to Supreme Leader. Min-ho nodded to the only other person in the room, the head of his personal guard detail, who took the weaker man by the elbow and escorted him from the room. Only when Min-ho was alone with the young man an ocean away did he cross the room and take his seat in front of the monitor. There would be no witnesses to the conversation. Min-ho trusted no one when it came to this project.

Even Lt. General Pak, who commanded a dozen men whose sole responsibility was to make sure the young man was never alone, had no idea why he'd been assigned this duty so far from home. If the hacker succeeded, the general and his men would be rewarded for their sacrifice. If he failed, they would share the hacker's watery grave. For four years, they'd lived aboard a yacht—another gift from the Iranian government—trolling the oceans while the hacker, who rarely saw the light of day, toiled at his computer.

As he listened to the hacker's report, Choi Min-ho thought perhaps he'd let the kid live. "What of the people on board? Could they have survived?" The last thing he needed was for the passengers to be picked up by fishing boats. Alive or dead, their bodies would tell a story he didn't want anyone to hear.

The map disappeared, and the hacker's image filled the screen. "They were dead long before the plane went into the ocean. Once I knew I had complete control of the plane, I cut off the oxygen supply. The carbon dioxide levels in the plane would have reached lethal levels within an hour, two at the most."

Choi Min-ho had been spending a lot of time with the pilots of the Chinese airliners, asking questions under the guise of wanting to learn to fly. He'd learned the cockpit had a separate emergency oxygen supply from the one provided for the passengers. "And the crew? What about their emergency supply?"

"Does it matter? The plane crashed into the ocean. They're all dead now."

He nodded, imagining the passengers gasping for air, their lungs working but coming up empty. It pleased him to think the flight crew had known what was happening and had been powerless to stop it. "The wreckage won't be found?"

"I doubt it. The plane went into the water along the Mariana Trench near Challenger Deep—the deepest point on the planet. Even if it didn't sink to the bottom, the water pressure at any point along the trench would crush the fuselage to dust."

"You had better be right. If not, your family will pay for your mistake."

As much as Min-ho coveted Boeing's big jets, he'd been willing to sacrifice this one for a good cause. In a few hours, Japan's prime minister would go on television to announce the loss of his beloved nephew aboard the fated aircraft. Min-ho didn't spare a thought for the hundreds of other passengers who had lost their lives this day. Collateral damage. That's what the Americans called it. More like good riddance. The Japanese prime minister would think twice before calling him a menace to society again.

Min-ho resisted the urge to laugh. It wouldn't do for this grunt to see how satisfied he was with his results. "There is another plane. A small jet will leave Washington, D.C. for Guam. It is to land in Pyongyang instead. No one is to be injured. I want all the passengers and crew alive."

The young hacker wisely said nothing. He was used to these orders. In the last three years, the North Korean Air Force had acquired nearly a dozen new planes. Not fighter jets. Everyone knew the days of dogfights were coming to a close. What Min-ho needed were planes big enough to carry cargo and men beyond their small peninsula. The passenger planes could easily be converted to bombers, spy planes, or troop transports. Thanks to his foresight and shrewd trading with the Iranians, he'd commandeered enough planes to make even the Americans sit up and take notice.

The time had come to make his intentions known.

Kwon Seul-ki
North Pacific Ocean
Monday 14:30 Zulu (Tuesday, 00:30 ChST)

The screen went blank, and Kwon Seul-ki wiped sweat from his brow with trembling fingers. The twenty-seven-year-old computer geek swallowed, forcing down the acid eating away at the back of his throat. A shudder ran down his spine. He'd dreamed of doing great things, of bringing honor to his country and his family. Instead, he'd become a murderer. And he'd just lied to Supreme Leader.

His family had been so proud when he'd been selected for Supreme Leader's special program to train the next generation of computer experts. They'd been told he would lead North Korea into the twenty-first century.

He'd been trained all right. Trained to kill. He looked at his palms, slick with sweat, and saw the blood of all the people he had murdered. They'd never stood a chance. Never knew what happened to them, most likely. Having given up on the existence of a benevolent god, he prayed to the universe that his victims hadn't suffered. The cockpit crew had tried multiple times to override his control but had failed. The very technology they'd depended on had allowed Seul-ki to end their lives. He'd cut off the passenger's oxygen supply, believing quick suffocation preferable to hours of terror followed by a fatal plunge into the ocean. But what did he know of death and dying?

Seul-ki thought of his family back home. Supreme Leader continued to hold family over his head, but Seul-ki suspected it was all a ruse. He hadn't seen them in the decade since the men from the government office of education had come for him. At twelve years old, he hadn't wanted to leave his home and family, but he'd been given no choice. With nothing but the clothes he was wearing, he'd been taken from his home near Haeju where his father worked in a cement factory to the port city of Hamhung. He'd shared a room with five other boys at the College of Electronics and Automation for the next six years. They were told their parents could come to see them anytime, but his never did. Once a year, on his birthday, he received a letter from his parents asking about his health and stating how proud they were of them. Year after year, they proclaimed they almost had enough money saved to come to see him, but the visit didn't materialize, and he wasn't allowed to leave.

By the time he'd left to attend college, he'd quit thinking about them every day and accepted there was a real possibility he might never see them again. He'd entered the California Institute of Technology with a South Korean passport. For four years, he did nothing but study under the watchful eye of his state sponsor. Attended no events outside of the classes chosen for him. He made no friends other than the few he'd met in the online hackers' club he'd belonged to for a short time. Knowing he couldn't continue his association with them once he left school, he'd broken off all contact during his final semester. He graduated with dual degrees in computer engineering and electrical engineering, with a minor in aerospace technology.

Shortly after graduation, Seul-ki's sponsor escorted him to the Port of Long Beach where he was put aboard a private yacht—the one he now thought of as his prison. He lived and worked below deck. Once a week, he was allowed to go above for fresh air, but only at night, and only if he remained beneath a canvas stretched overhead to protect him from the prying eyes of drones and satellites.

His captors refused to tell him where they were, but he'd managed to figure it out by tracking his own computer signals. For the most part, they stayed in international waters off the West Coast of the United States. Occasionally, they would rendezvous in the dark of night with a larger ship to refuel and take on provisions. As far as Seul-ki could tell, no one ever joined the crew, nor could he discern if anyone left. He'd counted a dozen people on board besides himself and General Pak who was with him almost constantly. Everyone on board was armed, except Seul-ki. If he ever gave a thought to escape, he would never make it.

His family was probably dead or as good as if they'd been transported to one of the work camps. They'd pinned all their hopes on him, and he'd let them down. Seul-ki wasn't foolish enough to believe Supreme Leader would let him live once he'd fulfilled his mission. He knew too much. Correction—he knew everything. As long as the orders continued to come, and he continued to follow them, he would live. This wasn't a revelation on his part. He'd known from his first day on the boat he was one mistake, one failure away from death. Watching a video of your predecessor's murder tended to get the point across.

From that moment on, Seul-ki had begun to make plans of his own. As much as his sponsor had tried to shield him, he'd learned a lot more than engineering while attending school in the United States. It was impossible not to. They could prevent him from attending social events. They could control what he saw and read at home, but they couldn't control anything he saw or heard in the classroom or walking across campus.

He had been trained to notice details, and that's what he'd done. He watched his fellow students, and though he'd complied with orders and didn't interact with them, he did listen in on their conversations. Seul-ki took every opportunity to eavesdrop on the evil Americans. He lingered when packing up his books at the end of class. He feigned indecision at the bank of vending machines in the hallway. He'd learned much from the other hackers he communicated with via the computers in the library. And on the rarest of occasions, he managed to eat the lunch packed for him in the student center where at least one television broadcast a twenty-four-hour news station. He'd learned the rest of the world held little regard for Choi Min-ho, calling him unpredictable and unstable. Over time, these views began to color the periodic conversations he had with North Korea's leader, and he began to see the truth in them.

Then he'd begun to formulate a plan.

Major Megan Sloan
Freedom Center, Herndon, Virginia
Monday 17:00 Zulu (13:00 EDT Noon – CDT)

"Turn that off," I ordered as I entered my office to find Sanchez perched on the corner of my desk watching the news coverage of the missing Global airliner on my television. I'd seen enough of it and others like it over the last few years to last me a lifetime. "Watching that won't make our job any easier."

Sanchez pointed the remote at the flat screen on the wall. The image faded to black, silencing the voices I'd heard before. Every time a plane disappeared.

Every incident was the same. The talking heads on television couldn't tell me anything I didn't already know.

First came the breaking news reports triggered by concerned family and friends awaiting the passengers' arrival. Confused when the plane didn't arrive, they began to reach out to airport personnel, seeking answers. Next would come the "in-depth" reporting. News crews across the globe would unearth "experts" on everything from search-and-rescue techniques to grief counseling. If I heard another shrink speculate on the mental health of the flight crew or another terrorism expert talk about the underwear bomber, I was going to scream. There'd be news conferences with airline executives, the NTSB, Homeland Security, TSA, and even the president would speak, conveying the country's condolences on the loss of so many lives. Speculation would run rampant. Airport security would be increased across the country.

Predictable. And all of them were wrong. Only we couldn't tell them they were.

When we'd begun poking around their passenger lists and crew records shortly after 2455 left Honolulu, Global had known their plane was in trouble, giving them plenty of time to formulate a press release and get support personnel in place at both airports involved. It hadn't made any difference in terms of media coverage. Like other airlines before them, Global refused to confirm the plane had gone down, sticking to the term *missing*. As if it didn't mean the same thing in this instance. Anyone with a passing knowledge of geography could tell you if a plane leaving Honolulu with enough fuel to reach Dallas didn't make landfall somewhere along the West Coast, and hadn't turned back to Hawaii, it wasn't going to put down safely anywhere else.

"Why do they have to interview the most distraught people they can find?"

I shrugged. "Because those are the ones who are too consumed by grief to fight them off, I suppose."

"How did your meeting go?"

I'd just spent two hours on a conference call with Global's top execs and Colonel Rodgers, attempting to explain how we, a task force whose existence and purpose we couldn't discuss with them, had known their plane had gone missing before they did. "I'm not sure we convinced them it wasn't some sort of military training situation gone wrong. They did agree to keep their mouths shut, for now. If we don't come up with the source of that signal, I'm not entirely sure they won't go public with their suspicions."

"Who would believe them?"

"Which planet do you live on?" I settled into my chair, propped my feet up on my desk, and closed my eyes. I was beyond tired. "Americans love a good conspiracy theory. All they have to do is plant the idea and *bam!* it'll go viral in a matter of minutes. Face it, more people would believe our own military accidentally shot down an airliner than believe a terrorist bomb took it down. We're always the first they blame."

"I could start the alien abduction rumor."

"Not helpful, Sanchez."

"Maybe not, but someone is going to say it sooner or later."

"Could be some truth to it," I acknowledged—a sure sign I needed sleep. "What are you doing here anyway?"

"I came to see if you wanted to go down to the cafeteria. How long has it been since you ate?"

"I had...I had..." Well, shit.

"Just what I thought." Sanchez knocked my feet to the floor. "Let's go. You won't be any good to anyone if you collapse from hunger."

"What if I fall asleep in my soup?"

"Or that either." He ushered me out the door. "Food first then sleep. I'll even guard the den, won't let any of the other lions in unless they come bearing good news."

"Sounds like a plan." Seeing as I didn't have a better one, I let Sanchez lead me to the trough where the hunger I'd been ignoring for too long caught up with me.

After my first decent meal, decent being a relative term since it was government cafeteria food, I went back to my office and stretched out on the floor behind my desk. With the lights off and the door shut, the room was pitch black. My mind was racing, sorting through the same information over and over and coming up with nothing—again. It took every bit of my training to empty my mind and will my body to sleep.

Major Megan Sloan
Washington, D.C.
Tuesday 14:00 Zulu (10:00 EDT)

I'd been twiddling my thumbs for over twenty-four hours when Reed Wilson stuck his head in my office doorway. "We've got a lead. The guy lives here in D.C., and he's agreed to talk to us. Want to come along?"

With no word or sightings of Global 2455, we knew it had either crashed into the ocean or run out of fuel, forcing it down. We were back to square one, and I couldn't say I was taking it well. We needed a break in the case, and we needed it now.

"Hell, yes."

At this point, I'd do anything to get out of the office. Having left my house before dawn the day before, it had now been nearly two days since I'd seen the sun. At this rate, I was going to have to get me one of those grow lights for my office or start mainlining vitamin D. I dropped the file I'd been staring at for the last hour onto my desk and holstered the Glock I kept in my top drawer when I was in the building.

"What's the rush?" I asked, trailing the FBI agent in the hallway. "Is he getting away?"

Reed slowed to let me catch up. "Sorry. This place gives me the creeps." Which explained why he spent as little time here as possible. Can't say I blame him.

"Where're we going?"

"Maryland. Ft. Meade." I stifled a groan. Traffic from Northern Virginia to Maryland could be a bitch this time of day.

"He's a state actor now?"

"NSA," Reed confirmed. "Recruited out of college. Been there ever since. Jefferson called ahead to make sure we could interview the guy."

We broke through the front doors to daylight like two convicts escaping death row. Reed pulled a pair of sexy aviator sunglasses from his pocket while I squinted and hoped I wouldn't suffer retina damage. The aviator glasses gave me hope, though. Maybe we were going to take the express lane to Maryland via one of the choppers resting at the distant helipad. No such luck. Good thing we weren't trying to sneak up on the witness. Nothing screamed FBI like a dark sedan with tinted windows.

I fiddled with the air conditioner while my host plugged our destination into a directional app on his phone. "Last time I used that app, it sent me through Anacostia to get to Georgetown," I said.

Reed shrugged. "Must have been a bunch of roads closed on your usual route. Happens all the time around here."

"What's it saying today?"

"Looks like the usual—495 to 95. Should be there in about an hour."

Forty-five minutes if I was driving. Damned FBI. Wouldn't break a traffic law to save their own life. "So, tell me more about the guy we're seeing."

"Remember the online hacker club I told you about? Well, this guy was one of the founding members."

"So, he was in it from the beginning."

"Yep. He says they were mostly white hats, looking for low-level Zero Day bugs in order to make a buck. Said some, including him, paid his way through college that way."

"A real entrepreneur," I said. "So why is he working for Uncle Sam? Looks like he could make more in the private sector."

"Not from Leavenworth."

"Oh."

Dressed in vintage jeans that looked like the real thing and a baby-blue dress shirt, no tie, sleeves rolled up to reveal tanned-and-toned forearms, Trevor Gates didn't fit with any image I had of a hacker. At over six-feet tall, he had broad shoulders, long legs and arms, and wide hands with long fingers. His hair was dark, his eyes an arresting shade of blue, and he had dimples when he smiled. As we shook hands, I got the impression he smiled a lot. "Nice to meet you, Major Sloan, Agent Wilson."

We'd been led to a small conference room where Mr. Gates had been waiting for us. I chose a seat facing the door. Reed sat across from me. Gates took the chair at the end of the table, slumped down in a casual pose, fingers laced across what I'd bet my vibrator were six-pack abs. I wondered what he'd done to get on the NSA's radar, so I asked. "What did you do to earn a life sentence in this place?"

His lips curved up on the corners, showing off his twin dimples. "Let's just say I got greedy. I got caught. It was here or Leavenworth. I chose here."

I nodded. "How's your greed? Cured?"

His smile vanished as he sat up, his posture rigid. "If you're asking if I'm committing treason, then this conversation is over."

"You're the one who said you were motivated by money."

"Not anymore. I was young and stupid. I'm an American, for God's sake. I'd never do anything to jeopardize national security. I put in seventy hours a week at my job. The other ninety-eight, I'm either sleeping or sailing. I've got a sloop I bought secondhand and fixed up myself. If I've got any extra money, any at all, I spend it on repairs and upgrades."

"I had a boat once," Wilson interjected as he flashed me a look that said, "Shut up." Maybe my interrogation skills were rusty, or maybe I just couldn't believe someone as pretty as Trevor Gates actually liked living within the constraints imposed by one of the most security-conscious agencies in D.C. Hell, in the world. I pressed my lips into a thin line and let Wilson continue. "Wife made me sell it, said she was tired of looking at it sitting in the driveway." Wilson cleared his throat. "Thanks for agreeing to speak with us."

"Anything I can do to help," Gates said.

"About the guy you mentioned," Wilson said, getting to the reason we were there. "You indicated there were a couple of people in the online group you ran when you were at MIT who might have been capable of hacking into an airliner's computer system."

"That's right. One of them I know for a fact has never done it, but he could."

Wilson beat me to my next question. "How do you know this person has never done it?"

"Because *I* haven't."

"Well, shit," I said. "And we're supposed to take your word for it?"

Gates stood. "We're done here."

Wilson bolted from his chair. "No. Wait. Major Sloan has been under a lot of stress. She won't say another word. I promise." The way his hand went to his empty holster led me to believe he wanted to shoot me. I'd like to see him try. Nevertheless, I nodded.

"Promise." I made a show of zipping my lips shut, locking and throwing away the key.

Gates' blue eyes bored into me as he dropped back into his chair. At least he was smart enough not to believe me. I gave him points for that.

Major Megan Sloan

National Security Administration, Ft. Meade, Maryland

Tuesday 15:15 Zulu (11:15 EDT)

"Who's the other guy you think is capable of hacking an airliner?" Reed asked our less than cooperative hacker.

"He went by Joe. People think hackers have cutesy names, but it's rarely the case with the ones who do it for a living."

"What was your hacker name?"

"Ray. My middle name is Raymond."

I wanted to laugh, but I didn't. Raymond was someone's great-uncle with thick-soled shoes and thicker glasses, not a young guy with laser eyes and all his hair.

"Tell us about the group. You mentioned to the agent who contacted you that you were mostly white hat hackers."

I had to give it to Agent Wilson, he'd zeroed in on Gates' weakness. We listened as the man went on about the group he'd founded on the Dark Web. All college students at the time, they'd been strapped for cash to pay for classes and books, not to mention the finer things in life like booze and women. It chapped me there hadn't been any women in his group, but statistically, most hackers were male. Statistically, more men than women are criminals. So there.

I learned more about hacking in the next ten minutes than I'd ever known or wanted to know. What stood out was that among Gates' merry band of hackers, there had been one who didn't fit the profile. "Joe didn't seem to have money trouble. When everyone else was talking about ways to find the biggest value Zero Day bug, he was asking questions about where to buy satellite time—off the grid. He was smart—crazy smart. You could tell from his vocabulary—from the way he phrased his questions. I'd chat with him occasionally about what he was studying. You know, making conversation. Hacking can be a lonely business. Anyway, I figured out he wasn't American, but he wouldn't say where he was from. His English was excellent. Better than any of the native English speakers in the group."

"Did he say what he was studying?"

"Aeronautical engineering and electrical engineering. He had a lot of computer science classes, too. He'd make comments sometimes about having to write code for a class the next day. I knew he was good because the kind of stuff he was coding takes most people days if not weeks and he was doing it in a few hours."

"What makes you think he could be our guy?"

Gates shrugged. "Like I said, hacking is a lonely world. I got the impression this guy was lonelier than most. Everyone else would occasionally mention going on a date or a movie they'd seen or a concert. They had a life, but not this guy. It was almost like he was in prison."

I sat up. So much for promises. "Could he have been? In prison?"

"No. I don't think so." Gates' brows met in the middle as he considered his answer. "Maybe prison isn't the right word. I know he took classes. He talked about them too often."

"But he didn't seem to need money."

"No. I always thought he was more interested in the group for the social angle rather than the purpose of the group—to help us pay our tuition."

"What happened to the group?" Wilson asked.

"Nothing. We sort of went our separate ways. The chat room is still active."

"When was the last time you checked in?"

"I don't know. A couple of years, I guess."

"How do you know it's still active?" I asked.

"I set it up. I'm the only person who can take it down, and, a few years ago, I was kind of busy—you know? The feds were after me. I forgot about it. Since I've been working here, I haven't had time, plus, it's part of my past. Until you guys started asking questions, I hadn't given it a thought."

Reed and I made eye contact. I knew what he was going to ask because it was exactly what I wanted to ask. "Can you still contact Joe through the chat room?"

"Maybe. I can't do it here, though. No personal business. We're not even allowed to check our outside email."

We'd handed over our cell phones and service weapons at the front door. Not because we wanted to, but because they weren't going to let us in otherwise. These people took their security seriously.

"We could get you out of here. How long would it take?"

"A few minutes to check the chat room. If you want me to try and track Joe down, that could take a while. A couple of days."

"You can track him?"

"Maybe. Depends on a lot of things. He was playing with satellites years ago, bouncing his signal all around. I never did know where he was, exactly. I kind of thought he was on the West Coast, but it was only a hunch."

Reed stood. I followed suit, while Gates remained seated. "We'll talk to your supervisor."

"Do you know how he's doing it?" Gates asked.

"We don't know shit," I said. "Not who or how or why."

"I know how I'd do it."

Reed and I both sat back down.

"How would you do it?" I asked.

Major Megan Sloan
Freedom Center, Herndon, Virginia
Thursday 12:00 Zulu (08:00 EDT)

"**I**t's been two days." Trevor Gates' supervisor had agreed to loan him to the task force, so Reed and I had set him up in Terrence Jefferson's office with a computer and our NSA liaison to keep an eye on him. It had taken him all of three minutes to figure out "Joe" hadn't logged into the group chat room since 2012. He'd been surprised to find several of the old group was still there. We'd left him mining for information regarding their old chat mate hours ago. I was going out of my mind.

"Wearing a trench in the floor isn't going to help find the wreckage," Sanchez said from his perch on the corner of my desk.

"The media hounds make me sick." It hadn't taken the reporters long to figure out another plane had gone missing—this one with the prime minister of Japan's nephew on board. They interviewed every grief-stricken relative they could find, followed by any official who dared open their mouth and aired the footage over and over again.

"You know they'll do anything for ratings."

As with the other unexplained disappearances, everyone demanded answers and assigned blame.

"I wish the explanation was as simple as alien abduction," I said, "but my gut tells me this is the work of someone right here on earth." Eliminating the suspects down to one planet in one solar system didn't make the hunt any easier.

"They might as well be Martians for all we have on them—which is nothing."

Sanchez was right. Whoever was responsible for the missing aircraft had covered their tracks, and, surprisingly, had yet to take credit for the misdeeds. In my mind, that eliminated the usual suspects—terrorist groups, known and unknown. The Islamic extremists were quick to take credit for what they'd done, and for a few things they *hadn't* done. In the name of Allah, of course, as if killing people in the name of God made it okay. The very idea confirmed why I wanted nothing to do with a deity who encouraged the murder of innocent people simply because they didn't believe. Seemed to me there had to be a better way to convince people to your way of thinking.

Forcing my thoughts to the matter at hand, I picked up the passenger and crew list on my desk. The FBI, in coordination with multiple counterparts in other countries, had compiled extensive bios on everyone on board Global 2455. The passengers ranged in age from six months to seventy-five years. Most had been American tourists, but not all. The Japanese prime minister's nephew had been among a group of young ambassadors on their way to Washington, D.C., to participate in a conference designed to promote cooperation between nations.

"I've been over the passenger list a dozen times. There's nothing here." I dropped the thick report onto the desk. "No one aboard had exhibited any behavior prior to boarding that would indicate a desire to do harm to themselves or the plane. Video from the airport security checkpoints reveals the usual number of people exasperated by the screening process, but not a single one fits the profile of a bomber."

"Doesn't mean one of them didn't unwittingly carry a bomb aboard or in their checked baggage."

"The preliminary report on the baggage screening process shows nothing but a few undeclared pineapples."

"Well, either the system failed or the terrorists have come up with a new explosive the current screening process can't detect."

Silence filled the room as we both chewed on that thought. I shook my head. "It doesn't add up. I can't see ISIS or Al Qaeda keeping quiet if they'd brought even one airliner down, much less the number we're talking about, but we haven't heard a peep out of them. They aren't the kind of people to pass up the opportunity to strike fear in the hearts of nonbelievers."

"You're right. It's not like them at all. Whoever this is has a different motive."

"And a means of keeping radical Islam from taking credit."

"That narrows the suspect list down considerably."

"Whoever it is, they're messing with the whole world, not just the United States." Planes from nearly every major international airline had gone missing, beginning with the most famous, Malaysia Airlines flight MH370. I'd been involved in the investigation from the beginning, analyzing satellite data to map the plane's movement. If the same person was responsible for all the others, they'd learned from the first one. For reasons still unknown, the flight crew of MH370 had ceased communication with the outside world, but their plane had not. Various instruments, including the engines themselves, had continued to send data via preprogrammed satellite transmissions, allowing investigators to track the plane's movement for several hours after the crew's final communication.

"If we're right, and MH370 was the first one to be virtually hijacked, then they've learned from their mistakes. They've managed to turn off or block every method we used to track MH370."

"There are people who would argue what you're saying is impossible."

"Yeah, well. Those are the same people who thought they'd never own a watch like Dick Tracy's."

Sanchez nodded. "True."

"Any news on the guy our hacker friend mentioned?"

"The FBI is still knocking on doors. Seems no one has seen or heard from the guy. His name is Seul-ki. He was set to graduate from the University of Southern California in 2012 but never showed up to collect his diplomas."

"Diplomas? Plural?"

Sanchez consulted his notebook. "He completed degrees in computer engineering and electrical engineering with a minor in aerospace technology. In three years."

Sloan whistled low. "How did he do that?"

"They tracked down some of his classmates. Talked to his professors. Consensus is, all the guy did was study. Never went to anything on campus other than classes. Kept to himself. Brought his lunch and ate outside or in the student union on the rare rainy day."

"And they can't find him?"

"Nope."

My cellphone played "The Ants Go Marching." I snapped it from the pocket of my jeans and pressed it to my ear. "Colonel?"

"I just got a call from PACCOM. One of their pilots on a routine training flight spotted debris about two hundred miles southeast of Guam. They're on the way now to investigate and recover."

"I'm on my way."

Kwon Seul-ki
North Pacific Ocean
Thursday 21:00 Zulu (Friday 07:00 ChST)

He'd barely slept since murdering the passengers and crew of Global 2455. He knew he should eat. But he'd been given another task—one that, though not impossible, certainly had unique challenges. He'd hacked a Gulfstream aircraft before, but never one belonging to the United States government. He'd need his wits about him to pull this one off. Who knew what kind of modifications the owner had made to the aircraft? On the other hand, if he missed something and they were able to track the plane, would that be so bad?

Supreme Leader had been in a rage. Pieces of the fuselage of Global 2455 had been spotted floating off the coast of Guam just hours after the plane had gone down. It was sheer luck, but he knew Choi didn't believe him when he'd said so. According to the news reports he'd accessed during the short breaks his watchdog took each day, he'd learned the U.S. Navy had also recovered several bodies.

If Choi suspected he'd brought the plane down in a manner that almost guaranteed pieces of it would be recovered, Seul-ki's days on earth were numbered. Supreme Leader would find someone else to do his murdering for him. That was fine with Kwon. He had enough blood on his hands. The time had come. One way or another, this plane would be his last. The Americans would find him this time, and the killing would end.

The Americans are too trusting. He hacked into the records of the Gulfstream Corporation as easy as a thief with a key. Everything he needed was there in their database, just waiting for someone like him to come and take them.

Major Megan Sloan
USS Ronald Reagan, 200 miles southeast of Guam
Friday 21:00 Zulu (Saturday 07:00 ChST)

I watched a group of seamen on a lower deck struggle to capture a piece of floating debris and drag it aboard. The gray slacks and matching jacket I'd chosen for the helo trip from Guam to the USS *Ronald Reagan* were serviceable and traveled well, but I'd overestimated their windbreak qualities. Tropical my ass. If I stayed out here much longer, I'd freeze my derriere off. "You know the difference between an ocean and a desert, Admiral?"

"One has water, and the other doesn't?"

I forced my gaze from the drama taking place below to the man standing beside me. At six-foot and change, Rear Admiral Harmon Reese didn't have an ounce of flab on his body. A bit of salt at his temples hinted more toward wisdom than age. Any facial flaws he might have were masked by a cloak of confidence only a man sure of his authority could wear. Command fit him like the proverbial glove. "There is no difference, Admiral Reese. None at all."

Arms casually folded, he flashed a smile. "This, I have to hear, Major Sloan."

I returned my attention to the action four decks below us where his crew risked their lives for a few hunks of scrap metal I had my doubts would yield a single clue as to what had happened at thirty-nine-thousand feet. "Both are vast, desolate," I said, "and inhabited by deadly creatures. And, they're both capable of swallowing up entire civilizations without leaving a trace."

"I can't argue with your logic."

No, you can't.

"Have they located the black boxes yet?" For the first time since anyone noticed planes disappearing from the sky, we had a chance to acquire the flight data recorder and the cockpit recorder from one of the missing planes. Having discovered the mysterious pings prior to the Global 2455 falling from the sky, we had more reason than ever to believe the plane had been remotely taken over. What we didn't know was how. Maybe the boxes would tell us. Maybe they wouldn't.

"Not yet, but we're on it."

"But you think you can recover them?"

"The wreckage is deep, but the crew of the submersible thinks they have a shot at it." He cleared his throat and shifted his feet.

Here it comes. I'd been waiting for it—the excuse for not recovering the single most important pieces of the puzzle. "Go ahead. Tell me. I'm used to disappointment."

"As of yesterday, the boxes were in a location accessible, or at least possibly accessible. As you know, the wreckage sits on a shelf, within reach of the submersible. The storm last night could have pushed it over the edge into the Challenger Deep. It would account for the amount of debris on the surface today."

I knew all about the Challenger Deep, having spent the long flight from D.C. to Guam reading everything I could find on the subject. At the southernmost part of the Mariana Trench, approximately two hundred miles southeast of Guam in the North Pacific Ocean, it was the deepest point on earth—nearly seven miles below the ocean's surface. "In other words, the plane is either breaking apart on its own, or it's gone over the edge, breaking apart in the process." Swallowed up by the sea. Not unlike the theory about MH370 being swallowed up by the Horizon Deep, part of the Tonga Trench off the coast of New Zealand and, coincidentally, the second deepest point on earth. Did I mention I don't believe in coincidences?

"Yes, ma'am. That about sums it up."

"When will we know for sure?"

"I've set up a tight perimeter. Five destroyers, three cruisers, and the *Ronald Reagan*, with the remaining two destroyers, the *Fitzgerald* and the *Stethem* standing guard above the wreckage. I'll let you know when I hear something from either one."

"The submersible?"

"Launched at dawn, ma'am. They're doing their best to find and recover the instruments, but if they went over the edge..."

"Then we're screwed."

"Yes, ma'am. Even if we had equipment capable of going down 35,000 feet, there'd be nothing to find when we got there. The pressure would crush the unprotected wreckage to dust."

I nodded. "Thank you. I understand. I appreciate all you and your crew are doing. I guess I'm too anxious. We've been hoping for a break, praying whoever is behind this would make a mistake."

"We'll do all we can."

I couldn't ask for more. "I was told you'd recovered some bodies."

"Three. We've got them on ice."

"You have an ME on board?"

"Commander Schneider is our ship's surgeon. She doubles as the medical examiner when the need arises."

"I'm bringing my own people in to assist with identification. We'll do the autopsies on board." I wasn't asking. Word had come down from on high, ensuring the admiral's cooperation before I was wheels up in D.C.

"I speak for Captain Hervey and myself. The ship and crew are at your service."

"Thank you, Admiral. I appreciate your cooperation. We'll get out of your way as soon as possible. This is the first time we've recovered bodies. We're hoping, in the absence of the black boxes, they can tell us what happened up there."

Major Megan Sloan
USS Ronald Reagan
Friday 21:45 Zulu (Saturday 07:45 ChST)

I saluted the MP standing guard outside the cooler holding the human remains retrieved from the ocean then followed Lt. Graves who had been assigned as my guide for the duration of my cruise. Twenty-four hours in the water, not to mention falling out of the sky, hadn't done the bodies any favors. The two women and one man weren't the first corpses I'd ever seen, but I hoped they were my last. "Has Dr. Schneider had a chance to take a look?"

The autopsies would wait until the FBI's forensic team arrived, but with a little luck, the ship's ME could give me something to go on. Anything.

"I'm not sure. I can take you to her office."

"Let's go."

Commander Leslie Schneider, M.D.'s office was more spacious than I'd anticipated but far less so than her counterparts in private practice. A few photos and mementos added a personal touch to the otherwise utilitarian space. The woman herself was everything I'd expected. Medium height and slender with brown eyes and brown hair, which was pulled tight in a regulation bun, she wore her khaki uniform well. No doubt, behind the cookie cutter outside lurked a first-rate mind and a spine of steel that commanded respect. It was the only way a woman got ahead in the military—by being smarter and better than the men vying for her job.

Lt. Graves made the introductions and, after promising to wait outside for me, left us alone.

"How was your trip out to the carrier?" Commander Schneider asked.

"Bumpy and loud. I hate choppers." As soon as we'd gotten word of this plane going down, I'd taken Colonel Rodgers up on his offer of transportation—a Gulfstream aircraft the Air Force kept at Andrews Air Force Base. It wasn't the newest model from the luxury-aircraft manufacturer but the brand new 650 model parked next to my 500 was being held for someone higher up the food chain than little ole me. I couldn't complain. The nonstop flight to Guam might have been the single best flying experience I'd ever had. A Sikorsky SH-60 Seahawk helicopter had been waiting to take me to the USS *Ronald Reagan* some 200 miles out.

The doctor smiled and relaxed in her desk chair. "Not my favorite method of transportation, either. But you made it safe and sound. That's what matters."

"True enough."

"Since I know you didn't put in for a luxury cruise on an aircraft carrier, I'll get right to the point. You've seen the bodies?"

"I have. What can you tell me about them?"

"Not much without an autopsy. Good news is, they seem to be intact—no missing limbs. The condition of the bodies might be a clue as to how the plane went down. I'm no expert on crash landings, but I would think there wouldn't be much left of them if the plane had dropped uncontrolled into the ocean from several miles up. Finding human remains in relatively good condition seems to indicate a less violent entry into the water."

"You could be right. Then again, depending on where they were seated and the angle of entry, the airframe itself might have protected them."

"One of the women was still strapped into her seat. The others were floating free in the water. I took some photos before she was removed and put in the cooler."

"Can you forward the photos to me?" I wrote my email address on a pad she slid across the desk. "My forensic team will be here shortly. I'm sure I can count on you to assist them with anything they need."

The woman nodded. "Those are my orders, and orders aside, I want to help in any way I can. Whoever is responsible for this and the other incidents must be stopped."

"Thank you. We've already got more to go on with this one than any of the others. With a little luck, we'll find something useful in the wreckage recovered, or maybe the bodies will tell us something."

"Like I said, anything I can do, just let me know."

Major Megan Sloan
USS Ronald Reagan
Friday 22:15 Zulu (Saturday 08:15 ChST)

After meeting with Dr. Schneider, I asked to see the wreckage up close. Lt. Graves led the way to the hangar deck where I was handed over to the person in charge of the recovery process.

"Welcome aboard, ma'am."

"Thank you, Master Chief Sherman."

"If you'll follow me? We've secured the debris near the elevator."

I trailed the senior enlisted man through a maze of aircraft, some being serviced, others with ordinance attached to their wings like giant birds of prey waiting to be set free from their cage. The elevator bay door was open, allowing in light and the bracing sea breeze. Wishing I'd taken time to change into sturdier clothing, I wrapped my arms around myself. I wasn't sure if the sudden chill settling into my bones had to do with the gaping hole in the hull or the ragged-edged pieces of fuselage paying testament to an unfathomable act of violence. Blank windows stared at me from the two largest pieces, both sections from what appeared to be the front of the plane. Perhaps the first and business-class sections. Wires and cables that once carried the lifeblood of the monster machine hung lifeless, severed most likely by the sharp aluminum skin as it ripped and tore on impact.

In my years as an Air Force pilot, I'd seen my share of aircraft downed by explosions, whether internal or initiated by external forces. Fire left distinctive marks not even an ocean of water could wash away. My trained eye saw nothing to indicate there had been a fire on board. Though even a small fire in the cockpit could have damaged the communications system and theoretically led to the plane going down without a single distress signal being issued. It was something to look at, anyway. I glanced around at the dozen or so smaller pieces of debris. Unfortunately, none of them appeared to be from the cockpit. Unless they recovered the flight data recorder and the cockpit voice recorder, aka the black boxes, any conclusions reached would be nothing more than educated guesses based on a dozen pieces of debris and three corpses. Not much to go on, but more than we'd had thus far.

I pulled out my phone, snapped several photos, and sent them to Jude in Virginia. In a matter of hours, trained investigators would sift through the debris with a fine-tooth comb. Every inch would be examined and catalogued before the pieces were packed up for delivery to a secure hanger on Guam where more experts would try to make sense of a senseless tragedy. I'd have access to every report, every finding...or lack thereof.

I turned my attention to the smaller pieces of the puzzle. Off to the side, a lone passenger seat sat crookedly on its broken frame. First class, judging by the size of it. Waterlogged, the leather cover was otherwise unharmed. The aisle-side armrest remained intact, but the seat had been torn away from the shared armrest. "One of the bodies was found in the seat?"

"Yes, ma'am. A woman, I believe."

I nodded and crouched to get a better look at the seat, willing it to tell me what had happened. *Maybe your passenger will.* I could hope. We needed something to go on, something to explain why otherwise perfectly good aircraft were disappearing from the sky without warning. Without a single cry for help.

I stood and threaded my way through the remaining pieces. A section of overhead bins. An empty cargo container, a couple of seat bottoms designed to be used as flotation devices, only no one had used them, apparently never having had the chance.

I snapped a few more photos and sent them off. I'd come all this way looking for answers, and all I had were more questions.

In high school, I'd taken some journalism courses—a backup plan, just in case I didn't get accepted into the academy. One thing I'd retained was that every story had to answer six key questions. Who. What. When. Where. Why. And, how. In journalistic terms, I had zip. No story.

Choi Min-ho
Pyongyang, North Korea
Saturday 03:00 Zulu (Noon KST)

C hoi Min-ho didn't trust the young hacker, Seul-ki. He'd said there wouldn't be any wreckage to find. He'd said the ocean would swallow the plane, crush it to dust. But the Americans *had* found the wreckage. They'd pulled *bodies* from the water!

Yes, he'd enjoyed watching the prime minister of Japan boo-hoo about the death of his nephew—a boy who, by all accounts, had aspirations of following in his uncle's footsteps. Good riddance, if that was the case.

It was possible the Americans had made the whole thing up in order to put an end to the questions about what had happened to the airliner. He laughed at the idea of the American public putting pressure on their weak leaders to explain the disappearance of so many planes over the last few years. They had no explanation; this he knew because he'd seen to it the aircraft and their passengers disappeared without a trace.

All except this one. Satellite photos showed the American carrier group was in the area, but he hadn't seen any debris in the water. Either they'd already recovered all there was, or there'd never been any in the first place.

The computer genius's explanation had a ring of truth, but Choi wasn't inclined to believe him. Not many had the balls to lie to Supreme Leader. None did and lived to tell about it. If he was lying, the truth would come out soon enough, then Choi would deal with him. He'd given him another task, one he could not fail at. The future of North Korea rested on the plans he'd made and carefully executed since taking over the reins of leadership upon his father's death.

Choi Min-ho's grandfather, Choi Min-jun, had once been a great man who had garnered the favor of the Soviet Union and China, and in his early years sought to elevate North Korea to its rightful place as a world leader. He'd spearheaded a nuclear program that would have secured their place among the great nations, but in his later years, after suffering a crushing defeat when he attempted to unify the Korean people, he'd caved to pressure from the United States and Japan. The economic sanctions they'd imposed on his country had broken the once great man, had clouded his judgment.

Thankfully, Min-ho's father had not agreed with Min-jun, and the older man had not lived to sign the nuclear agreement with the West.

His grandfather's weakness had cost the people of North Korea dearly. They'd suffered under the economic sanctions, but their suffering wasn't for naught. Min-jae had invested wisely in new alliances with nations who weren't afraid to stand up to the United States. He'd built up the military and expanded the nuclear program, all while masterminding the plan his son would ultimately carry out.

It hadn't been easy. Min-ho had met with opposition from the outset. Min-jae's trusted advisors had questioned his vision, but nothing was going to stand in Min-ho's way. He would not cave as his grandfather had done. Since assuming his rightful place as Supreme Leader, he'd systematically removed all opposition. As his uncle, Pak Jin-soo had learned, not even family were safe if they didn't see the same vision for the future as he did. Min-ho had executed Jin-soo and his entire family, and still, the message hadn't been heard by all. They would all go. Nothing would stand in his way. The world had underestimated North Korea for too long. It was time to send the United States a message they couldn't ignore.

"Is the launch ready?" he asked.

Lt. Colonel Rhee of the Academy of National Defense Science stood at attention. He'd been summoned hours ago. "We await your command, sir."

"You have the coordinates correct?" There would come a time when he would send missiles to every inch of American soil he could reach, but not today. He did want to send a message, though—one the United States and every other country who dared to laugh and sneer at North Korea could not mistake.

"I've checked them myself, Supreme Leader. They are correct."

If they weren't, the man and his family, as well as everyone under his command would pay for the mistake.

"The square is filled?" he asked his Minister of State Affairs.

The man bowed. "There are two hundred thousand people waiting to see you and to witness your great achievement."

"The screen has been tested?" He'd had a huge electronic billboard installed above the square so the whole country could witness the missile launch. And the Western press said North Koreans didn't know what was going on in their own country. This event was being recorded. After the successful launch, hackers would release the video to show the world that they knew nothing about North Koreans, just like the missile launch would show them their size meant nothing to him.

"Yes, sir. I oversaw the tests myself. The image you see here at your desk is the same one the crowd outside will see in a few moments."

Min-ho paused in front of the gold-framed mirror. He called for his stylist who rushed forward to make sure every hair on his head was in place and the medals he wore on his chest were straight. Satisfied with his appearance, he signaled for the heavy drapes to be opened, and strode out onto the balcony to accept the adoration of his people.

Min-ho smiled and waved at the crowd below. This was his due, and soon, people all over the world would recognize his greatness, too.

On his signal, the countdown began. The assembled workers grew quiet as the numbers flashed across the giant screen, the stately missile in the background. This was a great moment for their country. Anyone could see it. Min-ho watched along with everyone else as the green needle-like weapon launched in an awe-inspiring column of fire. The crowd cheered, turning their attention to the balcony where he stood.

His heart pounded in rhythm with the chants rising from the square. His dick throbbed. He'd never felt more powerful, more alive. With one last wave to the crowd, he stepped inside. There was only one thing to do with such power. "Everyone out," he shouted. "Except you." He nodded at his secretary who stayed behind.

"Bring two this time," he said. "And hurry." Alone, he unzipped and pulled his majestic sword out, stroking it to the chants filtering in through the open balcony doors. This was what power felt like. Moments later, he motioned the guards to bend the first woman over the front of his desk. Did she know how lucky she was to be the recipient of such power? He hoped so as he rammed into her slick cunt over and over again as the crowd called out his name.

Major Megan Sloan
USS Ronald Reagan
Saturday 21:00 Zulu (Sunday 07:00 ChST)

After dinner last night, the admiral issued an invitation to breakfast—no sleepover required. I politely declined, citing my need to sleep in this morning. Like most men, he swallowed the bullshit as typical behavior for a woman.

My body slept when I told it to, and not vice-versa. I'd gone straight to my quarters after our dinner, caught a couple hours sleep before I checked in with Colonel Rodgers. Assured a forensics team and the requisite FAA and NTSB investigators would arrive later today, I went up top to get a run in. Due to high winds, the flight deck was off limits to runners, so I headed to the gym. After asking about a dozen people for directions, I finally located the small space. All the treadmills were in use, so I settled for ten miles on a stationary bike. Somehow, I found my way to my temporary quarters, showered, and dressed in my ABUs, figuring the personnel on board might take me a bit more seriously if I wore the camo uniform. It wasn't as comfortable as my flight suit, which I still carried with me—just in case someone was inclined to let me fly something—but it wasn't as uppity either. I looked relatable—exactly the look I was going for.

If I'd had any love of the ocean, the Navy might actually have been my calling. Because the occupants of the floating city worked shifts, there was something available to eat around the clock. It didn't take me long to find the bacon and eggs I'd been craving since sitting down with the admiral for a meal of steak and lobster the night before. Maybe it was the sea air, but I ate like a sailor, finishing off my high-protein meal with a cinnamon roll as big around as my thigh. I

119

washed it all down with about a gallon of orange juice. No scurvy for me.

I'd just dropped my tray on the belt that would carry it to the kitchen to be washed when my cruise director caught up with me.

Lt. Graves gave me a weak smile. "Thank God. I was beginning to think you'd fallen overboard."

"Nope." If she knew how much I hated water sports, she'd know I wasn't going any closer to the sea than required. I tapped the wings sewn onto a blouse I rarely wore. "Air Force, remember? I don't do water."

She smiled at my quip, but it didn't last long. "The admiral said to find you and take you to the hanger deck ASAP."

"Why? What's up?"

"He didn't say, and I didn't ask. Follow me, please?"

Maybe they'd found the black boxes. As soon as the thought occurred, I dismissed it. We couldn't get so lucky. I fell into step behind her. We went down passageways and up ladders I'd never seen before, ending up on the same deck where I'd gotten my first good look at the recovered wreckage. My first thought was they must have cast a net out overnight. A mountain of debris blocked my view of the open hangar door and the ocean beyond. As my eyes adjusted to the harsh daylight streaming in, I picked out a few suitcases—some the old-fashioned hard-sided ones, but most were of the newer, lighter variety—plastic cases with wheels to make it easy on travelers running through airports to catch their flights.

"Admiral Reese is over there." Lt. Graves pointed.

I followed her outstretched arm to see a group of sailors huddled in silhouette against the light.

"Thanks," I said, stepping around the morbid pile.

Everyone except the admiral saluted as I approached. Outranking all but him, I returned their salute. "You wanted to see me?"

"Thought you might want to see this." Admiral Reese gestured at the deck. "The crew fished it out of the water about an hour ago."

Whatever it was, it wasn't the black boxes I'd hoped for. We studied the mishmash of materials at our feet. I recognized the individual components but couldn't make sense of any of it. "What is it?"

"Don't know. At first glance, it looks like some random debris got tangled up, but on closer inspection, it appears to be deliberate."

"If I may, Major?"

I nodded to the seaman. The young man knelt. Slipping an index finger beneath what appeared to be a shoestring, he pulled the string upward until the knot at its end was plainly visible. "This is no coincidence. Someone knew how to tie a knot and did it deliberately."

An icy chill having nothing to do with the wind coming off the ocean raced down my spine. I knelt to get a better look. "You're right." Waving my hand to encompass the entire object, I asked, "Is it all tied together?"

"Yes, ma'am." He let the string drop. "And there's this." He used one finger to lift a business-card-sized piece of plastic attached to what appeared to be a small lunch box. A black box, but not the one I'd been hoping for.

I leaned in to get a better look. *Holy shit.* My heart raced, and my brain shifted into overdrive as I read the name on the luggage tag. "Toby Bledsoe," I read aloud. "This belonged to the pilot."

"What do you make of it?" the admiral asked.

My legs trembled as I stood. "Someone went to a lot of trouble. Those are PBE's—Personal Breathing Equipment."

"Yeah. We have similar equipment on board in case of a chemical spill or leak."

As much as I wanted to see what was inside the lunch box, I knew we had to be cautious and document every step. We had no idea what had brought Global 2455 down. It could have been Toby

Bledsoe, and this might be his way of taking out a bunch more people, just for the hell of it.

I waved everyone away. "Get back. We have no idea what's inside."

The admiral directed the seamen to the far side of the deck then barked orders at them. One by one, they hurried off to accomplish their tasks until the two of us stood there alone, staring at the mysterious package.

"What do you think it is?" he asked.

"I haven't got a clue."

In a matter of minutes, a perimeter had been cordoned off using the Navy's version of crime-scene tape stretched between various pieces of mobile equipment brought in to serve as fence posts. Wishing I could just open the thing and find out what Toby Bledsoe had thought important enough to go to so much trouble to preserve, I had just enough instinct for self-preservation to keep my distance.

A sailor bearing the master-at-arms insignia arrived shortly. After I returned his salute, he indicated the camera bag slung over his shoulder. "Major Sloan? Chief Petty Officer Cory Adams. Admiral Reese said to follow your orders, ma'am."

I nodded. "Thank you. I need pictures of everything." I pointed to the tangled heap behind the yellow tape. "I don't think it's dangerous, but it's only a hunch. Nevertheless, no one is touching it again until we've documented what we can see."

"Looks like a pile of trash from here."

"I won't argue with your assessment, but it could be anything from a bomb to a chemical weapon. Or it could be the pilot simply didn't want his lunch to go astray."

We both eyed the debris for a few seconds. "It didn't blow up when they fished it out of the water."

"No, it didn't. And the sailors who brought it aboard are all fine, so if it does have some sort of chemical weapon inside, it doesn't appear to be leaking."

The master-at-arms nodded. "Okay, then. I guess I'll take my chances." He ducked beneath the warning tape. I followed. Having already stood over the makeshift vault for some minutes, I had nothing to lose.

I pointed at things I wanted documentation on, and, for the next half-hour, he took photographs from every possible angle. Because of the size of the thing, he requested a yardstick to serve as a reference. I had to hand it to these men and women; they knew how to hustle. Minutes later, not one but two yardsticks were made available, and the photographer began a whole new set of photos. When he'd exhausted every possible angle, he stood.

I shook his hand. "Stay around?"

"You going to open it?"

"Yeah. I guess I am. The admiral informed me we don't have bomb detection equipment on board, and it could be days before it got here if we requested it. As for chemical detection—well, that's a no-go, too. Not even a canary on board." My gut was telling me whatever was inside could hold the key to my investigation. I'd never bought in to the pilot-suicide theory. Maybe it had happened once, but not every few months.

"Guess I'll stick around." He patted the weapon holstered on his hip. "If they managed to trap an alien inside, maybe I'll put a slug into it before it eats its way through the entire Pacific Fleet."

His words brought to mind a popular sci-fi movie where aliens took over a spaceship. The graphics had been horrifying and way too believable. I laughed and put a hand on my own Glock. "Just stay out of my way, Adams."

He dipped his chin, acknowledging my move. "No doubt you're more likely to save my ass than I am yours." He squared his shoulders. "The admiral said your forensic team is on the way?"

"Should be here before lunch. With a little luck, whatever's in there"—I pointed to the lunch box—"will tell me all I need to know."

"Let's do it. Want to move it somewhere else or open it here?"

The admiral had sent a contingent of Marines to guard the box. They stood around the taped-off perimeter, their backs to us. A group of seamen rimmed the edge of the aft elevator, looking for more debris. "Might as well open it here. There's good ventilation." Short of an isolation chamber, our present location was the best we were going to do, and I'd be damned if I was going to wait until we could move the package off the ship.

"Let me change out the memory chip." He held his camera up. "Then I'm good to go."

"No problem. I'm going to see if one of these Marines can get me some rubber gloves. I doubt there are any prints left on the outside, but the inside might be a different story. Wouldn't want to compromise the evidence."

"Good idea. They'll have some in sickbay. Just ask him." He indicated the closest Marine. "That's Lt. Palmer. He'll make the call for you."

After speaking to Lt. Palmer, I returned to stare at the package. If what we thought had happened to all the missing aircraft, including Global 2455, proved correct, I had to wonder why this was the only one we'd ever recovered anything from? My gut told me Toby Bledsoe had gone to so much trouble for a reason.

Without moving anything, I could see he'd used at least four shoestrings and two neckties to secure the lunch box to a seat cushion. Either his copilot had already been dead or had given up his laces and tie willingly. I hoped for the latter but conceded the former might hold more truth. I wasn't sure what role the PBEs played, but tied the way they were, they looked like deflated Mylar balloons. My best guess was he'd somehow filled them with air, turning them into makeshift buoys. If he'd used the breathing equipment in order to make the seat cushion and lunch box more visible, his strategy had worked. The men who'd recovered the box said reflections off the shiny silver fabric had caught their attention.

Dr. Schneider arrived a short time later with a box of surgical-grade gloves.

"Better stay back. Better yet, get the hell out of here," I cautioned. "We have no idea what's inside."

"My money's on ham-and-cheese with mustard. Wanna bet?"

I smiled, snapped on a pair of gloves then tossed another set to Adams. "Our master-at-arms thinks there's an alien inside."

"Sure would beat my ham-and-cheese theory." The doctor smoothed latex over her slender hands.

In the short time it took to get our gloves on, I noticed a marked increase in the number of people standing around. I considered ordering them to get the hell out of here but thought better of it when I caught sight of another spectator headed my way.

"Carry on," Admiral Reese said, answering my unasked question.

I made eye contact with my two cohorts. "Let's open the patient up, shall we?"

Major Megan Sloan
USS Ronald Reagan
Saturday 21:30 Zulu (Sunday 07:30 ChST)

We gloved up more to protect the evidence than to protect ourselves. If there was some sort of chemical weapon inside, nothing was going to save us, so why bother? I said as much to the good doctor when she offered up what amounted to hazmat suits kept in sickbay in case something like Ebola found its way on board. I did offer to give her a head start if she wanted to get the hell out of here. My admiration for her went up a couple of notches when she declined.

Crouched over the tangled mess, I asked my crew of two, "Ready?"

Adams nodded and lifted the viewfinder on his camera to his eye. Dr. Schneider clenched and unclenched her latex-covered hands before nodding once.

I gave the PBEs a cursory inspection, figuring the payload would be inside the insulated cooler. My inspection turned up nothing, so I carefully isolated the small box. About eight inches by twelve, it had a pocket on the front and a zippered lid. I figured it would hold a six-pack or a couple of water bottles and the usual lunch—sandwich and chips—but not much more. I had something similar I'd used a few times when I'd been forced to endure classroom-type training. You could pick one up at any discount store for around ten bucks.

My fingers itched to open the main compartment, but I'd been trained to be methodical so I unzipped the front pocket first. I peeked in then held the empty pouch open so Adams could document the moment.

"Nothing," I said, "which means whatever we're supposed to find is in the main compartment."

"Agreed," Dr. Schneider said.

"Makes sense," Adams said.

I made eye contact with each one of them, and, with one hand on the bag to hold it in place, I reached for the zipper pull. Unaffected by its recent saltwater bath, the teeth on the nylon zipper parted with ease. I'd waited long enough to see what Toby Bledsoe had taken such pains to preserve. As soon as the zipper pull came to a stop, I flicked the lid open. The three of us leaned over to see inside.

"Would you look at that?" Adams said.

"Holy shit!"

I couldn't help but smile at the conservative doctor's whispered exclamation as I peered down at the contents. Seawater had leaked in through the outer covering. A couple of empty plastic bottles acted as fillers in the bottom. Sitting atop the water bottles was a sealed sandwich bag in which resided two perfectly dry and, it seemed, undamaged cell phones.

My heart raced so fast I wasn't sure if I was hearing my own blood rushing past my ears or the roar of jets taking off on the deck above us. My gut told me the phones belonged to Toby Bledsoe and his first officer, Skip Bernard. It was all I could do to keep from snatching the puffed-up bag before Adams could document the find. Finally, we had something to go on. I knew it like I knew the sky was blue.

"Take pictures, Adams." My command jolted the master-at-arms out of his trance. As he began to snap away, I waved the admiral over. He leaned in to take a look then straightened.

"You think?"

"I know. The flight crew found a way to communicate with us. I need the best technicians you have. I need to know what's on those phones, and I need it yesterday."

"Our resources are at your disposal." He waved a junior officer over, and, in less than a minute the younger man hustled off to carry out his orders.

"All done," Adams said.

I went down on one knee and, using my thumb and forefinger on the sealed edge, plucked the bag from the tiny saltwater pool. Adams snapped a dozen more photos as I manipulated the contents so he could document the two devices inside.

I'm no expert on cell phones, but these both looked just like mine—the latest Apple had to offer. Though they could have been older models for all I knew. They both appeared to be dry, a miracle given what they'd been through. I made a mental note to find out what brand of sandwich bags Toby Bledsoe had bought.

"Come on," Admiral Reese said. "Our best IT guys should be in my office by now."

I thanked the two people who'd bravely stayed by my side while I opened the box. I'd been reasonably certain they weren't risking their lives, but they hadn't been. It took real guts to stick it out, and I said so as I shook their hands. Despite their bravery, this was as far as they could go. Whatever was on those phones was a matter of national security. I wasn't even sure the admiral had high enough clearance to listen, and his IT people sure as hell didn't, but I'd take responsibility for any breach in protocol. In the field, agents often had to make decisions that skirted conventional wisdom.

"How far out is my forensics team?" We'd left a couple of Marines to guard the lunch box until it could be examined by people who knew what they were doing, then made our way through a rabbit warren to the upper reaches of the carrier. I congratulated myself for recognizing the short hallway leading to the admiral's office. If I stayed on this floating city long enough, I might actually learn my way around.

"I checked with Captain Hervey. They should be arriving on Guam about now. Another couple of hours to shuttle out here." He held the door to his office open for me and the bag I carried with both hands. A pair of seamen snapped to attention, saluting as we entered. The admiral returned the salute. I wasn't ready to let go of my charges, so I simply nodded. My rank wasn't lost on the recruits. Just about everyone in the military outranked these two. They appeared confused as for how to handle my curt nod until the admiral ordered them to stand at ease.

"Captain Hervey assures me you two are the best communications people on board," the admiral said as he took his seat behind his desk.

I sank into one of the plush leather visitor chairs facing him, cradling the package in my lap.

The two didn't miss a beat. "Yes, sir," they said in unison.

"Good." He waved his hand in my direction. "This is Major Sloan, Air Force Intelligence. Do what she asks and keep your mouth shut. That's an order."

Major Megan Sloan
USS Ronald Reagan
Saturday 22:00 Zulu (Sunday 08:00 ChST)

"**I**'ve got two cell phones here," I said, holding the bag up for them to see. "Someone went to a lot of trouble to make sure these survived the crash, which makes me think there's something on them we need to see or hear." The sailors both nodded, following my line of thinking. "I need you to find whatever it is, and I need it yesterday."

"Yes, ma'am." The one on the left, Seaman Pope, stepped forward. "Can we have a look?"

I glanced at the admiral. "I'd really like to fingerprint these first. Is there someone on board who can do that?"

He raised one eyebrow and reached for the phone on his desk. "I can find out."

"I won't take them out of the bag, promise." Seaman Pope held his hand out.

I should have asked Petty Officer Adams about the fingerprinting. He would have known. I don't know why, but I felt as if every minute counted, and I'd unnecessarily wasted too many already. If they didn't have fingerprinting capability on board, I had two choices—forget about it and move on or wait for my forensics crew to arrive. I had every reason to believe I knew who owned these two phones, but what if I was wrong? What if they *did* belong to the flight crew, but someone else had used them in the minutes or hours before the plane went down?

"Okay," I said, handing the plastic container over. As I listened with one ear while admiral Reese tried to pin down a fingerprint expert, the other sailor, Mitchell, according to his nametag, stepped up to examine the phones, too.

"If they're password protected, we're screwed," Mitchell said.

"We can pull the SIM cards. See what we can get from them." Pope turned the bag over. Seeing the scrap of paper at the same time the sailors did, I sprang from my seat like someone had lit my ass on fire. The three of us stood, heads together, over the package.

"I hope it's the passwords."

I silently agreed with Mitchell. These two might not be able to access the phones without the passwords, but I knew people who could. It might not be legal, but screw legalities. My gut told me lives were at stake and some invisible clock was ticking. These two getting the information off the devices might be the difference between preventing another disaster or not.

"Sure would make things simpler," Pope said.

"Chief Petty Officer Adams is on the way with his camera. He's bringing Petty Officer Rodriguez and her fingerprint kit with him."

Petty Officer Rodriguez was younger than I'd anticipated, with long, dark hair she kept in a regulation bun. She had a wide face with stunning eyes, full lips, and flawless skin. If she was lonely, it was because she chose to be. From the way Chief Petty Officer Adams looked at her, I guessed he had more reasons than just wanting to document this next step.

We all gathered around the admiral's conference table a few minutes later. Rodriguez had brought along a box of latex gloves, so we all gloved up, just in case. I slid one phone from the bag and handed it over. She worked quickly but, to my trained eye, missed nothing. When she finished with the first one, I handed her the other phone. We'd all decided the two four-digit numbers scrawled on the scrap of paper were indeed the passwords for the phones. The only thing they'd forgotten was to tell us which went with which. Luckily, we had a fifty-fifty chance of getting it right the first time, so we weren't likely to get locked out.

I handed the fingerprinted phone to Seaman Pope. In a few seconds, the black screen lit up. He tapped the screen, which brought up the password screen.

"Which one?" Pope asked.

I shrugged. "You pick."

Tap. Tap. Tap. Tap.

"I'm in!"

I leaned forward, eager to see.

"Well, look what we have here."

Liam Donovan

Gulfstream G650 over the North Pacific Ocean

Saturday 22:00 Zulu (Noon HST – 08:00 ChST)

Liam shifted, silently cursing a seat that had long since lost any cushioning qualities it might have had. He guessed he should be grateful his six-foot-two frame wasn't crammed into a steerage class seat on a crowded airliner. He'd been there, done his time with less "important" government officials who didn't rate a ride on a Gulfstream 650 but nevertheless were given a security detail. Several agents had actually offered to take his place on this trip, something he couldn't understand. Who the hell wanted to spend a day of their life enclosed in an aluminum tube thirty-thousand feet, give or take, in the air with a delegation of lawmakers who hated each other's guts? Then have the privilege of protecting them for a week from the crazy people they were scheduled to meet with—all of whom would rather kill them than hear a thing they had to say.

Yeah, it was a plum assignment. *My ass.*

He should have taken one of the other agents up on the offer to stay home, but the only thing he could think of worse than this gig was the tedium of working in the WFO, the Washington Field Office, assessing the deluge of domestic threats America's lawmakers received each day. Ninety-nine percent of them came from nuts who couldn't tie their own shoelaces, much less carry out an attack. Of the last one percent, 99 percent of those were already locked up. Didn't leave much to do but stand between them and their targets and hope to God you could pick the crazies out of a crowd and react before they got a shot off or blew themselves, and everyone else, up. When he looked at his situation from that angle, a ride to the tropical paradise of Guam on a private jet and a few hours of beach and sun time in exchange for the possibility of ending up dead sounded like a pretty good deal, or at least a better deal than the one responsible for him being loaned out to the Secret Service in the first place.

After his last mission in the desert, he'd needed a change of pace, and he'd gotten it. A day in the life of a Secret Service agent began slow and ended slower with a whole lot of boredom in between. When it got down to it, he'd become a professional traveler. His life consisted of airports and hotels, long, mind-numbing flights, and a steady diet of questionable food. His job was to stay alert and to protect his charges with his life, if necessary. What a gig.

He'd like to blame his current situation on someone else, but, like Jimmy Buffet, he'd gone through the stages of denial and arrived at the truth—he had no one to blame but himself. He'd screwed up and people had died—for nothing. He'd failed to accomplish their mission, possibly endangering more lives, and done the unforgivable—he'd left one of their own behind. Never mind he'd seen Sloan take a couple of rounds and had been convinced she was dead. He shouldn't have left her there, even if retrieving her would have meant they'd both be dead. He'd acted within the parameters of the mission when he should have ignored orders and done what he knew was right.

But he hadn't, and the decision had cost him everything he'd ever loved.

He deserved to be bored.

From his seat in the forward cabin, he had a good view of everything from the cockpit door to the rear of the aircraft. They'd left Andrews Air Force Base with two flight crews, two cabin attendants, and eight members of the Senate and House Armed Services committees as well as the deputy secretary of state. Add in himself and

Mike, and the Gulfstream 650 was at near capacity—thus the refueling stop in Hawaii. No one had left the plane, and no one had come aboard, which meant they were drawing closer and closer to the tipping point for civility.

Hearing a door in forward cabin opening, he looked up from the novel he'd brought along to keep his brain from turning to mush. Normally, monitoring this routine in-flight stuff would fall on his partner's shoulders while Liam kept an eye on their charges. They weren't going anywhere, but he'd seen occasions when too much togetherness got the better of even the most levelheaded travelers.

Politicians and government bureaucrats were the worst of the lot. He could hear them talking in mid-cabin where the bulk of them had decided to ride. It was only a matter of time before an argument broke out. They had the standard issue of assholes, one per, but when it came to opinions, they'd all been given more than their share and felt it their God-given right to force it on anyone within hearing distance.

Unfortunately, Liam's partner had come down with a stomach malady—probably the same one that had been running rampant through Mike's household the last few weeks. Every one of his four kids and his wife had succumbed one after the other. He'd begged for this assignment, saying he needed a break from cleaning up bodily fluids at home. Shortly after takeoff, he'd commandeered the lavatory in the forward cabin, coming out for short periods to rehydrate before going back in for another round.

The lavatory door swung open, and a pale Mike Woodrow emerged.

I swear to God if he gives me whatever bug he has, I'll personally toss his ass out over the ocean. Liam waved at his partner.

Mike gave him a weak smile then began rummaging in the galley compartments. The cabin steward, Jeannie, he thought, who had been taking a break in one of the seats at the rear of the forward cabin, rushed to help.

Thank God the advance team was already on the ground. All he had to do was get these people to Guam alive.

Major Megan Sloan
USS Ronald Reagan
Saturday 22:30 Zulu (Sunday 08:30 ChST)

"Whose phone is it?

"Says Toby Bledsoe."

"Check the photos." I'd had a few minutes to think about what I would do if I'd been in the pilot's shoes and determined to get a message to someone. "Maybe he made a video."

"Bingo!" Pope showed me the screen. Toby Bledsoe hadn't taken many photos, but he had made a video.

I snatched the phone from the seaman's hand. I wanted this to be the answer we'd been looking for, but it could be anything from a suicide note to his last will and testament. How much time had Bledsoe had to prepare this? Hell, for all I knew, he could have recorded this a week ago, planning all along how he'd get it into the right hands.

"All done with this one." Petty Officer Rodriguez leaned back in her chair. "What do you want me to do with the prints?"

I eyed the stacks of carefully labeled evidence. "Leave them. My team should be here soon. I'll have them take custody."

The young woman stood and began to pack her equipment. "Thank you, ma'am. If you don't have anything else for me, I'll return to my duty station."

Rising, I smiled and shook her hand. "I should be thanking you, on behalf of everyone on that plane."

"Glad to be of service, ma'am." With a smart salute for her superiors, she lifted the case she'd carried in and headed for the door.

"Want me to look at this one?" Seaman Mitchell pointed to the second phone.

I nodded. "Would you, please?"

He scooped it up and, after a quick glance at the piece of paper containing the passwords, tapped the screen a few times. "Battery is low on this one." He tapped some more. "Whoa. Lots of pictures. Looks like they're mostly of the cockpit. Switches. Screenshots."

"Any videos?"

"Looks like one." He paused while he tapped away again. "It's a short one. Less than a minute."

"Can you tell whose phone it is?" My gut told me I knew the answer, but the voice of reason in the recesses of my brain said I didn't know shit.

A few more taps and finger swipes. "Skip Bernard."

I let out the breath I'd been holding. The release of tension in my shoulders felt better than executing a perfect three-point landing. "Can you download everything to a thumb drive for me?"

"Sure can. It'll take a minute, and we'll need a computer. You want them both on the same drive or two different ones?"

"Different ones, please." My team could copy and distribute as needed, but, for now, I wanted to be able to access them separately.

"You can use my computer." Admiral Reese stood and stretched his long frame.

"Yes, sir." Seaman Mitchell hustled to the admiral's desk. "May I?" he asked, indicating the plush leather desk chair.

"Make yourself at home, sailor."

A big smile crossed the seaman's face. "Yes, sir!"

Seaman Pope joined his co-worker at the desk. After some consultation, he left on a mission to find a couple of empty thumb drives and the cords they would need to connect the phones to the admiral's computer.

"What do you think is on the videos?" Reese asked.

"I know what I want to be on there, but it could be anything." I went through the possibilities I'd come up with. I was itching to watch them, but I wasn't going to take any chances. I wanted copies made. I knew all too well how important it was to preserve evidence.

Pope returned a few minutes later. Judging from the sweat on his brow and his labored breathing, he'd double-timed it to wherever he'd gone and back. I appreciated his effort, and I said so. My anxiety increased with every passing minute, and my gut was telling me time was not on our side.

Admiral Reese settled on the wide, dark-leather sofa anchoring the casual conversation area opposite the conference table. Too keyed up to sit, I paced while the two communications experts did their thing. When they disconnected the second of the two phones from the computer, I stopped pacing.

"Here you go, ma'am."

I took the thumb drives from Seaman Pope's outstretched hand. "Thank you both. You can leave the phones on the desk."

"You're welcome, ma'am. If you need anything else, Admiral Reese knows where to find us."

"I don't have to remind you what you saw and heard today never happened." The admiral stood to return the sailors' salutes. The fresh-faced recruits hastily affirmed their ignorance of today's goings-on.

Halfway out the door, Mitchell turned. With a smart salute to me and a grin on his face, he said, "Nice to have not met you, ma'am."

He was as handsome as the devil, and, judging from his smirk, he knew it, too. Women probably fell at his feet. I wasn't going to be one of them. Returning the salute and a smile of my own, I said, "Likewise, Seaman Mitchell."

I was still smiling when Reese reminded me why we were there. "Want to watch those videos now?"

My fist was clenched so tight around the thumb drives, they were digging into my palms. This was the moment I'd been waiting for.

but I wasn't sure I really wanted to hear what the dead pilots had to say.

"Might as well." I gestured to his desk. "May I?"

Major Megan Sloan
USS Ronald Reagan
Saturday 23:00 Zulu (Sunday 09:00 ChST)

I paused the recording and slumped in the admiral's desk chair, letting Toby Bledsoe's message settle into my consciousness. After identifying himself and his first officer, he'd uttered the three words no pilot ever wanted to speak, "We've been hijacked."

"Is that what you thought he'd say?"

Reese had perched on the edge of his desk and angled his body so he could see the computer screen. I glanced up at him.

"Honestly? I thought there was a small chance he'd gone off his rocker and brought the plane down himself." I waved a hand at the pilot's face, frozen on the screen. "Still could be a ruse to cover up a suicide so whoever his beneficiary is can claim his insurance."

"Cynical, much?"

"I've seen people do some crazy shit, Admiral, so yeah, he's going to have to convince me."

"Let's see it, then."

I moved the cursor over the Play button and clicked Enter. The video continued. We watched it straight through twice before I accessed Skip Bernard's photos and video. The first officer didn't have much to add to Bledsoe's recounting of their situation. He'd let the photos he'd taken speak for themselves.

"Got to admire them," Reese said as Wilson's video ended. "They knew they were going to die, but they didn't go on about it. They were more concerned with making sure someone knew what had happened so no one else would have to go through what they were experiencing."

"Military," I said. "Both of them were Air Force before going over to the other side."

"Officers and heroes to the very end."

"Yeah." We were still pondering the admiral's statement when the phone on his desk buzzed. I stared at the image frozen on the computer while he answered the call. The tap of his foot on the chair I occupied got my attention.

"Your team just landed."

It was about time. I was hoping the investigators from the National Transportation Safety Administration (NTSB), who were supposed to be part of the group sent out from Washington, could glean something useful from the wreckage. I wanted to talk to them before they went to work. "Mind if they come here first?"

He spoke into the receiver again. "Have someone escort them to my office, ASAP." He listened for a few seconds then said, "Take them to the hangar deck. I'll be right there." He returned the handset to its cradle and stood.

"Something wrong?"

"Depends on your point of view. There's a chopper full of reporters coming in."

I grimaced. Whoever was behind this and the other disappearances had finally made a mistake, and the last thing we needed was for them to find out about the videos. I'd hoped we'd have more time before the camera-toting vultures found us. We needed to figure out what or who had brought Global 2455 down. "I don't need to tell you how much damage they would do if they got ahold of the pilot's videos."

"No, you don't. I'll keep them as far away from my office as possible. Any objection to letting them see the wreckage we've brought aboard?"

"I wish we could put them back on their chopper and be done with them, but I can only imagine the stories they'd write if we did."

"They're coming in a military transport, so someone up the chain of command authorized their trip. We've got to give them something."

He was right. Throwing them overboard wasn't an option. I nodded. "Show them the wreckage. No photos though. Not until the NTSB guys have a look. Better let them make the decision on what can be photographed and what can't." If I ever found out who had authorized the press junket, I'd put the fear of God into them. I sighed, letting my frustration go. The reporters were here. We were going to have to dance with them. "They're going to want details."

"I'll talk to them myself—give them some soundbites without saying anything." One corner of his mouth lifted. "In other words, bullshit them."

I smiled. "Do they teach you how to bullshit the media in admiral school?"

"They sure as shit do."

It felt good to laugh, even if it was strained. We sobered quickly. "Do you need your office? If you can point us to another place we can work, I'll get out of your hair."

"My office is yours, Major Sloan. Even if I didn't have orders from the Pentagon, this is the best place for you and your team to headquarter. The room's secure. My assistant, Lt. Franklin, will be at your disposal. Just tell him what you need."

I'd met the lieutenant when we came in. I had no doubt he was up to the task. Anyone who could keep a rear admiral in line knew how to get things done. "You're sure we won't be in the way?"

"I'm sure. Lt. Franklin will know how to find me if I'm needed."

A few minutes after Reese left, Lt. Franklin led my team in. I knew most of them, Jude and Sanchez had made the trip, along with several other analysts who had been hand-picked by Jude. A parade of people I didn't know introduced themselves as they filed into the office. The NTSB had sent four investigators. TSA had sent two, and the FAA had thrown in a couple of their own. I was glad I'd had a look at the video before they got here. Once they got their hands on it, God only knew how long it would be before anyone else saw it.

In addition, Col. Rodgers had sent one of the FBI's premier medical examiners, Simon Jefferies. We shook hands.

"Thanks for coming."

"It was quite a trip," Jefferies said. "This is my first time on an aircraft carrier. Takes some getting used to."

"If you go off on your own, best leave a trail of breadcrumbs," I joked.

"Or a blood trail? Follow the dotted line?" He mocked pricking his thumb, then laughed.

ME humor. I cracked a smile and turned to Jude. The team members knew we'd found the phones but hadn't heard what we'd discovered on the devices. Jude, bless his geeky heart, set to work so we could all watch at once on the large monitor mounted on the wall at the end of the conference table. In the meantime, Lt. Franklin arranged for coffee and sandwiches to be brought in. I didn't feel much like eating, but I knew better than to neglect my physical needs. It was like missing a foul ball with two outs. The mistake always comes back to bite you in the ass later on, so I forced down half a sandwich and got to know some of the newcomers.

A couple of the NTSB people were bomb experts and had worked some of the more prominent incidents. No doubt they were good at what they did, but they were wasting their time here. I kept my opinion to myself, knowing they'd come to the same conclusion soon enough themselves. Others were experts on the type of stresses capable of causing a plane to come apart in the air. Since I didn't know if the plane had come apart before or after hitting the water, I figured they might add something to the investigation from a manufacturing standpoint. Anything that made airframes sturdier was good by me.

The TSA folks seemed a bit defensive to me, and rightfully so. They were the Transportation Security Administration, *security* being the operative word. I knew for a fact someone or some organization had brought Global 2455 down, which meant they'd failed their primary mission somewhere along the way. They weren't happy when they arrived, and I didn't expect their attitudes to change once they saw the video.

All of them knew about our task force but, like most people, thought we were nutjobs who had found another creative way to spend the taxpayers' money.

I excused myself to check on Jude's progress. Once he had it all set up, I asked him to step outside with me while I made a CYA call to Colonel Rodgers. So far, only two people had seen the videos, myself and Rear Admiral Reese. I knew the colonel had cleared every last one of the people inside, but that was before the videos had surfaced. Even the colonel hadn't seen them.

Liam Donovan
Gulfstream G650
Saturday 23:00 Zulu (13:00 HST – Sunday 11:00 WKT)

It had been a matter of time, and, judging from the raised voices coming from mid-cabin, time was up. Liam stood, stretching as best he could in the confines of the plane. It was times like these when he regretted his career change the most. In his former line of work, an argument between co-workers could get the entire team killed, so, out of necessity and a will to live, they'd learned to listen, evaluate, and compromise. Out of habit, his hand went to his primary weapon, a Heckler and Koch HK45 with a custom-built grip. He had no plans to use it, but past experience told him it would be tempting. How, in the name of everything holy, were these people supposed to negotiate a nuclear arms treaty with a hostile nation if they couldn't get along with each other for a few measly hours?

"Boggles the mind," he mumbled as he made his way to the next cabin where most of his charges were engaged in a heated argument over God knew what. Could be anything from the arms treaty to which restaurant in D.C. served the best calamari.

Feet braced shoulder-width apart, he crossed his arms over his chest. His pose exposed the badge clipped to his belt and, beyond, the butt of his holstered weapon. As a Spec Ops team leader for over a decade, he'd developed a scowl his team members would have recognized as his *shut-up* expression, but not a single one of these people indicated they'd even noticed him. To them, he was the hired help. As invisible as the flight attendant who, at that very moment, stepped from the rear galley with a tray of fresh drinks for the group.

146

Airman Charlotte Williams, Charlie for short, glanced up and made eye contact. She raised her eyebrows in question, indicating the drinks on her tray. Liam tilted his head and shrugged. Wasn't any of his business how sloshed they got. As long as they didn't go for each other's throats with the toothpicks sticking out of the fancy little snacks they'd been munching on before the argument broke out, he didn't give a damn. He just wished they'd tone it down a little. The bickering was giving him a headache.

He couldn't stand here forever. Someone had to keep an eye on the cockpit door, and since he'd seen his partner duck into the forward latrine for the umpteenth time, the job had to be Liam's first priority. Charlie set the last glass down in front of the dude with the bad toupee, gathered his empty drink glass and straightened. He'd seen her before. He'd accompanied the vice president on an overseas trip and Charlie had been one of the flight attendants on the trip. At the roll of her eyes, Liam's lips quirked up on one side. He'd pretty much given up on relationships, but he hadn't given up on screwing. Maybe if there was time once they got these idiots to Guam, he'd ask her out for a drink. Hell, he'd even spring for dinner if it meant seeing her out of uniform. The smile she flashed him before turning and heading into to the galley with a bunch of dirty glasses made him think she might be open to his proposition.

As long as she didn't want more. He had nothing against relationships in general. In fact, he'd tried one once. Though it was officially over, having ended about as badly as was possible, he hadn't quite managed to purge it from his soul. A part of him would always belong to Megan Sloan, and, unfortunately, the part she owned was the part every woman he'd dated since said he didn't have. That's why his interactions with women were strictly of the physical variety these days.

He'd almost made it to his seat when Airman Jeannie Randall, the flight attendant from the forward cabin, approached. "Agent Donovan?"

He nodded. They'd been introduced before leaving D.C., but they'd had no reason to speak since. "Is Mike, I mean, Agent Woodward all right?"

"I don't know. I think so, but he's not the reason I'm here."

Okay. "You need something?"

"Not me." She pointed a thumb over her shoulder. "Captain Davis asked for Agent Woodward. I told him he was sick. He said to send you instead."

"Any idea what he wants?"

She shook her head. "None. He just said to bring you up to the cockpit."

Behind me, the argument continued. "I can find it on my own. Why don't you go see if you can give Charlie a hand? Mike and I can take care of ourselves."

Her grimace said she'd rather feed a pond full of gators than help out with this group of passengers, but wisely, she didn't argue. "Yes, sir." She eased past him. "Just tap on the door. They'll let you in."

He gave his partner the one-finger salute as he passed the forward lavatory. The man had excellent timing, though being sick on a trans-Pacific flight ranked right up there with the things Liam could live without experiencing. He considered dragging Mike's ass out to deal with their undignified dignitaries. He'd do it if it didn't mean exposing himself to whatever wicked germs the man had. It would serve their passengers right if they caught whatever plague the agent had brought on board. Maybe they could pass it on to Choi Min-ho. There was a bastard who deserved a plague.

At his knock, the first officer opened the door. Liam felt like a giant trying to squeeze into a troll's house. There was barely enough room for the two pilots in the confined space. He'd met these two when he came aboard, but introduced himself again anyway. "Agent Liam Donovan—Secret Service."

The one in the left seat glanced at him before returning his attention to the instrument panel. "Steve Davis," he said. "And this is Todd Wilkerson."

"You wanted to see me?"

"You know anything about flying?" Davis asked.

"Used to be Air Force Intelligence before I left the field. Took this gig with the Secret Service. Haven't flown much since. Why?"

"We have a situation."

Liam Donovan
Gulfstream G650
Saturday 23:05 Zulu (Sunday 11:05 WKT)

Liam's hand tightened on the back of the pilot's seat. "Exactly what kind of situation are we talking about?"

"It seems we've lost control of the aircraft."

Liam's attention shifted from the pilot to the first officer who had delivered the bad news. His gaze swept the console awash with colorful digital displays. At first glance, everything appeared perfectly normal. "What are you talking about?"

"About ten minutes ago, we drifted twenty-two degrees off course," Captain Davis said. "I disengaged the autopilot in order to make a correction, but the aircraft didn't respond to my commands. We tried reprogramming the FMS, the Flight Management System, but it seems we've been locked out."

"You've been on autopilot for how long?"

"Since we reached cruising altitude about ten minutes after clearing Honolulu tower."

"You're sure the correct flight plan was fed into the computer?"

"Checked and double checked. We were headed for Guam up until a few minutes ago."

Liam wiped his sweating palms on his pant legs. "Where are we headed now?"

"North Korea," Major Wilkerson said.

"You're kidding me, right?"

"I wish we were." Captain Davis pointed to a longitude and latitude displayed on one of the computer screens. "Those coordinates are for Pyongyang."

He wouldn't call what he felt fear—more like dread. What the hell? Choi Min-ho really had gone off the deep end if he thought he could get away with hijacking a plane full of United States officials on a diplomatic mission. "Are you sure?"

"Positive."

"And you can't change course?"

Both pilots shook their heads. "We've tried, and we'll keep trying," Davis said. "What we want to know is what to tell the passengers, and who's going to do the telling."

"Well, shit."

"My sentiments, exactly," Wilkerson said.

Liam studied the console. It had been a while since he'd occupied a cockpit, and he'd never flown a Gulfstream. Davis and Wilkerson were excellent pilots or they wouldn't be flying congressmen around. Instinctively, he sought out and scrutinized the various instruments pilots relied on for accurate data—data that meant the difference between life and death. As best as he could tell, everything was normal except for those damned coordinates.

"What's the fuel situation?"

"It's pushing the envelope, but if we remain at cruising altitude, we should make it."

The Air Force had taught him to fly anything with wings or rotors, all part of their version of spy training, but he'd spent more time on the ground than in the air. Most of Liam's ground time had been in various desert countries. His experience with oceans amounted to flying over them, and those times had been few and far between. "If we can override the computers, is there anyplace to land this thing?" He knew shit about the Pacific.

"Wake Island," Davis said. "We overflew their airspace about an hour ago."

"Did you contact the tower there?"

"We did, but we tried to hail them just before you came in. Either no one was in the tower or our radio is out of commission."

"Don't they have someone in the tower around the clock?"

"Not on Wake. They don't get a lot of traffic, just military on the way to Japan and the occasional airliner having trouble."

"See if you can raise them again. We're in a shitstorm of trouble here."

His mind raced while both pilots futilely sent Mayday calls out to Wake Island and anyone else who might be in hearing range. "What about the waypoints?"

"What about them?" Wilkerson asked. "The data link sends our position information at the required intervals."

"Assuming it's working, what happens when we fail to report the next scheduled waypoint? Or we report an unscheduled waypoint?"

"In a perfect world, we'd get a nastygram from Oakland directing us to return to our previous course," Davis said, "but this is far from a perfect world."

They were about to test the Big Sky Theory, which stated two randomly flying objects were unlikely to collide given their size relative to the space occupied. In other words, the chances of two tiny aircraft flying around over the vast North Pacific Ocean colliding with each other was astronomical. He zeroed in on the altimeter. *Jesus, 45,000 feet.* The altitude certainly lessened the chance of a midair collision. Most aircraft cruised at a much lower altitude. "Any way besides our non-functioning radio to contact the outside world?"

Wilkerson looked up from studying the instrument panel. "This thing is state-of-the-art. All the bells and whistles, but they're all automated, computerized. All we do is sit here and look pretty. We used to fly planes. Now we're the backup system in case the computers fail."

"What, exactly, happens when you disengage the autopilot? Does it show to be off? Could the switch have malfunctioned?"

"Let's show him, Dave."

Captain Davis gripped the yoke with a firm hand while the first officer flipped the offending switch to the Off position. "Here goes," he said as he eased the yoke to the right. The plane should have banked but remained perfectly level and on its prescribed course.

"Want me to re-engage the autopilot?" Wilkerson asked.

"Doesn't seem to be any reason to," Donovan said.

Davis rested his hands in his lap.

"Still could be the switch. Or a circuit breaker of some sort."

"Neither of those would account for the change in direction." The captain pointed at the latitude and longitude displayed on the computer screen. "The computer didn't just pick those out of thin air."

He had a point. Given the nature of our human cargo and the mission they were on, their new destination couldn't be a coincidence. Besides, he didn't believe in coincidences. No one in the intelligence community did. "My partner has a satphone. Unless something is jamming us, we should be able to call someone, but we need to find a way to override the computers before help gets here."

"Why?" Wilkerson asked.

"Because there's no way in hell the president is going to let North Korea get ahold of the people on board this plane. Unless we can bring this thing down safely on our own, we're all going for one last swim."

Liam Donovan
Gulfstream G650 over the North Pacific Ocean
Saturday 23:07 Zulu (Sunday 11:07 WKT)

"The tower at Andersen will be expecting to hear from us soon."

Donovan let Capt. Davis' statement sink in. Lots of folks were expecting them to land at Andersen Air Force Base on Guam. Their no-show wouldn't go unnoticed. The country had been on a collision course with North Korea for years, and nothing the administration tried had changed the status quo. It looked like they'd become a pawn in the latest game between the rival nations. All communications built into the aircraft had been disabled.

"They'll start looking for us soon. They've got Global Hawks at Guam." The unmanned ISR planes were capable of searching a wide area and would probably be the first option, followed by manned SAR, search and rescue aircraft. Once they were located, he fully expected they would be shadowed by armed aircraft.

Davis' head bobbed up and down.

"And when they find us," Liam continued, "all hell is going to break loose." He could see it now—an international incident destined to make the Bay of Pigs look like a friendly game of chess—and they'd be the pawn both sides fought over.

"You think they'll shoot us down?" Wilkerson asked.

"Not immediately, no." Liam stood, hunched over in the cramped space. "If they haven't noticed we're missing, they will soon. With a little luck, the satphone we brought along will work. We need to let someone know what's going on. I'm sure they'll try diplomatic channels first, but I can guarantee you one thing—we'll never set foot on North Korean soil. President Gilchrist will never let it happen."

He was certain Choi Min-ho didn't want them, either. If he reprogrammed the computer once, he could do it again, only the next time he might dump them in the ocean—just to prove he could. Liam had no doubt this was just another one of the insane leader's games, like the missile launches and hydrogen bomb tests he'd been conducting with increasing frequency. He was nothing more than a street bully, flexing his muscles, daring someone to take him on. This time, he might have succeeded. Gilchrist had been rattling his sabers about North Korea for months. Something like this might be the excuse the president needed to grind the little bastard under his heel.

"I'll be right back." Liam exited the cockpit and was surprised and relieved to see his partner sitting in the seat Liam had vacated hours ago. "You're looking better."

"I think I might live. Sorry to desert you for so long."

Glancing toward the rear of the plane, Liam said, "The natives seemed to have calmed down a bit, but we've got bigger problems." He pressed his lips into a thin line for a moment. "Grab the sat-phone, will ya? And come with me."

Mike's smile faded. He grabbed the hard plastic case resting beneath the seat and stood. "What's going on?"

"Not here." He gestured toward the cockpit. "In the office."

In a matter of minutes, they'd filled Mike in. The veteran agent, already pale from his bout with a stomach virus, went ghost white as their situation sank in.

"Our phone should work." Liam popped open the waterproof case designed to protect the heavily encrypted phone and every gadget they could possibly need including a solar charger and a watertight bag for the phone itself then removed the phone from its slot in the foam-rubber liner.

"Who you going to call?" Mike asked.

There were a few key phone numbers programmed into the device. Liam stared at them, his thumb hovering over the keypad while another number flashed across his brain—one he'd tried to forget. One the owner probably hoped he'd forgotten. If there was anyone in the world who could get them out of this mess, it was Megan Sloan.

From the minute he'd understood what was happening, he'd known she would be brought in on this. Might as well cut to the chase—go directly to the person most likely to help them.

He'd tried to forget her. He'd tried to forget the way she felt in his arms. Tried to forget how it felt to move inside her. Tried to tell himself he was better off without her. She sure as hell was better off without him. It was the one truth he clung to even as he followed her career. It wasn't difficult to do. Like him, she'd retired from field-work, but unlike him, she hadn't given up on the mission.

Christ! He'd left her for dead. Every step he'd taken away from her had been like a Hellfire missile straight to his heart, but others had depended on him, and, by God, he'd seen her take several rounds to the gut. Rescuing her would have meant endangering the rest of the team. It was his call to make, and he'd made it. And lived with the guilt ever since.

God only knew how, but she'd survived—and like a phoenix, she had risen from the desert floor and made her way across the border. A roving patrol had found her. They'd been miles and days away from medical help, but the medic they had with them had kept her alive long enough.

Liam was one of the few people who knew what she'd gone through, and the only one who knew what she'd lost. What they'd lost.

He'd earned her hatred, but as much as he still loved her, a part of him hated her, too. He'd never have let her go on the mission if he'd known. The mission had been doomed from the beginning. If they'd only had to contend with the Iranian army, they would have recovered the technology and gotten the hell out of there. Relying on the intelligence they had, they'd walked into a situation they weren't prepared for. Mercenaries had taken possession of the package they'd come to get. Well-armed and even better trained, they weren't going to give it up. And they hadn't.

He'd lost two team members besides Sloan on the failed mission, and barely escaped with his life. He'd served the last few months of his contract stateside. Megan had been transferred to Walter Reed Medical Center in D.C. He'd made a pest of myself, asking to see her every day after his CO cut him loose, only to be turned away. He'd finally given up when a couple of MPs met him at the door one day and escorted him to the base commander's office. He'd been forced to accept she didn't want to see him. Thank God she wouldn't recognize the phone number.

She wouldn't piss on him if he was on fire, but he knew Megan. She wouldn't let the rest of the people on this plane die—not if there was a chance in hell of preventing it.

Mike nudged him with a fist to his arm. "I said, who are you going to call?"

"The last person on earth who wants to hear from me."

Major Megan Sloan
USS Ronald Reagan
Saturday 23:10 Zulu (09:10 ChST)

Jeffries summoned me to the sickbay where he'd been given access to an operating room in order to conduct the autopsies. If he wanted to see me, it meant he'd discovered something. As I followed Lt. Graves through the ship, I could only hope the FBI's top forensics man had found something useful.

Commander Schneider was waiting for me in the outer office. I knew she'd agreed to assist Jeffries, so her navy-blue scrubs didn't surprise me. "Major," she said. "Thanks for coming so soon."

"Your assistant said it was urgent."

She nodded. "I don't know about urgent, but it's definitely something we thought you should know about sooner rather than later. You up for seeing this, or would you rather I tell Jeffries you're out here?"

I didn't want to see a corpse mid-dissection, but I also didn't want to take Jeffries from his work. "I'm good. Lead the way."

This wasn't my first rodeo, but the smell was something I could have done without. I should have taken the good doctor up on her offer to fetch Jeffries for me, but it was too late. I buried my nose in the crook of my elbow, and, keeping my gaze glued to the man wielding the scalpel, I soldiered on. "You rang?"

Simon Jeffries took one look at me and smiled behind the Plexiglas shielding his face. "Eau de dead body. You won't see it on any store shelf, so enjoy it while you can."

Medical examiner humor again. I rolled my eyes to let him know how unappreciated his comment was since I had no intention of lowering my arm so he could see my frown.

"Okay," he relented. "I won't keep you. Just wanted to let you know these folks didn't drown."

I raised my eyebrows. I'd sort of assumed they'd been knocked unconscious when the plane hit the water and drowned. Guess that was what I got for making assumptions.

"There is no obvious trauma to the bodies to indicate death by a sudden stop. It's amazing what smacking against an immovable object can do to bones, not to mention soft tissue. The ocean surface wouldn't be any more welcoming to a body dropping from thirty-thousand feet than a concrete sidewalk—thus I expected more trauma."

I'd had much the same thoughts before I knew the pilots hadn't had any control over the plane, so if the airliner had glided into the water, why hadn't at least some of the passengers and crew made it out of the fuselage before it sank and began to break apart?

Jeffries continued. "I'm not an expert on plane crashes, but I've seen what's left of humans who fall out of the sky, and I'll tell you, these aren't typical."

"Okay," I said, signaling with my free hand for him to get on with it. The arm covering my nose and mouth had nearly reached its limit. I made a mental note to hit the free-weights harder next time I went to the gym.

"So, I asked myself, why didn't they make it out of the plane before it sank? All three corpses seem to be more or less able-bodied. Unless they were unconscious when the plane hit the water—in which case, they would have drowned. Only they didn't drown."

My blood felt like ice water circulating through my body. A shiver raced down my spine. If they'd been conscious, they and others would have tried to escape. If they'd been unconscious, they would have drowned. I connected the dots. "They were dead before they hit the water?"

"Looks that way. Any number of things could have happened to them—drugs, poison, either ingested or inhaled, depressurization of the cabin leading to asphyxia."

I thought about the sections of the fuselage I'd seen so far. If the cabin had lost pressure, the oxygen masks in the overhead compartments would have deployed, but they hadn't. On the pieces I'd seen, even the luggage compartments had still been closed—another indication the aircraft had experienced a relatively soft landing. Someone—whoever was responsible for taking down this plane—had not only managed to murder all the passengers in flight but had brought the plane down in a manner that virtually assured we would find the wreckage. I turned the new information over in my mind, but it made no sense. Who would do such a thing? And why?

Needing oxygen myself, I dropped my arm and filled my lungs with air. Putrid air being better than none at all. Every pilot knew the dangers of low oxygen levels. I'd been through the training, experienced the beginning stages of hypoxia, euphoria, tingling sensations, gasping for air, and hadn't fared well. I'd turned blue, vomited all over myself, and passed out. Thank God they'd gotten me out of there quick, or I might have suffered severe brain damage. Just thinking about the experience still gave me the chills. Thinking about a whole planeload of passengers deprived of oxygen made me sick to my stomach. "Crap."

I thanked him and got the hell out of there.

Major Megan Sloan
USS Ronald Reagan
Saturday 23:20 Zulu (Sunday 09:30 ChST)

Eager to hear what the team thought of the new information I'd gotten from Jeffries, I nodded at the admiral's gatekeeper as I passed his desk in the anteroom. I was halfway through the door when he stopped me.

"They're putting a call through for you. You can take it out here if you want."

"Can you forward it to the admiral's desk?"

"Yes, ma'am. I'll put it right through."

Sanchez was reaching for the phone when I finally made it through the door. "That's for me," I said. My assistant picked up the handset, handing it to me as he vacated the desk. I sank into the soft leather chair. "Sloan," I said.

"Megan."

The familiar voice from my past shot right past my defenses, and, in an instant, I was back in Iraq, face down, breathing sand while my life, my future, painted the desert crimson.

I tightened my hand on the handset and let my chin sink to my chest. It was a good thing I was sitting or the abdominal pain my therapist said was all in my head would have brought me to my knees.

"Megan. Are you there? It's me. Liam."

Like I wouldn't know his voice. Straightening, I took a deep breath and wished I'd taken the call at the lieutenant's desk. I didn't want any witnesses to this conversation, but no one gets everything they want. If they did, the man on the other end, Liam Donovan, would be dead. "You have some nerve," I said into the phone.

"I know I have a lot to answer for," he said. Understatement of the century. "But this is important. I need your help."

Rot in Hell. "I'm in the middle of something. Gotta go."

Before I could end the call, he spoke the only words guaranteed to keep me on the line. "Drone Theory."

I pressed the phone to my ear again. "What did you say?"

"I said, The Drone Theory isn't a theory anymore."

Had someone leaked our discoveries to the news media? Had he heard a report and, out of some misguided memory of our past, thought he should let me know? "What makes you think so?"

"I need your help, Meg. I'm on a Gulfstream 650 somewhere north of Wake Island, and we've lost all control over the aircraft."

A jolt of adrenaline hit my system, and I bolted from the chair as Liam's once-beloved voice continued on, explaining his predicament in detail. Several members of the team were seated around the conference table. With a slash of my hand and a fierce expression on my face, I called for silence. Sanchez, knowing me as well as anyone, instantly recognized my frantic gesture and gained me the quiet I needed.

"Hold on," I said into the phone. "My team is here. I'm going to put you on speaker." Then I spoke to my team. "Everyone, listen up. This is Liam Donovan. He's Air Force Intelligence." I tapped the speakerphone button. "Liam. Start from the top again."

Sanchez slid a notepad and pen to me. I wasn't the only one making notes as my former lover reeled off details about their current position and the state of the aircraft he was on.

"Who's with you?" I asked.

"We've got the nuclear arms negotiating team on board. We're due to land at Andersen in an hour. All hell's going to break loose when we don't show up."

A chorus of expletives rose from my team members as Liam's words sank in. We all knew about the talks scheduled to take place in a few days. When I'd landed at Andersen on my way here, they'd been preparing for the influx of world leaders and their delegations.

"I need your help," Liam said. "*We* need your help."

Well, screw me sideways on Sunday. If Liam Donovan had been the last male on earth and drowning, I wouldn't have thrown him a rope. Leaving me for dead in the godforsaken desert was the least of the things I held against him. But he wasn't alone, and though he had to know how much I detested him, he also knew he could count on my honor to save the others if I could, even if it meant saving his sorry ass in the process. So he'd called me instead of his chain of command.

He'd always been a rule breaker. It was part of what had made him an excellent field operative—able to think on his feet and change course with the wind. It also made him an asshole.

"What the hell are we going to do, Meg?"

I felt the weight of a half-dozen eyes on me. No one called me Meg. No. One. I was Major Sloan or just Sloan. Even my mother called me Megan. The use of his pet name for me made the pain in my abdomen which, according to medical science, wasn't really there, even more acute. I pressed a hand to my stomach and let my gaze float over the pale faces ringing the table. "We're working on it," I told him, and hoped to God I'd spoken the truth.

Wait. How the hell was he calling from a hijacked plane when none of the others had been able to? "Are you on a satphone?"

"Yes. Encrypted. Secret Service issue for this mission."

My sources had told me he'd been loaned out to various intelligence groups since returning stateside. I hadn't cared enough to ask which ones. As long as our paths didn't cross, I was okay with living in the same city as him. As they say, know where your enemies are. "What's the status of your communications equipment?"

"Out. All of it. We've tried everything. If our signals are getting out, we can't hear their response."

"Give me a minute then I need to know everything."

I covered the mouthpiece with my hand. "Someone get Colonel Rodgers on the horn."

Jude's fingers flew across his laptop keyboard—doing what, I had no idea. I took a deep breath, willing my nerves to settle.

I dropped my hand. "Liam? My guys are on it. I know you don't want to see fighters, but we need eyes on you. If we know your location, it could help us locate who or what has taken control of your aircraft."

"You and I both know the president isn't going to let us land in North Korea."

"Yeah," I said. "Copy that."

His concerns were valid. Having a fighter escort would only underscore their fate if we couldn't figure out how to override whatever or whoever had hijacked their computer system.

"We haven't told our passengers yet."

"Better tell them before your escort gets there." I could only imagine what kind of shitstorm the news was going to churn up amongst his charges. Couldn't wish that kind of chaos on a more deserving guy. According to the list he'd given us, he'd have his hands full with a variety of reactions ranging from hysteria to, "Get out of my way, asshole. I'll fix this."

"Yeah. We'll get right on it. In the meantime, I'll leave this phone with the flight crew. They can tell you more than I can. Oh, and feel free to solve this little problem of ours before one of these distinguished dignitaries does something stupid."

"We're doing our best," I assured him. "It won't be much consolation if we fail, but tracking you in real time is the best break we've had yet."

"Glad to be of service."

I cringed at the saying, dripping with sarcasm. Early on in our relationship, I'd made the mistake of thanking him for a particularly spectacular orgasm. "Glad to be of service," had been his reply. It became a joke between us, guaranteed to make us both smile whenever he said it. As I listened to him instruct the pilots before he and his partner left the cockpit, I wondered if he'd used the phrase deliberately, or if it had just slipped out. My bet was on the former.

"Captain Davis speaking. Who's this?"

I identified myself then asked him to tell us everything from the moment they took off until now. Sanchez and I scribbled notes and asked questions while Jude tapped away at his keyboard. I knew from experience he could listen and work at the same time, so I didn't worry he'd miss something crucial. He stopped once to ask a question, proving my faith in him hadn't been misplaced. When the flight crew ran out of steam, I thanked them for staying calm and assured them we were doing everything we could to help them.

I took the call off speakerphone and handed the receiver to Sanchez. "Find someone to monitor this line. And call Gulfstream. Find out if they have a backdoor built into their systems. We need a way in. Someone else found one. We need to find one, too." If the president ended up shooting the plane down, he probably wouldn't want the world to know he'd done it. All the general public would know was the plane had gone missing like so many others had done lately, never to be heard from again. America would mourn the loss of their elected officials, but they'd move on as soon as the next crisis came along. "Make up something, anything, but whatever you do, don't tell them the real reason you're asking."

President Shane Gilchrist
White House, Washington, D.C.
Saturday 23:45 Zulu (19:45 EDT)

"What the hell do you mean, their plane is missing?" Shane Gilchrist sat up in bed, and rubbed sleep from his eyes.

The man on the other end of the telephone line, Chief of Staff Brett Loren, placated, "Mr. President, I'm just repeating what the base commander at Andersen told me. The plane carrying the members of the Senate and House Armed Services committees to Guam for the Asia-Pacific Nuclear Arms Summit never made contact with their tower. They should have checked in an hour ago. There's no sign of them, and they aren't responding to radio transmissions."

"Scramble some fighters." He swung his feet to the floor. "And find that plane!" Slamming the receiver down felt good, took some of the edge off the anger and, yes, fear flooding his system with adrenaline. If he was going to make it through the next twenty-four hours, he needed to calm down. He'd learned a few things since taking office a year ago, and one of them was not to make emotional decisions. Taking a deep breath, he held it to a count of ten before exhaling in one quick burst. Panic on his part wouldn't do anyone on the missing plane any good.

"Something wrong?" Meredith, his wife of twenty-five years, asked. She'd taught him the art of controlled breathing when he'd been Governor of Kentucky and had to deal with a series of coal-mine disasters. It was about the only thing she'd ever taught him. A former Miss Kentucky, she looked the part of First Lady, and as the daughter of a federal judge, she possessed the political savvy to play the role. She also knew the meaning of discretion and when to *not* see what was clear as crystal.

Nevertheless, it seemed he'd used the breathing technique at least once a day since taking office. If it wasn't one thing driving him to the brink of a panic attack, it was another. Why he'd ever wanted this bitch of a job, he couldn't imagine. Maybe he was a sadist. No, those were the ones who liked to hand out the punishment. Masochist. He was a masochist. Why else had he stayed married to Meredith the Merciless all these years?

No. Just thought I'd go for a fucking midnight walk. Damn, for such a smart woman, she could be clueless as hell sometimes. "Yeah. It'll be okay. Go back to sleep."

"I'm sorry."

"For what?" He slid his feet into his slippers. No matter what he did, his feet always seemed to be cold in this old house. He'd complained, but the structural engineers had said short of tearing the White House down and starting over, there wasn't anything more they could do to the old mansion. He'd just have to live with it. Three more years—seven if his bad luck held—then he planned to retire somewhere in the Southwest. Arizona or New Mexico, maybe. Or Hawaii. He could buy a few acres on Molokai and grow pineapples. If the Secret Service didn't want to come along, too bad. And if Meredith didn't want to come along, well, he'd find some sweet Polynesian thing to play house with.

"I don't know. Whatever is wrong?"

Shane slipped his arms into the heavy terrycloth robe he kept nearby and tied the belt in a loose knot. "Like I said, it'll be all right."

The lie slipped out easily—a politician's trick he'd honed during his first campaign to be mayor of Louisville. If you said it with conviction, the populace would swallow anything. Absolutely nothing about this situation was going to be all right. Ever since the Malaysian airliner had disappeared over the Indian Ocean a couple of years ago, planes of every description had been vanishing without a trace, over oceans, over whole continents, and nobody had a clue where they were going.

There were theories by the dozens. The one he liked most suggested aliens were snatching them out of the air, taking all the humans for interstellar lab rats and crushing the planes like empty soda cans. The theory went on to describe how the new space junk eventually fell out of orbit and entered Earth's atmosphere as flaming balls of fire, evidenced by a few recent incidents of space junk creating brief but spectacular light shows.

However, he suspected, if foul play was involved, it was more likely the work of earthlings. He'd rather deal with Martians. He wouldn't be surprised if they threw green shit at the fan, but humans? They never ceased to amaze him with the ways they found to screw up the world.

Leaving his wife behind, he tried to recall exactly who he'd sent to try to talk some sense into the North Koreans. The secretary of state, Harman Adams, had weaseled out of the trip, citing an inability to travel all the way to Guam. He'd even produced a doctor's note, like some kid trying to get out of gym class. In his stead, Deputy Secretary Jessica Cho had gotten the job. A certified bitch from California, she bore a remarkable resemblance to Choi Min-ho. Shane wouldn't be at all surprised to learn they were first cousins, if not long-lost brother and sister.

In addition to the deputy secretary, the chairpersons of the Senate and House Armed Services committees, Charles "Chuck" Hastings and Chris Sanderson, respectively, were on the plane. Both Republicans, and, unlike that liberal whack-job, Cho, they could be counted on to take a hard line with the Pacific Rim nations.

A few members of both committees had gone along as support and to show the United States meant business. Among them was Senator Shelby Conrad from Georgia.

If Jessica Cho was lost, he'd dance at her memorial service. As for Hastings, Sanderson, and whoever else had wanted the free tropical vacation, they'd be missed, but Shelby? Just thinking about not seeing her again, not holding her in his arms, not making love to her, caused a pit to open up and swallow his heart. He'd tried to talk her out of going, but with her seat up for re-election during the midterms, she'd said she needed the street cred her attendance at the summit would provide. He'd acquiesced, knowing she spoke the truth. Her opponent, the Democratic Representative for a heavily black district in Atlanta, had a formidable war chest and solid support from his constituents, thanks to his affiliation with the Black Lives Matter folks. Being a white woman with a pedigree straight out of Who's Who of the Daughters of the Confederacy, Shelby's only hope of keeping her job was to pit her years of political experience against her opponent's lack thereof.

Five minutes later, Shane stood at the head of the conference table in the secure Situation Room, several stories below the Oval Office, and scanned the assembled, familiar faces. Yanked from, he assumed, their cozy homes, the Joint Chiefs of Staff of the various Armed Forces, and the heads of an assortment of national security and intelligence organizations looked like they'd been found passed out at an all-night costume party and dragged here under duress. He felt the same way every single day.

He collapsed into his seat, the one bearing the crest of the president of the United States. "Someone tell me where our plane is," he demanded. He rapped his knuckles on the conference table. "And where's my coffee?"

President Shane Gilchrist
White House Situation Room
Saturday 23:50 Zulu (19:50 EDT)

A mug bearing the presidential seal appeared on the table in front of him. President Gilchrist took his first sip of coffee, savoring the bitter taste. He knew better than to drink the caffeine-laden liquid on an empty stomach, but desperate times called for desperate measures. As he took his second sip, his gaze wandered around the room again, marveling at how twenty people confined together in what amounted to a secure bunker could remain isolated in their own little worlds. If he hadn't witnessed the rise and fall of their chests with his own eyes, he'd think he was in a room full of stiffs. Eyes downcast, no one spoke, no one moved—except one. At the far end of the conference table, a single man sat tall in his seat, his gaze steady.

The president swallowed and felt the stimulant hit bottom. The clock read 7:50 p.m. *Almost 10 a.m. in Guam.* His stomach churned. He ignored it and got down to business, zeroing in on the only man in the room who looked alert. "General Stadler. Tell me what we know."

Marcus Stadler, known to his close friends as Viper, stood six-feet-two-inches tall, had a full head of dark, close-cropped hair and hawk-like eyes. He also had a reputation as a man who made the impossible happen. A wild kid from some corn crib in Kansas, his uncle, who happened to be a Senator, had pulled strings to get him into the Air Force Academy. Stadler had almost flunked out of the academy his first year due more to his inability to walk away from a fight than his lack of brains. No one knew how he'd done it, but he somehow managed to turn things around late in his second semester. From there, he'd graduated near the top of his class. After pilot training, he'd been assigned a coveted position as a fighter pilot where he'd distinguished himself in a couple of minor skirmishes. A chest full of medals guaranteed him any spot the Air Force had to offer. He'd chosen an almost invisible post in Oklahoma, training young pilots to assume the role of flight commander. Over the next decade, he'd quietly climbed the ladder of command to the very top. There wasn't a person in the room who didn't respect his opinion or who had the balls to challenge the man on anything—including Shane Gilchrist.

The Air Force general consulted a small notepad he drew from the inside pocket of his dress uniform and began reciting. "Mr. President. The plane carrying the U.S. delegation left Naval Air Station Pearl Harbor at 10:00, local time. Flight time to Guam was estimated at seven hours, twenty-six minutes. Last known contact was with the tower at Wake Island. No recording was made of the conversation, but the air traffic control specialist by the name of Mark Tinker said the pilot hailed Wake for a friendly exchange. Nothing unusual was said. Seems Davis had spent a night on Wake early in his career and has fond memories of the place. Tinker said nothing seemed amiss, just the usual conversation. The plane should have contacted the tower on Guam around three hours later. Repeated efforts were made to contact Captain Davis but went unanswered. That's when our man on the ground there gave us a shout."

"Where the hell did they go?"

"Mr. President." Stadler cleared his throat. "There's someone waiting outside who has information pertinent to the situation."

"Who the hell is he, and why isn't he in here?"

"It's Colonel Clint Rodgers. He heads up The Drone Theory project. His clearance doesn't extend to the Situation Room."

Shane Gilchrist's heart and lungs felt like lumps of concrete. The cowards he relied on to help him run the shit-show had their eyes trained on him. His brain projected into the future—a decade, maybe less—they'd all document this moment in their biographies. They'd want the world to know they were here, in this room, at the exact moment the commander in chief of the greatest military in history... Did what?

He'd been briefed on The Drone Theory. It sounded like sci-fi bullshit to him, but what if it wasn't? If he embraced the theory and it turned out to be a joke, he'd look the fool. But if he dismissed it without hearing what this Colonel Rodgers had to say and it turned out to be true, history would call him an idiot.

The decision weighed heavily on him, but the fact remained—his mistress was on board the missing plane. He couldn't afford to dismiss any possibility.

"He has a team in the field now, aboard the *Ronald Reagan*," the General added.

"The airliner that went down." The president nodded, recalling the investigation. "You think the two incidents are connected?"

"Colonel Rodgers is better able to answer your question, sir."

"Get him in here."

Colonel Clint Rodgers
White House Situation Room
Saturday 23:55 Zulu (19:35 EDT)

Colonel Clint Rodgers entered the room, pausing to salute his superiors, which tonight included the president of the United States who casually returned the salute without rising from his seat.

"General Stadler says you have information with some bearing on this situation."

"Yes, sir. I do." He glanced at an empty chair.

"Go ahead, have a seat," the president said.

Clint placed the leather portfolio he'd brought with him on the table and sat. "As you all know, Global Airlines flight number 2455 went down earlier this week about two hundred miles off the coast of Guam. Shortly before the plane ceased communication, one of my team detected an electronic signal sent from a land-based station to the aircraft. This wasn't the first time this analyst had noted such a signal, but it was the first time he was able to trace it to a particular aircraft. Moments after he'd isolated the signal to Global 2455, the aircraft disappeared. We immediately scrambled fighter jets to search for the plane in and around the last known coordinates. We also alerted every asset in the Northern Pacific region to be on the lookout for an unidentified aircraft in their airspace. There was no sign of the plane until two days later when a Navy pilot on a routine training flight noticed debris floating in the ocean. The USS *Ronald Reagan* Carrier Strike Group was deployed to search for survivors, secure the site, and recover debris. In the process, they recovered three bodies, which I'll discuss in a moment—"

"What does this have to do with our missing Gulfstream, Colonel?"

"If you'll bear with me, Mr. President?"

"Go ahead, but make it quick."

"Yes, sir." Rodgers consulted his notes again. "In addition to the bodies, they have been able to recover some large sections of the fuselage and a small mountain of miscellaneous debris. Among this flotsam was a rather unique object. By this time, my lead investigator, Major Megan Sloan, had arrived on board. She made the decision to inspect the object, which turned out to be a lunch box belonging to the pilot, Toby Bledsoe. The box contained Captain Bledsoe's cellphone as well as the cellphone belonging to his first officer, Skip Bernard. Further inspection of the phones revealed a video recorded by the flight crew. In it, they documented everything from take-off until what we believe was less than an hour before the plane went down."

"What exactly did they say?"

Colonel Rodgers consulted his notes. "Shortly after the plane checked in with San Francisco Radio, the flight crew lost all control over the operations of the aircraft. Someone had reset the autopilot for a point near where the debris was located. According to the flight crew, and as demonstrated on the videos they recorded, nothing they tried resulted in them being able to change course. I've seen the video, and, in my opinion, they did everything they could to recover control of the aircraft."

"Wait." The president sat forward. "Are you saying someone on the ground was in control of the plane?"

"At this time, sir, it appears to be the case."

"That's impossible!"

Rodgers swiveled to look at Vice President Schmidt who sat at the opposite end of the table from the president.

"Conventional wisdom agrees with you, Mr. Vice President," Rodgers continued. "But my team has been operating on the theory it is possible, and someone has figured out how to do it. As you all know, we operate UAVs, unmanned aerial vehicles, from earthbound stations around the clock. UAVs are some of the most effective tools in our arsenal, and we believe the technology behind them has been corrupted and is being used against us. To what aim, we have no idea." He held up his index finger. "But, if you will allow me to continue, I might be able to shed some light on the subject."

A murmur rose from the gathered dignitaries as they talked among themselves. The president let it go on for a minute before his voice rose above the din. "Gentlemen. Let's hear him out."

"Thank you, sir. Now, as I was saying, we were convinced the signal we intercepted had something to do with the disappearance of Global 2455, but the video testimony and the still photos the two pilots went to pains to provide us, even while they knew there was little hope of survival, confirmed our suspicions. A side note to this particular investigation relates to the bodies recovered from the crash site. Preliminary autopsy results suggest the passengers were all dead before the plane hit the water."

As he knew it would, this bit of information set tongues wagging. Colonel Rodgers sat back in his chair as the discussion raged around him. A few minutes later, the president called for calm again.

"Colonel Rodgers. You've told an incredible story. How long have you known this, and when were you planning on bringing this to our attention?"

Clint straightened his shoulders. "The information is hours old, sir, and the situation is fluid. I've kept General Stadler apprised of every development. However, I just got off the phone with Major Sloan a few minutes ago, sir. There's been a new development."

"I've yet to see how any of this relates to the plane currently missing. You know, the one carrying United States legislators and cabinet members to a nuclear arms summit? Are you going to get to that sometime soon?"

"Immediately, sir. If I may?"

"The floor is yours, Colonel."

"Within the last hour, Major Sloan received a satellite communication from an associate of hers at Air Force Intelligence, Agent Liam Donovan, who is now assigned to the Secret Service. He is also one of two agents aboard your missing flight, sir."

"And? What did Agent Donovan have to say?"

"He said, sir, their plane has been hijacked."

Liam Donovan
Gulfstream G650
Saturday 23:35 Zulu (Sunday 11:00 WKT)

The last thing Liam Donovan wanted to do was tell his charges their plane had been hijacked, but like any mission, everyone involved needed to know every detail and understand the risks they would be taking. He doubted anyone on board could help the situation, but he did need their cooperation.

"Hey, folks." He stood in the aisle blocking passage to the forward cabin. "Can I have your attention, please?"

A couple of them looked at him as if they'd never seen him before while the others kept right on doing what they were doing. He'd pursued invisibility his entire career and apparently had achieved it.

He cleared his throat and placed his hands on his hips. Raising his voice, he tried again. "Heads up, everybody!"

One by one, they turned their attention his way.

"In a few minutes, you'll see a couple of F-18s on our wingtips. They'll be monitoring our movements and are here to provide a layer of protection."

"Protection? What's going on?" Senator Cho snapped. The woman seemed to wear a permanent scowl that matched her nasty personality. How in the world she got elected year after year was beyond him.

"Sometime after we left Wake Island airspace, someone on the ground managed to reprogram the autopilot for a destination within North Korea." He glanced from one stunned expression to another until slowly his words sank in and they began to fling questions like they were the press corps and he was the White House press secretary. Shaking his head, Liam then held his hand up, requesting quiet. "If you'll bear with me, I'll answer as many of your questions as I can. As far as we can tell, we aren't in any danger at this time. The flight crew has lost control over all aspects of the aircraft, including the communications system. We have no idea who is behind this, or what their goal is. Using the satellite phone agent Woodward and I brought aboard, we have requested assistance from the U.S. Military. The escort planes will provide personnel on the ground with the information they need to track our progress while they work to figure out how this has occurred, and execute a plan to return control to our flight crew. In the meantime, we need you to remain calm. We're doing everything we can to ensure your safety."

"Has the president been informed?"

The question came from Shelby Conrad, the Senator from Georgia, and, according to his friends in the Secret Service, the president's mistress. "I don't know for certain, but I imagine he was at the top of the call list."

To the woman's credit, she simply nodded and turned to look out the window.

Senator Chuck Hastings shifted in his seat. "No way in hell Choi is going to get by with this."

"We don't know he's responsible." Senator Cho sent the Chairman of the Senate Arms Services Committee a quelling look. Liam had been too busy the last decade protecting life and liberty to pay much attention to politics, but the animosity between these two was legendary. They'd been at each other's throats for almost as long as Liam had been alive.

"We don't know who's responsible," he said, hoping to head off a battle no one would win.

"Who's working on this?" Liam appreciated the sane question from the secretary of state, Harman Adams, and he said so.

"Good question, Mr. Secretary. You're all familiar with The Drone Theory task force headed by Lt. Col. Clint Rodgers?"

Heads nodded. A few curses flew and opinions were tossed out. Donovan waited until the cabin grew quiet again before he continued. "Whether you believe in the task force's mission or not, they're in the best position to help us right now. The core of the task force is aboard the USS *Ronald Reagan* as we speak, investigating the downing of the Global Airlines flight southwest of Guam. I've spoken with the officer in charge, Megan Sloan, and been assured every asset available is being directed at our situation."

Mike Woodward had been hunched over looking out the window. He straightened. "They're here."

"To shoot us down." The bald, but potentially accurate statement came from Representative Christopher Sanderson, Chairman of the House Armed Services Committee, and opened up another heated round of debate.

"Whoa! Quiet!" Liam held both hands up, trying to quiet the passengers. Nothing good could come from arguing at this point.

"You know it's true." Sanderson directed the comment at Liam.

"I'm not paid to speculate on the president's intentions, and an order like that would have to come from him. Mike and I need you all to stay calm and let us do our job." Liam cocked one knee and cast his gaze at the floor. Blowing out a sharp breath, he raised his face, focusing on a point on the wall above their heads. "Look, I know Major Sloan. She's one of the best intelligence agents I've ever worked with. If anyone can get us out of this mess, it's her."

Major Megan Sloan
USS Ronald Reagan
Saturday 23:40 Zulu (09:40 ChST)

I spoke with the flight crew aboard the Gulfstream briefly, letting them know we would be monitoring the open line. "If anything, and, I mean anything changes, let us know." Assured they would keep us informed, I muted the conversation on my end. They didn't need to hear we didn't have a single clue how to help them.

I stood, stretching muscles that had grown tighter throughout the conversation with Liam. "Tell me we have something—any-thing—to go on here." The statement was met with silence and blank stares from the few who had the courage to actually look my way. The sharp pain Liam's voice had brought on was now a dull ache. I put my hand on my hip, a move I hoped looked casual and not like the desperate attempt it was to focus the pain into something worthwhile. I let my gaze linger on each person at the table. "Unbelievable. We don't have even one thread to pull?"

Jude, one of the few who had the balls to meet my gaze, spoke. "We've got our hacker guy at HQ. He said he thought he could do this—hijack a plane in flight—maybe we should see if he can."

The hacker had said as much, but I'd dismissed his comment as hubris. But what if it wasn't? I knew he wasn't the source of our present dilemma or the previous ones either. We'd had him under lock and key, with constant surveillance for a week, and, before we got our hands on him, he'd been at the NSA. You couldn't scratch your-self inside their headquarters at Ft. Meade without someone making note of it. He wasn't their nemesis, but he might be the key they needed to solve the puzzle.

"Read him in on the situation. See if he can find a way in. Maybe we can override the system ourselves or, at the very least, find the bastard who's at the controls now and shut him down."

"I'm on it, boss." Jude stood, laptop in hand. "I'm going to the communications room. Lt. Franklin said they'd hook us up with a secure line to anywhere."

"Keep me informed." I turned to the rest of the team as the door closed behind Jude. I pointed to the handset resting beside the admiral's desk phone. "We're the only thing standing between those people and death. Give me something. Anything, to go on."

These were support people. They analyzed fingerprints and cobbled together MOs. They scoured computer files and phone records to map a path taken—past tense. None of them had the ability to recognize a clusterfuck before it happened but could document with precision the number of phallic thrusts used to get the job done—after the fact. Useful in preventing a similar disaster in the future, but useless when it came to stopping one in progress. They'd come here to investigate a plane crash, not prevent one. Nothing they'd discovered so far did anything to lessen my anxiety or give me any hope we could stop another tragedy from happening.

Colonel Clint Rodgers
White House Situation Room
Saturday 23:40 Zulu (19:40 EDT)

"Hijacked? By whom?"

The colonel had been expecting the question. "We don't know, sir, but the new coordinates programmed into the autopilot are for the airport in Pyongyang."

It was as if someone had sucked the sound out of the room then, as quickly as the silence had descended, pandemonium broke loose. Everyone talked at once. Questions flew at him, at the president. Curses bounced off the soundproof walls, circling the room like birds of prey looking for a place to land. Rodgers sat, his gaze trained on the commander in chief.

Shane Gilchrist clamped his jaw tight before the thoughts streaming through his brain spewed out. He had every intention of letting them fly, but not here. He'd wait until he was alone before he let the universe know what he thought of the little twerp who called himself Supreme Leader of the People's Republic of North Korea.

In the last few months, Choi Min-ho had done some pretty stupid things, but this took the cake.

The president sat for a moment, collecting his thoughts and allowing snippets of conversations happening around the room to register. It seemed the only sane person in the room was the one who had dropped the bomb in the middle of the table. Gilchrist stood and slapped both palms flat on the table. "Silence!" When the group didn't shut up fast enough for his liking, he slapped the table again. "I said—silence!"

When the only sound in the room was the sound of the men squirming in their seats, the president trained his gaze on Colonel Rodgers. "Do they have enough fuel to make it to Pyongyang?"

"They believe they do—with proper flight maintenance."

"Explain proper flight maintenance."

The colonel briefly spoke about the dynamics of fuel consumption depending on certain variables. "They refueled at Pearl Harbor, so if they maintain their present altitude and airspeed, they should be able to coast in."

"Or, the son of a bi— I mean, the hijacker could drop them into the ocean."

"Or redirect the flight over water until it does run out of fuel. Or, as we suspect happened with Global 2455, the hijacker could kill everyone on board at any time. Unless someone contacts us with a demand, we can only guess at their next move."

Shane Gilchrist dropped heavily into the big leather chair with the Seal of the President of the United States emblazoned above his head. "Christ Almighty." The weight of the office had never felt heavier on his shoulders. "Do we know where the plane is?"

"Agent Donovan is keeping the task force informed. Fighter jets from Andersen are on their way to intercept as we speak."

"Good." The president nodded. "Good. Keep an eye on them in case... Hell, I don't know. What can we do?"

"As you know," Rodgers addressed the president directly, "The Drone Theory task force was formed after the disappearance of Malaysia Flight 360. As far back as 2010, when the Iranians claimed to have brought down a UAV belonging to the CIA, DOD has been concerned about someone using the technology to essentially turn any aircraft they want into a drone. It's why we sent operatives into Iran to get or destroy the computer components of the downed UAV. The mission turned out to be a disaster. We lost two CIA agents and nearly lost the rest of the team."

"I was chair of the Senate Intelligence Committee at the time," Vice President Schmidt said. "If I recall correctly, the two Air Force Intelligence officers involved were Megan Sloan and Liam Donovan. Is it a coincidence they're both front and center of this shit-show, too?"

Colonel Rodgers clenched his fists beneath the table. "If you are in any way suggesting Major Sloan and her former partner are conspiring with North Korea, then you are sorely mistaken. Might I remind you Donovan left Major Sloan for dead in the godforsaken desert, smack in the heart of enemy territory!"

"Yet, here she is, alive and well, and up to her eyeballs in yet another international incident."

Chaos erupted around the table again. It was all Clint Rodgers could do to remain in his seat when his fingers itched to choke the life out of the vice president.

Gilchrist's fist came down on the table. *Thump. Thump. Thump.* When quiet reigned again, he directed his comments to everyone, but his gaze was fixed on Schmidt, who had been chosen by the party, not by Gilchrist. "Everyone in this room has read the report on the failed mission to recover the drone computer. Americans died trying to recover the technology. Let's not forget that. Donovan and Sloan have both answered questions before the House and Senate Intelligence committees and no misconduct was determined. We will not question their loyalty to this country. Are we clear?"

Schmidt looked like he was about to have a coronary, which would have suited Rodgers just fine. He made a conscious effort to relax his fists as heads nodded in deference to the president's edict.

"As you were saying, Colonel Rodgers?"

Rodgers cleared his throat before continuing. "Yes, sir. The task force has been looking into the possibility someone has taken drone technology to the next logical step—the ability to intercept a plane in flight from a fixed command center, much like the centers from which we remotely launch and control our military UAVs. If someone has developed this technology, it will change aviation as we know it."

"How so?" The question came from Brett Loren, the president's chief of staff who'd remained relatively quiet at his boss's side.

"It's simple, Mr. Loren. Nothing that flies would be safe."

Major Megan Sloan
USS Ronald Reagan
Saturday 23:45 Zulu (09:45 ChST)

Knowing my team was doing everything they could, I decided to get some fresh air. Lt. Graves was waiting for me in the outer office. After asking directions to the nearest mess, I assured her I could find my way there and back. It was a lie, but she was only a phone call away if I changed my mind. Right now, I wanted to be alone to think. And, I needed a cup of coffee.

The mess was right where she'd said it would be. The recovery effort had dwindled to one sailor on the lookout for floating debris, so the Navy had returned to business as usual. If I wanted peace and quiet, I'd have to find another place, but, in some perverse way, I welcomed the sound of the catapult and the roar of jet engines on the deck above. White noise to the extreme, I guess, but it helped me block out everything but the one thing I needed to focus on.

I went over my conversation with Liam, word for word. He was absolutely correct. There was no way our president was going to let their plane land in North Korea. He'd order it shot down himself before it got anywhere near the peninsula.

Since the destination coordinates had been changed to North Korea's capital city, and given the nature of the human cargo aboard, the logical conclusion was Choi Min-ho was behind the hijacking. But to what end? Did he plan to take the committee members hostage in order to demand some sort of ransom? He should know better. The official stance of the United States remained—we don't negotiate with terrorists. But who really knew? It was up to the president to make the decision. In fact, there was precedence to make a deal. The previous administration had bargained away a handful of

Gitmo prisoners in return for an American soldier who had somehow found himself the guest of the Taliban.

I'd hoped there was a good reason for wanting the American back, like he was really an intelligence officer who had been detained by design in order to obtain information—something I wouldn't put past the DOD or the military intelligence community. They were all crazy bastards—myself included.

However, the returned soldier had recently been court-martialed and found guilty of deserting his post. Seemed he'd believed we should all just sit down and talk out our differences—a stance the former president had voiced on the campaign trail. The comment had won him the votes of every old hippy who still believed in making love, not war. The former president had soon learned the error of his ways, but on occasion did something stupid, like swap dangerous terrorists for deserters.

Last I'd heard, the released prisoners, who had agreed not to associate with any of their previous American hating, murderous friends, had all returned to their previous lives. I suspect we haven't heard the last of them. In the meantime, the do-gooder soldier was looking at a long vacation in a federal pen. Couldn't have happened to a nicer guy. He'd left his post in the middle of the night, leaving his fellow soldiers at risk, and though he was nothing more than a grunt, no telling what he'd told his captors. I'm certain he gave up more information than he got, meaning we gained nothing from the exchange. Stupid, but water, or sand, under the bridge. I had other things to worry about, like a plane full of elected officials and cabinet members presently headed to North Korea.

If Choi's goal was to gain the upper hand in the nuclear arms negotiations, perhaps President Gilchrist would be open to talking. Or not.

Choi was the logical culprit in this instance, but trying to look at this from all sides, I had to wonder, what if he wasn't?

I started in on my second cup of coffee. I probably didn't need any more caffeine, but I did need the simple, familiar routine. Like the rhythmic sounds coming from the flight deck, it allowed me to think.

What if Choi Min-ho wasn't behind this? What if someone was dicking with both countries? If by some miracle, the plane made it into North Korean airspace uninvited, no doubt batshit crazy Choi would shoot it down himself and declare the breach of airspace an act of war. God only knew what he'd do afterward, but any smart person wouldn't rule out nuclear retaliation. He'd been showing off his rockets and boasting about his nuclear capability like a playground bully spoiling for a fight. Which made me think perhaps he might be drawing the plane into his airspace for that very purpose. If we couldn't prove he was behind the hijacking, we couldn't blame him for shooting it down. We'd look like the aggressors to anyone who didn't know better, and there were plenty out there who would see only what they wanted to see.

We'd have World War III on our hands.

Shit.

Major Megan Sloan
USS Ronald Reagan
Saturday 23:50 Zulu (09:50 ChST)

My hands were shaking so hard I was afraid I'd drop my mug if I tried to drink from it, so instead, I wrapped my arms around my midsection and willed the pain to go away. I was on my second deep-cleansing breath when someone joined me at the table. I looked up into the concerned eyes of Dr. Schneider.

"You should let me check you out," she said as she lifted a mug to her lips.

"It's nothing," I lied and grabbed my cup. I was glad to see the tremors had stopped. The good doctor had already seen too much.

"Doesn't look like nothing to me." She sipped then held the steaming cup in both hands. "Want to tell me about it?"

"No." My tone held a finality I know she heard because she sighed.

"Okay. It's your call, but if you don't want to be ordered to get medical attention, you need to do a better job of hiding whatever it is."

She was right, but there wasn't a person within a thousand miles who had that kind of power over me. Knowing I was safe from prying and well-meaning eyes, I'd let my guard down. I wouldn't do it again. "Point taken. I'll be more careful."

Our gazes locked and held for a moment. She was a doctor first and a military officer second. As either one, she could contact my superiors. I hoped she wouldn't, and I let her see the concern in my eyes.

"Do you know what it is?" she asked.

I nodded. "I took a couple of rounds a few years ago. Messed some stuff up pretty bad. They patched me together. Said I was good to go."

"The pain?"

"Is all in my head."

The good doctor raised one eyebrow. "Sounds like bullshit to me."

"Could be," I said. "I'll have it checked out again when I get home."

"Home is D.C.?"

"Yeah."

"I have a friend at the Bethesda Medical Center. She's good."

"Thanks. I'll email you for her contact information."

She nodded. We both sipped our coffee. When enough time had gone by, she asked, "How's the investigation going?"

I didn't know what kind of security clearance she had, but I was pretty certain it didn't extend to the level of national security my present situation had risen to. "Nothing new." I told her the truth. "I'll be out of your hair soon."

I needed to get off this tub, if for no other reason than to preserve my sanity. In many ways, the aircraft carrier was no different than my little section of the Freedom Center complex. The offices didn't have windows, and most were below ground, or, in this case, below sea level. It wasn't the narrow tunnels they called passageways or the cave-like rooms. Knowing I was surrounded by water got to me, so maybe I wouldn't have made a good sailor after all.

"I've got to go." Dr. Schneider stood. "I just needed to get out for a while."

I smiled. "Same reason I'm here. Needed a change of scenery."

She reminded me to stay in touch then she walked away. She stopped at the giant coffee urn to refill her mug before leaving the mess without another look my way. I didn't have many women friends. My job sort of made it impossible. I guessed the doctor was in the same boat, so to speak.

I stared at the last, cold dregs in the bottom of my mug and wondered what I would do when my tour of duty ended. I'd sort of told myself I'd stay until this project had either been resolved or died a natural death. If we were successful here, The Drone Theory project would come to a conclusion soon, as would my latest contract with the Air Force.

I knew a few people of my kind who had entered the private sector. Personal security was big business across the globe, and several had successfully made the transition. Others had joined what were laughingly called private security firms, but were, in fact, private military operations. Mercenaries, to use a more familiar term. More and more, the government was hiring out the dirty work to these companies. Deniability was the name of the game, plus, these private contractors weren't bound by the same rules and regulations that often tied the hands of the military. They could go places, do things as private citizens U.S. military personnel simply couldn't. I'd worked with a few over the years. Some were good. Some, not so good. It depended on their motivation. Money drove them all—why else would they risk their lives? But the good ones also respected what America stood for and kept their country front and center while they pocketed Uncle Sam's cash.

As I made my way to the admiral's office, I pushed retirement thoughts from my mind. Now wasn't the time or place to think about anything but the immediate future. If I could end this threat against our country, I could walk away with a clear conscience.

I had to consider the possibility there were other likely players in this deadly game besides North Korea. There were any number of other countries who would like an excuse to wipe us off the map, and most weren't above creating an excuse. On the other hand, it could be some middle-aged guy with a grudge or some deranged computer geek who'd spent too much time with his hand around his own joy-stick. It could be anybody with a computer, and every person on the planet owned one.

That was the reality I had to consider.

Major Megan Sloan
USS Ronald Reagan
Sunday 00:45 Zulu (10:45 ChST)

"**M**ajor?" I turned to see Lt. Franklin standing in the doorway. "There's a call for you in the comm center. They want to know if you want to take it there or in here."

I glanced at the still silent phone lying on the desk. We were the only hope they had. I didn't want to put them on hold for even a second. I stood. "I'll take it there." Tapping Jeffries on the shoulder, I put him in charge of listening for the flight crew or Liam Donovan to come on the line. "Lt. Franklin will know how to reach me," I said, raising my eyebrows at the officer in question.

He nodded at the FBI agent. "I sure will." Turning to me, he said, "Lt. Graves will show you where the comm center is."

I spied Jude as I entered the secure room. He'd been given a small space to call his own and a hands-free headset he was using to communicate with our hacker in our D.C. offices. He was deep in conversation, so I scooted past him to a seaman standing in front of a door at the rear of the room. As I approached, he opened the door, revealing what I assumed was a soundproof room containing a padded desk chair on wheels and a small metal shelf about desktop height. An old-fashioned plastic handset hung from a metal hook on the wall.

"Just lift the handset, ma'am. I'll patch the call through immediately. Replace the handset when you're through."

I thanked him and sat. He closed the door, leaving me in what amounted to a phone booth. I lifted the receiver.

"Patching the White House through, ma'am. Please stay on the line."

The line clicked a few times before I heard someone breathing on the other end. "Major Sloan," I said, letting whoever it was know I was there.

"Sloan. Colonel Rodgers here."

I breathed a sigh of relief and, realizing I was practically sitting at attention, relaxed into the chair. "Sir. What can I do for you?"

"Major, I've got you on speaker. Can you hear me okay?"

"Clear as a bell, sir."

"Good. Good." He cleared his throat. "I've just briefed the president and vice president regarding the situation with the negotiating committee. Can you tell us what is being done to gain control of the aircraft?"

At the mention of the commander in chief and his second-in-command, I tried to muster the energy to straighten my spine but couldn't find any. No one could see me. I gripped the handset tighter and brought my unseen audience up to date.

"I wish I had better news," I said, "but the truth is, we're still working on it."

"What, exactly, are you working on?"

The voice of the president of the United States did what the colonel's couldn't—straightened my spine. I jumped to my feet, found I couldn't pace in the space given me, so I stood, clutching the handset in a white-knuckled grip. "Mr. President, sir. Our best analysts are going over everything we know so far, looking for anything we might have missed before. We've got assets at the NSA combing the universe for any communication with the flight in progress. If we can intercept even one communication, we could perhaps trace it to its origin."

"What if the origin is in North Korea?"

My blood ran cold at the implication. I'd known Liam was right—President Gilchrist was not going to let Choi Min-ho get his hands on his nuclear arms negotiating team. If the origin of the signals turned out to be within the boundaries of North Korea, he'd have little choice but to shoot the plane down himself. Even if the CIA had assets in the tiny country, which I had no way of knowing, the timeline to get to the source and neutralize it would, at best, be a couple of hours. Not to mention, taking the source out would be a suicide mission for the agents involved. Choi Min-ho would certainly retaliate, and it wouldn't be pretty. We were talking Nuclear with a capital N. I answered the only way I could. I lied. "I don't know, sir."

"Every military and intelligence asset is at your disposal, Major. We would prefer to acquire the technology in question, but if destroying it is the only means of saving the people aboard the plane, I'm prepared to make that call."

In other words—he'd nuke North Korea if he had to. There were less extreme options, a guided missile delivered with pinpoint precision to take out the target, for example, but such actions would only lead to a volley, perhaps out of proportion, which would lead to another from us until nuclear warheads were flying all over the place. Better to cut to the chase. Nuke the son of a bitch first, and thoroughly. How the hell had I gotten in the middle of something like this?

I knew how. I'd screwed up and let the Iranians make off with the drone technology. The unholy alliance between Choi Min-ho and the Iranians was no secret. American intelligence agencies had known for years the two countries were trading intelligence. North Korea needed oil, and Iran needed an ally. It was a match made in hell. God only knew what Choi had traded to get his hands on the drone technology. It could have been anything from uranium to slaves from his prison camps. If the United States nuked North Korea, would their buddies in Iran stand with them?

God Almighty. Wiping North Korea off the map was one thing. Starting a nuclear war with Iran was something altogether different.

We needed to get our hands on the technology, and preferably the person or persons operating it. As long as it was out there, we stood on the brink of a nuclear confrontation.

I hadn't been the one who let the Iranians get their hands on the CIA's drone, but I had been a part of the team sent to recover it. We'd failed, and, like one of the hounds of Hell, it was poised to take a bite out of our asses. Karma was a bitch.

"I understand, sir."

"I need a target, Major."

"Yes, sir."

The line went dead. I stared at the receiver. When my hand quit trembling, I carefully placed the device on its cradle. Like Atlas, the weight of the world rested on my shoulders. With one hand, I braced myself on the metal shelf/desk. I placed the other hand on my abdomen where a tiny platoon armed with bayonets were at war with my insides. If this really was all in my head, I should be locked up somewhere, not out in the middle of the ocean trying to save the world from nuclear destruction. If I lived through this, I'd tell the government's shrink where she could put her psychosomatic pain theories. Then I'd find a real doctor.

After a few minutes of deep-breathing exercises, the pain eased enough I thought I could walk without assistance. Jude signaled me as soon as I stepped out. His eyes were bright with the same kind of excitement I'd seen in them over a week ago when he told me about the ping he'd intercepted. I needed good news, and I hoped he had some. "You got something?"

"I think so. Maybe."

He looked around at the sailors surrounding us, doing whatever it was they did. Their security clearance amounted to being warned about loose lips sinking ships, but I didn't give a damn. I knew of only two private places on this boat—the bunk I'd been assigned and the tiny room I'd just left. One I couldn't find without an escort, and the other wouldn't accommodate two people at once. I hustled Jude into the hallway and shut the door. I could feel the clock ticking. We were running out of time, so the hallway would have to do.

"Tell me," I said.

Jude nodded and launched into his explanation. "The new guy—"

"Gates."

"Yeah. He's good. Really good."

High praise from Jude. I raised both eyebrows. "How good is he?"

"He found a backdoor into Global's system. We know how they isolated the aircraft, and how they got inside the computer system."

"Impressive, but how does it help us with our current situation? This is a Gulfstream."

"We contacted Gulfstream. They swear the only way into their system is through the front door. Gates is working on their system now, looking for an entry point similar to the one he found at Global. I've got our team listening for any signal that pings the Gulfstream's computer system. If we can intercept one—"

"We can trace it to its origin?"

He shrugged. "Maybe. Depends on how many satellites it bounces off. It's like chasing a rubber ball. The possible directions it could go are infinite with every bounce. If you blink, you lose sight of it."

"Don't lose it, Jude. For God's sake, don't lose it."

Major Megan Sloan
USS Ronald Reagan
Sunday 01:00 Zulu (11:00 ChST)

Lt. Graves was nowhere to be found, so I left Jude to do what he did best and went to check on the crew of the Gulfstream. I found my way to the admiral's office without incident, which meant I'd been on the carrier way too long. I was starting to recognize places with distinguishing characteristics or markings I could see. Yep. It was definitely time to get off this tub.

I picked up the phone, took it off mute, and identified myself to whoever was on the other end. It turned out to be Liam. Just my luck. I couldn't count the number of times over the last few years I'd dreamed of holding his fate in my hands, but in all of my dreams, he was alone, not babysitting a bunch of politicians. As much as I wanted him dead, I couldn't let the others share his fate. Not if I had a choice. I might not have a choice, but, as always, I wasn't ready to accept defeat.

"How's it going?" I asked. "Is your escort there yet?"

"They're here. Two F-18s flanking us. Two more on our tail. They came fully loaded."

He wasn't talking about the pilots, but hearing him confirm the armaments sent a chill down my spine. Every passing second was another one closer to their last one. The hell of it was, even if my team did locate the origin of the signals, there might not be a damned thing I could do about it. Even with a SEAL team at my back, a ground assault on a target in North Korea was out of the question, both from a time and a logistic standpoint.

The truth was, there was little I could do way out here in the middle of the ocean. If my team did find the source of the signals, any physical takedown would belong to someone else.

"Look, Sloan," Liam said. "You and I both know what's going on here, so let's cut the bullshit."

"No bullshit," I said. "You're deep enough as it is."

"Look, everyone on board knows the score. They've asked me to pass on their desire to attempt to negotiate—if we land somewhere."

I resisted the urge to sigh. "It's not my decision, Liam."

"I know. Just pass the request on to the White House."

He knew as well as I the official policy of the United States was not to negotiate with hijackers or terrorists. The lawmakers on board were well aware of the policy, too, but I couldn't blame them for wanting to try. "I'll pass the request along, but tell them not to get their hopes up."

"They understand what they're asking goes against official policy, but you can't blame them. It's easy to be noble and brave when you don't know the hostages. It's completely different when you *are* the hostage."

"I'll pass the message along."

"Any progress on finding the source?"

"As a matter of fact, we've got a guru in D.C. who thinks he found out how the person has been gaining control of the planes." I'd promised him the truth no matter how awful it was. "We're getting closer, Liam, but I don't know if it will be in time to help you."

"Is there any way we can override the computer system? Block the signal?" He sighed, and I envisioned him running his fingers through his hair—something I'd seen him do countless times when he was frustrated. I wondered if he'd cut his hair to fit in with his new assignment, or if he'd kept it long as he had when we'd worked undercover in the sandbox.

"We're working on it," I said.

"Can you work fast? Please?"

Neither one of us were blessed with an abundance of patience, and neither one of us had inherited the come-rescue-me-while-I-sit-on-my-ass gene. It's one of the reasons we'd gotten along so well in the beginning and, ultimately, part of the reason our relationship had gone down in flames. I could tell by the strain in his voice how much his inability to act was killing him. Less than an hour ago, the thought would have brought a smile to my face, but I was actually beginning to sympathize with the man.

"We're doing all we can, Liam. I promise." He was a smart man. He knew how I felt about him. How could he not? I'd refused to see him so many times when he'd come to the hospital after I'd returned stateside, he'd finally quit coming. Our personal relationship had been on the rocks, but not over, for a long time before he'd left me for dead. I'd lived, but what was left of our relationship had suffered a mortal wound. Our professional relationship had died the minute he'd made the decision to save his own ass. With all this history between us, I wondered if my promise meant anything to him or if he saw the irony of the situation. I knew he was counting on my honor, just as I'd counted on his. I thought I would enjoy watching him suffer, but it was ripping my insides apart—a feeling I knew all too well. "I mean what I said. Failure isn't an option here."

"You don't owe me anything."

Was he trying to apologize? Maybe, or maybe not. It didn't matter. People facing death often wanted to make amends—just in case it mattered on the other side. At least he had an opportunity to set things straight. It was more than I'd had. But I hadn't died, had I? And he wouldn't die today if I had anything to say about it.

"I know." I glanced up to see Lt. Franklin trying to get my attention. "Look, I've got to go. I'm going to mute on my end, but we're still listening."

"Fix this, Sloan."

I hit the mute button without answering him. "What's up, Lieutenant?"

President Shane Gilchrist
White House Oval Office
Sunday 01:00 Zulu (Saturday 21:00 EDT)

"That bastard Choi is behind this."

"We can't be sure, Mr. President." Gilchrist's national security advisor, General William "Bill" Haywood, leaned forward, his elbows resting on his knees, hands clasped tight. He glanced nervously at the grim faces of the men who, like him, had been summoned to the Oval Office to discuss the situation.

President Gilchrist, pacing behind the *Resolute* desk that had witnessed nearly every crisis since 1880, turned to the director of the CIA, Henry Rotham. "Henry?"

Rotham cleared his throat. "At this point, it would be premature to jump to any conclusion. Choi is certainly capable of this kind of treachery, but to what gain? He's already agreed to sit down and negotiate the nuclear arms issue."

"I'll tell you what he has to gain." Secretary of State Harman Adams, looking fit as the proverbial fiddle, stood. "I wondered why he would agree to send a delegation to the talks when he had absolutely nothing to bring to the table. We'd all agreed, there wasn't anything he could offer to convince us to let him continue to develop a nuclear arsenal, and we also knew he wasn't going to agree to dismantle his nuclear program. He's got something to bargain with now, doesn't he?"

"We don't negotiate with terrorists." The president's chief of staff, Brett Loren's voice sliced across the room.

Gilchrist clutched the back of his leather desk chair. "I'm inclined to agree with Harman, except no demands have been made. Yet."

Haywood raised his voice. "We'd be crazy not to look at other possible perpetrators. The Iranians were the ones who got their hands on our drone technology to begin with. I wouldn't put it past them to use it to force a confrontation between us and North Korea."

"For what reason?" Brett Loren asked.

"Hell, when have those camel jockeys ever needed a reason?" Haywood smirked.

"He has a point," the secretary of state said. "Any number of hostile states would do something like this if they could. Iran is one of the few with the money and possibly the technical expertise to pull it off. Think about it. They provoke a confrontation between us and their buddy Choi. Americans die and, have no illusions, Americans would die, while the Iranians sit on their hands and watch. We're innocent, they'll say, but look at the United States! Warmongers!" Haywood shook his fist in the air. "We might eliminate Choi and his regime, but with no proof he's behind this, we could start something we can't finish."

"I'll put our military up against any other force out there," Fred Ames, Chairman of the Joint Chiefs said. The seasoned Army general shook his fist in the air. "We'll wipe the lot of them off the map if they try and mess with us."

"Calm down, Fred." Gilchrist forced his fingers to release their grip on his chair. "We're getting ahead of ourselves here." He pointed at the uniformed man standing with his back to the windows overlooking the south lawn. "Sherman, what are your people hearing? Anything that could shed some light on this?"

Admiral Richard Sherman, (DIRNSA) director of the National Security Agency looked up from his contemplation of the cream-colored carpet beneath his feet. He shook his head. "Nothing so far. We're assisting The Drone Theory team as much as possible. Thanks to their analysts, we know what to look for. Capturing the signal the hijackers are using is the equivalent of trying to snatch a single spoken word out of the air from outer space and trace it to the exact person on the planet who uttered it. But, like I said, we're working on it. I'd put our analysts up against any in the world. If it can be done, they'll do it."

"You'll keep me informed?"

"Certainly, Mr. President."

Gilchrist nodded as he paced to stand before the ornate fireplace. "Harman? What about diplomatic channels? Can we contact Choi? Or at least contact the Chinese? See if they know what their little buddy is up to?"

Before the secretary of state could answer, DIRCIA Chrisman spoke up. "I wouldn't reach out to them, sir."

"Why the hell, not? Who knows how much time we have? You heard Col. Rodgers. These people don't have any problem dropping an airliner full of innocent people into the ocean."

"He's right," DIRNSA Sherman said. "Chrisman, I mean. We could be playing into the terrorist's hands if we open up a dialog with anyone. Not to mention what a shitstorm of chatter it would initiate within the intelligence world. It would be impossible for our analysts to sort the idle, curious chatter from any actual conversation taking place regarding the incident."

Gilchrist clenched his fists on the table. "So, we sit here with our heads up our asses and act like nothing's wrong? For how long? Can any of you tell me that? How long do we sit here blowing fart bubbles?"

Major Megan Sloan
USS Ronald Reagan
Sunday 01:15 Zulu (11:15 ChST)

I was pretty sure I could find my way on my own, but, for once, my gut was telling me not to waste time, so I followed Lt. Graves to the ship's comm center where they'd set Jude up with a dedicated line to our NSA hacker in D.C. According to the admiral's assistant, Jude needed to see me, and I needed to pass the message from the passengers on to the White House. I didn't think the president would give a shit what they wanted, but I owed it to them to make their wishes known. Negotiating a nuclear arms deal where everyone at the table had more or less the same power was one thing. Negotiating for a life when one person held all the cards was different. Still, I'd pass their message on. These kinds of decisions were, thankfully, far above my pay grade.

"I need to talk to Jude first thing," I said to my guide's back as we traversed the tunnel like passageway. "I also need to make a phone call. Can you talk to whomever? Get them to patch me in to the White House?"

"Yes, ma'am. Did your earlier call came from there?"

"Yes."

"Then I'm sure it won't be a problem."

"Thank you."

We arrived at a metal door I recognized. Graves held it open for me. Call it premonition or intuition, but I had the feeling everything was about to change. I paused to take a deep breath and let it out then told the lieutenant, "Don't leave. I might need you again soon."

Jude was standing in front of his assigned station, looking like a live wire dancing on wet pavement. The second our eyes connected,

205

I felt the current flowing between us and knew he had something. This evil game we were playing was about to change—hopefully, in our favor. "What have you got?"

"A location."

Adrenaline pumped through my system, and I willed myself to calm. Like any mission, timing was everything. There was no stopping the adrenaline rush, but I'd learned to control it—to a degree—so it would be there when I needed it, not before. I looked over my shoulder. "Lt. Graves?"

The woman stopped mid-conversation with the communications tech who had assisted me earlier. "Ma'am?"

"Hold off on my call." I turned toward Jude. "Where?"

"Gates looked up the coordinates. It's in the middle of the ocean, for crying out loud."

"Which ocean?"

"This one. He says it somewhere north of Guam. It could be nothing—some kind of misdirection to send us on a wild goose chase."

Or, it could be everything. I faced Graves. "I need to see Admiral Reeves and Captain Hervey. Is there a chart room around here?"

"Yes, ma'am." She spoke to the same sailor she'd been talking to earlier, instructing him to alert the quartermaster to expect company and to notify the senior command to meet us in the chart room.

I added, "I need Colonel Rodgers on the phone. Patch him into the chart room?"

"Yes, ma'am. On it."

"Let's go."

Captain Hervey was waiting for us when we arrived. To his credit, he didn't seem the least bit annoyed at being summoned by a guest on his own ship. I took his pleasant demeanor as a good sign and assured him we would be out of his hair as soon as possible. In truth, I had no idea when we'd be leaving, but I needed his continued cooperation and that of his crew.

"Jude has some coordinates. We need to pinpoint the location."

The captain nodded to the quartermaster who had been standing by for orders. I waved Jude forward. "Show him what you've got."

Jude handed over the notepad he'd scribbled the location on. After a quick glance, the quartermaster passed the pad off to one of the sailors occupying a computer console along the wall. "Bring this up on the screen."

Admiral Reese joined us, and we all moved to the glass chart occupying the center of the room. Quartermaster Campbell pointed out a red dot in the middle of nowhere, North Pacific Ocean style.

"What the hell?" I asked.

Captain Hervey called out, "Show me every ship within a hundred nautical miles of the location." A few seconds later, several more dots appeared on the screen, but none were near the coordinates given.

I already knew the answer, but I had to ask, "Could any of those have moved that far from the location in less than an hour?"

"Not unless they have wings," the admiral said.

Quartermaster Campbell cleared his throat. "Excuse me, ma'am, sirs."

"What is it?" the captain asked.

"Just because there isn't a tracking signal coming from the location, doesn't mean there isn't something there. If it's a private vessel, it's easy enough to turn off the transponder. The only way to be sure is to get eyes on the area."

"He's absolutely right," the captain said. "Going dark is pretty easy. Ships regularly traversing pirated waters often turn off their transponders so the pirates won't know where they are."

I didn't want to get my hopes up, but what he said made sense. Hijackers and pirates were both cut from the same malignant cloth.

Two-thirds of the Earth's surface was made of water. Where better to hide than in the vast openness of the North Pacific?

I glanced at the admiral. "Can we get eyes over the location?"

Admiral Reese deferred to Captain Hervey. "What are our options?"

"I'd recommend sending a flight of fighters. They're fast, can go the distance and remain high enough not to attract too much attention." The captain spoke directly to me. "If they find something, they can blow it to smithereens while they're there."

President Shane Gilchrist
White House, Washington, D.C.
Sunday 01:15 Zulu (Saturday 21:15 EDT)

S hane Gilchrist sat hunched over, elbows atop the desk in his private office adjacent to the Oval Office. His head, resting on his upturned palms, felt like it weighed a ton. The sun had yet to rise on what was shaping up to be the worst day of his life and, possibly, the last day of his political career. The decisions he made over the next few hours would meet with admiration and approval or sink his administration to the depths of historic failure.

"I can't let our plane land on North Korean soil," Gilchrist spoke frankly to his chief of staff, Loren Brett.

Gilchrist had been an idealistic kid, eager to make a difference in the world and naïve enough to think he could actually do it. Loren, only one year older than Shane, was the campaign chairman for the favored candidate running for mayor in the small town outside of Boston where he'd lived while attending Harvard Law School. They'd met when Shane volunteered his time to the campaign. The two men had hit it off and had been friends ever since. Gilchrist often credited Loren with the success of his political career. There was no one he trusted more.

"You can't shoot it down, either."

Shane's head snapped up. "You aren't suggesting I hand those people over to Choi Min-ho, are you? The American public would crucify me!"

"And the entire world will crucify you if you order American military aircraft to shoot down a plane full of innocent people. Not to mention, the death of the people on the plane would force special elections in their jurisdictions and could affect the balance of power in both houses. From a political standpoint, you can't be seen as having anything to do with a decision of this kind." Loren shifted his position in the antique armchair facing the president's desk. "This is a no-win situation unless Major Sloan and her task force pull off a miracle."

"I don't believe in miracles."

"Neither do I, but if, by some miracle, Sloan manages to disrupt the signal and return control of the plane to its crew, even if it ends up crashing or ditching in the ocean, you're going to owe her for saving your political career."

"You're right. I hadn't thought beyond finding the source and eliminating it. The longer the plane is in the air, the less likely it is to land safely—anywhere." Shane thought about the lives on board. Some were friends. Others, not exactly enemies, but certainly not friends. Then there was Shelby Conrad.

He reached for the mug of coffee his personal valet, Joshua, had so thoughtfully placed there, but retracted his shaking hand before he accidentally doused his desk, and himself, with the hot liquid.

Shelby Conrad. He wondered for the millionth time what his life would have been like if he'd met her before embarking on the path he now traveled. Would he still be president? Would she be First Lady instead of Meredith the Merciless? Or would he have settled for a more sedate life, out of the political arena?

How would he endure the endless nights without time with Shelby to look forward to?

"Goddammit, Brett. There has to be something we can do."

"We aren't going to confront Choi. He'd deny any involvement. I can just see him laughing his head off at our dilemma while he tells the world how you set up this entire situation to draw him into a confrontation."

"No one would believe him."

Loren raised one eyebrow. "Maybe. Maybe not. But you can bet every person out there with anti-American sentiments, and every American who opposes your policies regarding a strong military and defense spending will jump on the bandwagon. You'll destroy what credibility you have among our friends in the international community and destroy whatever chance you have at re-election in three years. Not to mention, you won't do anything to help the people on board the plane. In fact, Choi would probably ditch the plane somewhere off the coast of North Korea as proof of your deceit. So, no. You aren't going to initiate contact. If Choi is holding these people hostage, we'll hear from him soon enough."

"Shit!" The president shoved his chair away from the desk and stood, his gaze blindly directed at the curtains drawn tightly against the darkness.

Major Megan Sloan
USS Ronald Reagan
Sunday 01:25 Zulu (11:25 ChST)

Captain Hervey's offer of firepower was tempting, but I shook my head. "Hold off on blowing things up. Our orders are to recover the technology, but if we can't accomplish our mission, we'll take you up on the offer."

The captain issued orders to the quartermaster. "Send those coordinates to the air operations officer. Tell him to expect me in five minutes."

"Tell them to be careful," I said. "If there is something there, we don't want to let them know we've found them, and we have no idea if these people are capable of controlling multiple aircraft at one time, or even how they're doing it."

"Not a problem. No one will know our planes are there unless we want them to know."

I hoped he was right, but who the hell knew what kind of technology these people were using? I thanked him, and he left.

"Ma'am? There's a call for you."

I took the handset from the sailor who also offered me his chair. Too keyed up to sit, I waved him off. "Sloan," I said.

"Colonel Rodgers," a familiar voice replied. "You called?"

I smiled at the casual greeting. We both knew I never bothered my commanding officer unless I had a good reason, so I told him what Gates had discovered and passed on to Jude. I filled him in on the location we thought might or might not be a red herring, pardon the pun, and what we were doing to determine its validity.

"We should have eyes on the location within the hour, Colonel."

"If there is a ship there, what are the chances of reaching it in time?"

"I was just about to ask Admiral Reese for his assistance in that regard. I'll let you know when we have a plan."

"He's under orders to cooperate fully, so if you have any trouble with him, let me know."

"Understood, sir." I filled him in on the conversation I'd had with Liam. He ended the call by agreeing to pass the passenger's wishes along to the president, but I could tell from the sound of his voice he didn't expect a positive response or any response at all. I turned to the admiral who had been carrying on a conversation with the quartermaster. "Can you get me there?"

"Let's see what kind of reception the surveillance planes get. If there is a ghost ship there, getting you to it won't be a problem."

The wait would be hell, but necessary. There was no point in planning any kind of mission until we knew what, if anything, was there. Nevertheless, the logistics of boarding what, no doubt, would be a heavily secured ship raced through my mind. One thing I knew for sure, I couldn't do it alone. "I'll need a team."

"Not a problem."

I followed the admiral to the communications center where we expected to view the aerial surveillance footage. As much as I wanted to find the person or persons behind the hijacking of these planes, I had plenty of reservations about mounting any kind of mission against a floating target. There was a reason I joined the Air Force and not the Navy. I can swim, but there are better ways to get wet and none of them involve splashing around with sharks.

While we were waiting for the surveillance planes to send back images, I checked in with Jude for the latest update from Gates. "Anything new?"

"He thinks he may be able to follow the path they used to get into the aircraft's computer system. If he can, he thinks he can override their programming."

"How long will it take?"

"No idea. Could be minutes. Could be hours or days."

"We don't have days. We may not have hours." I could only imagine what the passengers and crew on the Gulfstream were going through. The uncertainty, the waiting. "What's their status?"

"I spoke with the pilots a few minutes ago. Nothing has changed. They're still headed for North Korea." The fighters shadowing them would have reported a change in course. I was more worried about how the passengers were coping. "Any word on the passengers?"

"Nothing, which I took to mean they were behaving themselves."

I let him know what was happening on my end, and where he could find me for the next few minutes, then let him return to his work.

"Admiral. We have visual confirmation."

At the sailor's announcement, we all turned toward the large, flat-screen mounted on the opposite wall where we were treated to a view of the vast North Pacific Ocean. A distinct voice filled the room. "There's something down there," the pilot said. "I'll make another pass. Hold on."

I've never been disoriented in the pilot's seat, but watching the live feed was like being on some amusement park ride—realistic, but not at the same time. I glanced away long enough to establish my equilibrium again. When I looked up, I zeroed in on the tiny speck in the center of the screen.

"Appears to be a pleasure craft," the pilot said. "A big one. Want me to get closer?"

I felt all eyes on me. The last thing I needed was to mount an all-out assault on a private citizen out for a little R&R. Nothing good could come of that. Whoever was behind this might have somehow fed us those coordinates, hoping we would go cowboy on the boat. It could be Choi Min-ho down there or some other world leader for all we knew. I didn't want to be responsible for starting the next world war. "Can we tell any more about it from what we've got? It could be some rich dude who just wants to be left alone."

The flight commander nodded. "One more pass, Wilcox." He issued orders to bring the aircraft into a tighter circle around the target while remaining out of visual range.

A few minutes later, myself, Admiral Reese, and Captain Hervey stood shoulder to shoulder looking at the latest images from the surveillance aircraft.

"It's a private vessel of some sort. They aren't flying any flags, and the GPS is still off. Whoever it is doesn't want to be found," the captain said.

Admiral Reese frowned. "Turning off their locator doesn't necessarily make them criminals."

There was only one way I could think to get better images—a geosynchronous satellite. I had no way of knowing for certain, but I'd long suspected we had one parked over the region to keep an eye on Choi, and perhaps the Chinese, too. "I need to talk to Colonel Rodgers. And I'll need to use your fancy phone booth again."

The admiral's gaze met mine. He and I were on the same wavelength. With a nod, he broke the connection. "Captain? See to it her call goes through ASAP, and keep eyes on that boat until I say otherwise."

Major Megan Sloan
USS Ronald Reagan
Sunday 01:50 Zulu (11:50 ChST)

"**N**otify Lt. Franklin when the new images come in. He'll know where to find me," the admiral said.

I took faith in his words. If anyone on this ship knew of the existence of a spy satellite monitoring the region, it would be him. "Will do, sir." As soon as he was gone, I turned to the captain. "Comm center?"

"Right this way, Major."

While the same sailor who'd helped me before placed yet another call to the mainland, I filled Jude in on what we'd seen, emphasizing we needed better intel before we could act. He wasn't happy, but I told him, "Get me something solid to go on, and I'll get you to the boat, I promise." I didn't give a damn who was on it, Mrs. Choi or the blessed queen of England. If the signal was coming from that boat, I was going to stop it.

"Colonel Rodgers is on the line, ma'am."

"Get me something, Jude," I said as I stepped into the small but secure booth. "Colonel Rodgers, sir. I need your help."

"Admiral Reese sent us the images from the surveillance planes," he said without preamble. "It's not enough to go on, Major."

"I know, sir, that's why I'm calling. I was hoping we have a better set of eyes in the area. Perhaps a satellite?"

"It's possible. I'll see what I can do."

"Time's running out, sir."

"Without being 100 percent certain, the president will not approve a military action."

I'd known this all along, but hearing it didn't make it any easier to digest. I took a deep breath and replayed the comment in my head, understanding now what he hadn't said. There were plenty of other options out there, none of which involved the use of U.S. military forces. I'd worked with several private "security" teams in the desert. If I'd been caught or killed, the administration would have disavowed any knowledge of my existence. Whatever paper trail could lead to discovering my military service would have vaporized. No doubt there were similar forces available to us now.

"I'm going aboard, sir," I said. "One way or another."

"Roger that, Major. Let me see what I can do about the satellite imagery. Be prepared to go wheels up at a moment's notice."

"Yes, sir."

The line went dead. I held onto the receiver for a few seconds before replacing it on the wall-mounted cradle. It had been years since I'd seen action, but I was more than ready to return to the field. I wished there wasn't an ocean involved, but I'd do anything necessary to end this person's reign of terror.

I checked in with Jude again before making my way to the communications center on my own. Captain Hervey remained where we'd left him, watching the latest images come in from the planes he'd sent out. They were good, no doubt about it, but I'd hoped the intelligence community had better eyes in the sky.

"Anything new?"

"Nothing."

My only connection to Liam and the Gulfstream was through the line to the admiral's office. Since I hadn't heard anything from the people I'd left to keep tabs on them, I excused myself. After a stop at the head, I entered the office. Lt. Franklin sat at his desk, as usual. I wondered if the guy had duty twenty-four/seven or if he even got to eat or take a leak.

"Any change?" I asked as I made my way to the connecting door.

"Nothing. The line is still open. I checked a few minutes ago."

"Thanks."

"Are they going to be all right?"

I appreciated his concern for the hijacked passengers, but, unfortunately, I didn't have an answer. "I wish I knew," I said before stepping into the admiral's inner sanctum. All eyes turned my way. Questions started flying. Hand in the air, I called for quiet. "One at a time, but, first, have we heard anything from the plane?"

Sanchez, whose task was to listen for any communication from Liam or the pilots shook his head. "Not a peep, but I can hear them talking. Sounds like the passengers aren't happy with our lack of progress."

"Believe me, I'm not either." I glanced around the table. Most of these people didn't want to be here any more than I wanted them to be. "Does anyone have anything new? Any scrap of evidence you think might be helpful?"

The silence and averted eyes sent a chill down my spine.

"Okay, then," I said. These people had been brought here to investigate the downed airliner, and they'd had ample time to collect the information they'd come for. "I'll arrange transportation for you to Guam. Pack up and be ready to go in the next half hour. If you have questions or need assistance, talk to Sanchez."

On my way out, I asked the admiral's assistant if he could switch the open line with the plane to the communications center.

"Not a problem, Major. Just tell me when."

"Thank you." A couple of team members shuffled past me to the hallway. "You can tell the admiral he can reclaim his office, and thank him for letting us invade."

"You're leaving?"

I mentally counted heads as the team members filed past. "Just them." Unless I missed someone, the office was empty now. I peeked inside, just to make sure. "Give me a minute, will you? I need to check in with the plane then you can transfer the call."

"Take your time, ma'am. Admiral Reese's office is yours until he tells me otherwise."

"Thanks." Taking a deep breath, I shut the door behind me. I was acutely aware this might be the last opportunity I had to speak to Liam without an audience. I didn't know what I was going to say to him, but I knew I needed to hear his voice. Dropping into the fleet commander's leather desk chair, I picked up the receiver, brought it to my ear, and pushed the button to take the call off mute.

Colonel Clint Rodgers
White House Situation Room
Sunday 02:00 Zulu (Saturday 22:00 EDT)

"**A**bsolutely not." President Gilchrist shook his head. "I want the technology in our hands as bad as the next person, but we aren't boarding the boat until we have some indication who it belongs to."

The president's position wasn't unexpected. He'd proven over the year he'd been in office to be a cautious man when it came to military action, but once he'd decided on a course, he didn't hesitate.

"That's why I'm here, sir." Clint glanced at the men gathered in the White House Situation Room. Everyone he needed was seated around the long conference table. A few didn't look any better than they had when they'd been summoned from their sleep to deal with this crisis. The president had changed out of the shabby-but-comfortable-looking bathrobe he'd worn earlier. Dressed in a dark suit tailored to his slender build, blue shirt, and striped tie, he appeared very much in command. Only the firm line of his lips and the dark circles beneath his eyes hinted at the strain he was under. "We need to get a better look at the boat. It's a ghost, sir. No name to trace. No flag. No transponder. It didn't get where it's at and drop anchor all by itself. Someone is on board, and if we're going to get our hands on the technology they're using, we need to get aboard, too. We understand your position, sir. You don't want to incite an international incident, and we don't want to send a boarding party in without knowing as much as possible about who, and what, they might encounter."

"You still intend to recover the technology?"

"Yes, sir. I've spoken with almost everyone here, and we all agree, recovering the technology is crucial and a top priority."

A man wearing a rumpled charcoal-gray suit and a navy-blue tie with little airplanes on it leaned forward. "If I may, sir?"

The president waved his hand dismissively. "Go ahead, Simmons."

"Thank you, sir. Colonel Rodgers is right. We need to get our hands on this technology. Our experts at Homeland Security have been trying to do something like this for several years. We've run some moderately successful tests on grounded planes, but we're years away from being able to completely control a plane in flight. We need to deconstruct this thing. Find out how this is being done so we can figure out how to stop it from happening again."

He nodded his agreement. "Sir, this may not be the only unit out there. In fact, I'd be surprised if it was."

The president rocked back in his chair. "Anyone disagree with what Simmons and Colonel Rodgers have said?" When no one spoke against their assessment of the situation, Gilchrist asked, "What do you need, Colonel?"

"Satellite imagery, sir."

Gilchrist pointed down the table to a man Rodgers had met several times, Retired Army General Stephen Butler who was Gilchrist's secretary of defense. "What about it, Stephen? Can we get Rodgers what he needs?"

Butler pushed his chair away from the table and stood, tugging the hem of his blue service uniform into place. "Give me a few minutes, sir, to contact Cooper at NGA (National Geospatial-Intelligence Agency)."

"Go ahead," Gilchrist said. "Take Rodgers with you."

The two men were nearing the door when the president's voice stopped them. "Rodgers. No one boards the boat until I say so. Are we clear?"

"Yes, sir."

Butler directed him to a small office adjacent to the Situation Room. "There's a secure phone in here." He waved Rodgers to a seat. "Take a load off. This shouldn't take too long."

They didn't have long. Hours? Minutes? It would take time to get any kind of team together. More time to get them out to the boat's location. Even more time to make their way aboard. It was anyone's guess if the mission could be accomplished in time to save the people on the plane.

Major Megan Sloan
USS Ronald Reagan
Sunday 02:00 Zulu (Noon – ChST)

"Hello? Anyone there? Agent Donovan?"

A voice came on the line. "Just a minute, ma'am."

"Thank you." I heard him tell someone to get Liam. "How's it going?" I asked.

"We're still in the air," he said. "Guess it could be worse."

Knowing the perpetrator had cut off the oxygen supply to the Global passengers, I knew how much worse their situation could be, but I kept it to myself. No use heaping more worry onto their plate. If they reported hypoxia symptoms, we'd deal with the issue then. Hard decisions would need to be made, and I wasn't sure anyone aboard would get a vote. Hell, they weren't being given a vote now. "Just so you know, everyone from the president on down is doing everything possible to get you safely on the ground."

"We appreciate everything you're doing, ma'am."

I heard Liam's voice in the background. "Is that Major Sloan?"

"Here's Donovan, ma'am."

Before I could thank him, Liam came on the line. "Megan?"

I knew I shouldn't have asked to speak with him. The sound of my name rolling off his lips made my stomach cramp. A familiar and unwelcome pain stabbed at my insides while my stupid heart bled for him. "It's me," I said, swallowing hard. "How are things going there?"

"Not good, as you can imagine. I think the only thing keeping some of the passengers from jumping out is the lack of parachutes, though if a couple of them don't shut up soon, I might shove them out the door myself."

We both chuckled, though we knew he was only half kidding. Opening a door at their altitude was physically impossible, but, knowing Liam, he'd puncture the fuselage himself before he'd let one of our own shoot them down. "Don't open the can yet. We have a lead. It's being checked out at the highest levels. If it pans out, this could be over soon."

"I'll hold off on the drastic measures, for now, but some of these people are losing their shit."

I could only imagine. "Do your best. Let them know we haven't forgotten them." *Or you,* I left unsaid. He'd been dead to me for years, which had suited me just fine, so now, with his life on the line, *my line*, I couldn't say I welcomed the heartache of knowing this could be our last conversation.

"I'll tell them."

The silence between us was loud enough to damage my hearing. I pulled the handset away from my ear while I searched for the right words. Part of me wanted to tell him to rot in Hades for putting me through hell on earth all those years ago, and now. But another part of me hated knowing he was helpless. He was the kind of guy who decided if *you* lived or died, not the other way around. Poetic justice, maybe? I should have been thrilled about his situation, but I wasn't. I set the troubling thought aside to examine later when this was re-solved. I had no intention of letting a planeload of people die or be-come Choi Min-ho's hostages if I could help it. The fact one of those people was Liam Donovan shouldn't factor into the equation. Didn't factor in. Didn't.

"I'm going to have Lt. Franklin transfer this call to the commu-nications center."

"You'd only be there if you had a visual on the target."

I heard the hope in his voice, and though I didn't want to squash it completely, I couldn't let him go on thinking the situation was un-der control. "A potential target. Nothing is certain yet."

"I have faith in you, Megan. If there's a way out of this for us, you'll find it."

I'd heard those same words from his lips once before, and then, like today, I knew they revealed more about who he was than any other words he'd ever spoken. Bile burned its way up my throat, the acid eating away at whatever kind thoughts my memory tried to dredge up regarding this man. *Like you found a way out?* Recalling what the therapist told me to do when I had still been in the hospital, the hate and anger doing more to hinder my recovery than the injury itself, I took a couple of deep, cleansing breaths, forcing the anger out with each exhale.

"Don't get me wrong, Liam. If you live through this, it will be because you aren't alone. Are we clear?"

I didn't know how, but I'd taken him by surprise. I could hear him breathing on the other end. In the utterly calm voice he used to mask emotion, he said, "Roger that, Major Sloan."

Was he pissed or hurt? I didn't know, and I didn't care. As long as he knew where we stood. I would do my job despite him being a possible beneficiary.

"I've got to get back to work. As I said, Lt. Franklin is going to transfer the call. We need to keep the line open." *So don't hang up.*

"Roger that. I'll stay on the line for the lieutenant."

I pressed the hold button with enough force it was a wonder the plastic didn't shatter. *Goddamnit.* I took a few more calming breaths. This time, I was angry with myself for letting him get to me. He always could push my buttons, but there'd been a time when he pushed the good ones better than anyone else ever had.

Colonel Rodgers waved his magic wand and, low and behold, a GEO satellite appeared in the heavens. It took a few minutes longer to direct it to the coordinates of our mystery ship, but the deed had been done. After my conversation with Liam, I was ready to kick some ass, and I didn't care who my accomplices were. Hell, I didn't even care if I had accomplices. The anger and hate I'd internalized since our fateful day in the desert were burning a hole in my gut. I needed to vent, and I couldn't think of a better place to do it than on that boat.

Standing shoulder to shoulder with Admiral Reese and Captain Hervey, I stared at the wall-mounted screen. The techs did their thing, zooming in until a tiny white speck became visible, growing larger with each click of the mouse until we had our first good look at the watercraft in question.

"No visible markings," the captain said. "No sign of life."

"There isn't a square inch of deck visible from the air." Someone had gone to a lot of trouble to stretch canvas above all the open decks.

"It could just be someone who values their privacy or needs protection from the sun." This from Lt. Franklin who'd joined us at the admiral's request.

"Or it could be someone who doesn't want to be seen or found," I said.

We all stared at the image, looking for anything to indicate the kind of people aboard. I could only imagine the diplomatic shitstorm that would result from mounting a military action against some influential person's private yacht. We had to be sure we weren't being set up.

"Look!" Admiral Reese pointed to the screen where a lone man had stepped out from under the aft canvas.

"Can we zoom in on him?" I asked.

"Yes, ma'am. Close-up coming right up."

As the image grew larger and larger, it was clear the man wore a military uniform. An automatic weapon hung from a strap over his right shoulder as he puffed on the cigarette he'd come outside to smoke. Leaders of even small countries traveled with military protection, so the fact this guy was in uniform, and armed, didn't tell me a thing.

"That's a North Korean Army uniform." Captain Hervey pointed to the screen. "He's an officer. See the stars on the shoulder boards?"

It took me a second or two longer to make out the distinctive stars, but he was right. If we could get a look at his face, maybe we could put a name with it. It was the best chance we'd have of determining who else might be on the boat. Hell, it could be Mrs. Choi out for a little vacay for all we knew. "We need to see his face."

"Unless he looks up..." the captain said.

I nodded, silently willing the guy to let us get a good look. *Come on. Come on. Come on.* "There!" I leapt toward the screen. Maybe he was checking out the clouds, assessing the weather, or maybe he was wondering who was watching up there. I didn't give a shit. We could now see his face. I watched as the tech zoomed in close enough to see a mole on the guy's chin and question the quality of dental care in North Korea. The technology was amazing and alarming at the same time.

Captain Hervey barked, "Freeze it right there." We were left with a perfect snapshot of the guy.

Before any of us had a chance to do anything more, one of the sailors occupying a computer console held up his phone. "Major Sloan? There's a call for you."

I grabbed the receiver and identified myself.

"We've got it, Sloan," Jude practically shouted. "The plane just changed course. The signal definitely came from those coordinates."

I willed the adrenaline pumping through my system to stand down. This was the best news I'd heard in a long time, but I knew I'd need the rush later on. "You're certain?"

"Absolutely."

I noticed both senior officers were on the phone now. Shit was happening.

"Stay with it, Jude," I said. "Let me know if anything changes."

As soon as I handed the receiver over to the sailor, Admiral Reese waved me over. "Understood, sir. She'll be wheels up in fifteen." He handed off the phone with a polite thank you to the sailor. "Lt. Franklin. See to it the major's bag is packed and topside in fifteen. We'll be in my office."

"Yes, sir." The lieutenant snapped off a salute before he left, presumably to pack my bags for me. I didn't know where I was going, but I was going there fast.

Captain Hervey ended his call. Turning to the admiral, he said, "There will be a C2 ready and waiting in ten. If you don't need me for anything else?"

The admiral smiled. "Just get the plane ready, Captain."

These two worked well together. I could see it in the economy of their speech and hear the respect in their voices. I was in good hands, no small relief knowing I'd soon be putting my life on the line. We left at the same time, the captain peeling off to go do what he did best while the admiral and I made our way to his office in the tower. My gaze landed on his phone, the buttons blank now and I realized I should have updated Liam—only I didn't have a clue what to tell him.

President Shane Gilchrist
White House Situation Room
Sunday 02:15 Zulu (Saturday 10:15 EDT)

Shane Gilchrist, who had been slumped in his chair to watch the live satellite feed, sat up, alert now, as a man stepped from the cover on the mysterious boat anchored in the waters northwest of Guam. Amazing, he thought, as the image appeared, what we can see from a camera in space. Incrementally, details grew clearer as the camera zoomed in on the man, the computer digitally enhancing the image until there could be no mistake. The man smoking a cigarette as if he hadn't a care in the world wore a military uniform.

SECDEF Butler cursed, "Christ, almighty! He's wearing a North Korean uniform."

"Are you certain?" Gilchrist asked.

CIA Director Henry Rotham spoke. "I look at photos of these assholes on a daily basis. He's North Korean Army. See the two large stars on the shoulder boards? He's a lieutenant general." As if he'd heard my prayers, the man turned his face to the sky. Or maybe he was just observing the spattering of puffy white clouds dotting the sky. "Holy shit! It's Pak. He's one of Choi's insiders. Or, he was. No one has seen him for the last year or more. We were beginning to think he'd fallen out of favor, been sent to the mines, or worse. Choi doesn't treat his enemies kindly."

"He's not Navy?" the president asked.

"Nope," Rotham answered. "Army. Choi's pets. He'd never trust something this sensitive to his Navy."

"And he wouldn't send a lieutenant general to guard a family member," the president surmised.

229

"It's not likely. He doesn't care about his relatives."

"What about the boat? What can we tell about it?" Gilchrist asked.

Joint Chief, Admiral Walter Wright answered. "It's definitely a pleasure boat, but the satellite antenna on the roof of the bridge isn't what you'd normally see on a vessel that size. Hell, half the ships in our fleet don't have antennas as big."

Gilchrist squared his shoulders. "We're all agreed, this is no ordinary pleasure craft?" His gaze swept the room, stopping briefly on each face to receive their answer. "Colonel Rodgers," he said, "instruct Major Sloan to board the boat. She'll find all the assistance she needs at Naval Base Guam. Tell her she's to recover the technology if at all possible. Resistance is to be answered with extreme prejudice."

Rodgers stood. "Yes, sir."

"Wright?"

"Yes, Mr. President?"

"If Major Sloan fails to secure the technology, be prepared to blast the boat to bits."

"Yes, sir, Mr. President." Admiral Wright pushed his chair back and stood. "Come with me, Colonel. You tell me what Major Sloan needs, and I'll see she gets it."

Major Megan Sloan
USS Ronald Reagan
Sunday 02:30 Zulu (12:30 ChST)

As soon as we entered his office, the junior officer who had been babysitting our open line with the plane stood and snapped off a smart salute while holding the receiver in his other hand. "Admiral, sir. I've been trying to reach you."

Reese nodded. "Tell them we're aware of the course change and things are developing here. Assure them I'll fill them in shortly."

We moved to the conference table. Behind me, the young man talked to Liam in a firm, authoritative tone. The people on the plane must have been going batshit crazy wondering when they were going to die. Not on my watch. As committed as I was to the thought, I had to be realistic. Whoever was behind this was good. Good enough they could be leading us on a wild goose chase certain to ignite a world war. And, if my instincts were right, I could be the spark. I'd put all my faith in Jude and Gates, a hacker I didn't know shit about other than he was NSA.

The admiral's voice was low, pitched for my ears only. "I just spoke with Colonel Rodgers. The president has authorized you to board the yacht. There will be a C2 waiting to take you to Naval Base Guam in a few minutes. You'll meet up with a SEAL team who will provide support for the mission. By support, I mean personnel and equipment. Another aircraft will be standing by to give you and your team a ride to a drop point a few miles from the target. From there, you'll regroup and proceed to the target. You'll be entirely on your own from the moment you leave the plane. Colonel Rodgers assures me you understand the mission is to recover the technology first. Disabling it and returning control of the plane to the pilots is

231

secondary to capturing the device, and/or the person or persons operating it."

I nodded. "Understood." My gaze shifted to the officer on the phone then again to the admiral. "They've changed direction."

"I know. Our escort pilots reported the turn."

"Any idea where they're headed now?"

Admiral Reese shook his head. "None."

I suddenly felt the weight of everyone aboard the plane resting on my shoulders. "I promised we would keep them in the loop."

"As soon as you're wheels up, I'll speak with Agent Donovan myself."

"Can I ask a favor?"

"Sure."

"Don't let them shoot the plane down. Give me a chance to get to the source."

"It's not my decision."

"I know, but can I count on you to at least argue for more time?"

"I want those people safe on American soil as much as you do, Major. I'll do everything I can to make it happen."

"Thanks." I glanced at the clock on the wall. "Better not keep my ride waiting."

"It's been a pleasure working with you, Major. Godspeed."

"Same, Admiral."

Lt. Graves stood when I entered the outer office. I nodded to her before turning to Lt. Franklin who was once again behind his desk. "You'll make sure Jude gets to Guam when this is all over?"

"Yes, ma'am. I'll see to it he gets VIP treatment while he's here."

"Thank you, and thanks for putting up with us."

"It has been my honor, ma'am. I hope you nail these bastards."

"Me, too, Lieutenant. Me, too."

Lt. Graves led me to the flight deck where a couple of guys wearing helmets, ear protection, and white shirts escorted me to a waiting plane. They made sure I was strapped in and assured me my duffle bag was on board. Above the whine of jet engines, they wished me a safe flight. As they closed the door, I donned my headset and listened to the pilot's conversation with the launch team. I'd never piloted a plane off an aircraft carrier, but this wasn't my first time as a passenger. However, as the aircraft shot down the flight deck and the g-forces took over, I hoped it would be my last. Pilots, as a rule, are crazy-ass people, but the ones who did this for a living were certifiable.

I'd wondered how the selection process went for these people. Once they weeded out the sane people, did they narrow it down to the ones who checked the box beside "Do you often have thoughts of suicide"?

I was sure they'd say the same thing about my line of work, but these guys thought this was fun. I guess it was their way of coping with the fear. I preferred to look fear straight in the eye and thumb my nose at it. I'd do my laughing when we were all safely home. Not before.

A cheerful voice came through my headset. "You okay back there, Major?"

"Just dandy. How long until we land?"

"If you're in a hurry, we can return to the carrier."

"No!" God, no. "In Guam. How long to Guam?"

"Not long, Major. They said to get you there ASAP, so we're taking the shortcut. We might have to dodge some artillery, but there's nothing for you to worry about."

As far as I knew, we were reasonably friendly with everyone in this region, save North Korea. The peninsula was beyond out of our way, and even those crazy idiots up in the cockpit knew better than to fly into Choi's airspace. I hoped. "Thanks," I said. "I appreciate it."

"Our pleasure, ma'am. It's a great day to fly, isn't it?"

I rested my head against the webbing behind me and closed my eyes for the first time in nearly forty-eight hours. "Roger that."

Liam Donovan
Gulfstream G650
Sunday 02:35 Zulu (12:35 ChST)

"Calm down, everyone!" Liam braced himself against the galley opening to address the passengers. "It's just a turn. No need to panic."

Representative Sanders, his face ash white, yelled out, "We're going to crash!"

The irrational declaration spurred a chorus of similar panic-laced comments from the other passengers. Liam noticed only Senator Shelby Conrad kept her mouth shut. He didn't know if she recognized the turn for what it was or if she was silently praying, and he didn't care. She got points in his book for her silence. He could use a little more quiet from the rest of the passengers right now.

"We are not going to crash!" he said over the melee. "The plane is leveling out. Feel it?"

The cabin quieted to a low grumble as the delegates realized the truth in Liam's statement. The plane was leveling out on its new course. Wherever the hell that was.

"What's going on?" Senator Hastings asked. "Why the turn?"

His patience with this group was thinner than the toilet paper in a federal building and twice as fragile. A less than diplomatic response sat on the tip of his tongue, but his partner beat him to it. "We don't know, Senator," Mike said. "We've had no communication with the person behind this. All we can tell you for certain is this change in direction is taking us away from Pyongyang. I'm sure we can all agree the new heading is an improvement."

"Sure as hell is," Senator Hastings said.

Mike's little speech seemed to calm their charges, so Liam took the opportunity to disappear into the cockpit to see what the pilots could tell him about their new heading.

"Any idea where we're going now?" he asked.

Captain Davis tapped the screen where the new compass heading was displayed. "As best as we can tell...nowhere."

"Nowhere?"

"Nothing but ocean ahead," First Officer Wilkerson said. "If we had enough fuel, we might be feet dry in Okinawa, but it's a long shot."

"Impossible," Davis said. "Our tanks will be dry long before we make it to Okinawa."

"Well, crap."

"I wouldn't tell them." Davis hooked a thumb over his shoulder. "The less they know about our present course, the better."

"You heard the freak out over the turn?"

"Yep. How could we miss it?"

"I agree with you. There's no point in telling them where we're headed. Whoever is doing this could change their mind and set us on course for North Korea again or God knows where. No sense getting them all worked up over something we can't do anything about."

"Any word from our ground support?"

Wilkerson said, "I told them about the turn, but our escorts had already filled them in. Maybe you can get something more concrete out of them?"

"I'll give it a try. Hand me the phone."

Wilkerson handed over the satellite phone. Liam settled into the jump seat and pressed the device to his ear. "Hello? Anyone there? This is Liam Donovan."

After a few seconds of silence, a voice came on the line. "Agent Donovan? This is Rear Admiral Reese on the USS *Ronald Reagan*. How are you doing up there?"

"We're hanging in there, Admiral. The passengers are concerned about the new direction. My understanding is we're headed to the middle of nowhere. Can you confirm?"

"Nothing but ocean ahead, Donovan."

As Liam nodded, his heart raced. He'd hoped their escorts had a brighter outlook on their compasses since he wasn't inclined to believe anything on their own instrument panels. "Roger that, Admiral. Any word from the person responsible for this?"

"Negative. No one has claimed responsibility or demanded anything from the president. However, we do have a bit of news."

"Good or bad?"

"Depends," the admiral said. "We've isolated the source of the satellite signals. The president has authorized military action to recover the technology."

"Is that the good news or the bad?"

"The good."

"Then what's the bad news?"

"The source is a private yacht anchored about two-hundred miles northwest of Guam."

"A yacht? Who owns it?"

"No idea, but satellite imagery confirms there are North Korean military aboard."

"Shit."

"You know as much as we do now, Agent Donovan. We could be looking at World War III here if this isn't handled right."

"You said the mission was to recover the technology? Is that military double-talk for disabling the signal controlling our aircraft is the secondary goal?"

"I see you're well-versed in military jargon."

Liam ran his free hand over his scalp and blew out a frustrated breath. "Who are they sending to recover the technology?"

"Major Sloan will be accompanied by a SEAL team out of Naval Base Guam. She's on her way to the island as we speak."

"How big is the yacht? How many people are guarding this technology?"

"The boat can hold about sixty people, I'm told, but we don't have any way of knowing how many are actually on board."

The SEALs had a reputation for being the best of the best, but Liam didn't like the odds. If it was up to him, he'd just blow the boat out of the water, and he said so.

"As I said, Agent Donovan, the president's first priority is recovering the technology. We have no way of knowing if there are other devices out there, so it's imperative we get our hands on this one so our people can dissect it. Blowing it up would solve our immediate problem but could endanger others down the road."

"Understood, Admiral."

"We haven't forgotten you, Donovan. Major Sloan is committed to recovering the technology as well as disabling it. Advise Davis and Wilkerson to be on alert for any change in the instruments. Once the device is disabled, they'll have to resume control of the aircraft immediately."

"They'll be ready, sir."

Major Megan Sloan
Naval Base Guam
Sunday 03:30 Zulu (13:30 ChST)

I woke to the grind of landing gear moving into place. I switched out the ear protection for the headset that would let me communicate with the flight crew. "Are we home?"

"It's American soil, so yeah, we're home."

The wheels touched down. Not a bad landing, but any landing you walk away from is a good one, right? "Nice job," I said as we taxied to a hangar at the far end of the runway.

"We have our moments, ma'am," came the reply. "It sure would be easier, though, if they'd float these runways."

The stab at the Air Force made me laugh. The rivalry was real, but when it came down to it, we were all on the same team. I was grateful for their help, and I said so as I exited the aircraft. "Stay safe."

"You, too, ma'am. Give 'em hell."

I nodded. "I plan on it."

Just past the unidentified hangar sat a C-130 with the cargo door open. With the sun setting behind the giant building, I could see only a few feet inside. Somewhere in the dark, cavernous building were the men who had been chosen to get me onto the boat and, hopefully, keep me from getting killed while I located and disabled the computer system. As I approached, a tall man wearing blue-and-gray tactical gear came out to meet me.

"Major Sloan, I presume?" He offered me his hand. "Chase Harper. Most people call me LT."

His grip was firm, as I would expect from six feet of dangerous lean muscle. Startling blue eyes framed by deep lines assessed me while I returned the favor. His skin was a shade of golden brown only achieved by too much exposure to the sun. I'd never been a fan of the military, high-and-tight hairstyle, but on him, it worked. Maybe it was the serious expression on his face, but I got the impression this guy didn't have a sense of humor. Not a problem. There was nothing funny about what we were about to do. "Lieutenant."

"Ready to go for a swim?"

"As ready as I'll ever be," I said, which was to say, no. "Did anyone fill you in on the mission?" Trusting Harper wasn't going to lead me straight into a wall, I followed blindly as my eyes adjusted to the dark interior.

"Admiral Reese said we're to get you aboard a boat that doesn't exist and protect your six while you recover something that also doesn't exist," he said as we made our way deeper into the building.

"Sounds about right," I said.

"Piece of cake."

The rest of the team was in the far corner. They'd already suited up in wetsuits and were going through their checklists—a reminder of how fast the clock was ticking on this mission. There wasn't a second to waste. Whoever was in control of the Gulfstream could decide to ditch it in the ocean at any moment or cut off the oxygen supply as they'd done with the Global flight. Once we were airborne, I'd get a status update, but no matter what happened to Liam and the rest of the people on board the plane, my mission was clear—end this once and for all.

"Look alive," Harper called out as we approached.

Five sets of eyes turned my way. Even though I outranked all of them, no one saluted, and I couldn't have cared less. For the time being, we were a team. My life wasn't worth any more or less than any of theirs. As a group, they moved toward me, hands outstretched.

The guy on the far left stepped forward. "Pleased to meet you, ma'am. Name's Augustus Simon. Everyone calls me Guts." My hand disappeared in his big mitt. He was the biggest of the bunch but still retained the lean, muscular physique I associated with Navy SEALs. I wasn't sure I wanted to know how he got his nickname.

"Guts," I said, moving on to the next guy.

"Lance Adams." His eyes sparkled with amusement as he took my right hand in both of his. "These guys call me Lancelot, but you can call me anytime you want."

I smiled at his playful Southern drawl and pointed to the black band on his left ring finger. "What would Guinevere say about that?"

His cheeks flushed an adorable red. "Ahh, shucks, ma'am. She'd love you, too."

"Lancelot has only been married a month," Harper said. "Sometimes he forgets."

"Never," Lance argued. "Emily's unforgettable. Nice to meet you, ma'am."

"It's my pleasure," I said before moving to the next outstretched hand.

"William Brooks, ma'am. Glad to meet you." The smallest of the bunch, he was still a good six inches taller than me, and though his smile was genuine, there was something dark lurking in the depth of his gaze. He might as well have had *Sniper* tattooed on his forehead.

"What do they call you?"

"Kid, mostly."

Harper stepped in. "Kid is short for Billy the Kid."

Yep. Sniper. I moved on to the next outstretched hand. "Diego Martinez," he said as he took my hand in a firm grasp, "but you can call me Cookie like everyone else."

"As in that's the way the cookie crumbles?" I asked.

He shook his head. "Nope. As in, if it weren't for me, these other wise-asses would probably starve."

"He could open his own restaurant," Guts said, "but he prefers to be shot at."

"Well, I wouldn't go that far," Martinez said with a laugh, "but dinner is on me when we get home. Deal?"

"Deal," I said.

The next guy in line introduced himself. "Angelo Gaetano. They call me Angel."

"Nice to meet you, Angel."

"Angel's in charge of our communications. If you want to talk to God, he's your man."

"Only if God is here on earth," Angel added. "I'm not a miracle worker."

"Too bad," I said. "I could use a miracle about now."

"We'll get you on the boat, Major." Harper reached for a duffel bag and handed it to me. "Didn't figure you brought your own wet suit, so we got one for you. Admiral Reese said he asked your man on the *Reagan* about the size."

"I'd better see if it fits." I'd trust Jude with lots of things, but guessing at the size of my clothing wasn't one of them.

"You can change in the office." He pointed out a solid door flanked by windows with the blinds closed. "We're almost done here. Wheels up in ten minutes."

Major Megan Sloan
Naval Base Guam
Sunday 03:45 Zulu (13:30 ChST)

With no time to waste, I headed for the office but stopped at the sound of Harper's voice. "You have jumped before, haven't you?

More than I wanted, I thought, but nodded and said, "A few times."

Everything in the bag was black, from the insulated undergarments to the outer neoprene layer. I stripped down and wiggled into the outfit. Jude did a good job sizing me up. I couldn't decide if I should speak to him about it later on or just let it go. Stuffing my discarded clothes into the bag, I toted it out with me.

"Drop it anywhere," Angel said. "It'll be here when we return."

"Everybody ready?" I got the feeling Harper knew the answer to the question or he wouldn't be asking. No one replied. In what appeared to be a well-choreographed move, the team hefted their packs and moved as one toward our ride waiting outside on the tarmac. Hanging back, the lieutenant pointed to a lone pack. "That one is yours."

I wasn't sure what was inside, but a helmet, goggles, and swim fins hung from the sides. "I need all this stuff?"

"Not if this is a suicide mission."

"It's not."

"Then, grab it, and let's go."

The damn thing must have weighed fifty pounds, but I managed to lift and sling it over my shoulder without grunting or collapsing. Harper nodded, and his lips lifted slightly on one side. He fell into step beside me. "Cookie packs our chutes. He's never messed one up, so no worries there."

Like most skydivers, I'd prefer to pack my own chute, but there was no time, and it had been so long since I'd packed one, it was probably better this way. "Good to know."

"This will be a HAHO—high altitude, high open jump. You okay with jumping last?"

"Works for me." I was sure there'd be a jumpmaster aboard to give me a shove if my feet refused to move.

"I'll jump right before you. Count to ten then follow me. Just follow us down, nice and easy. By the time you hit the water, we'll have the Zodiac inflated and be ready to go. Guide yourself down as close to it as possible. When your feet hit the water, release the chute. We'll come to you, so don't sweat it."

Sweat it? Was he kidding? I was dressed all in black and would be jumping out of a perfectly good aircraft over an ocean. My target would be a black rubber rectangle about the size of a bass boat. Nothing to worry about.

As soon as we were wheels up, Harper, who was sitting in the jump seat next to mine, unhooked his harness and dragged my pack out from under my seat. Everyone else had unstrapped and were busy putting on their helmets, goggles, and breathing masks. The cabin was pressurized, but once the cargo hatch opened, we'd need the oxygen. I released my harness as well. Harper helped me get my feet in the swim fins, adjusting them so they wouldn't fly off when I waddled out of the plane. Once my flippers were on, he handed me a tactical vest. "Put this on and stand up so I can hook your oxygen bottle to it."

The armored vest and the oxygen tank accounted for most of the weight in the pack, but I didn't complain. I needed both.

"Put the mask on," he said. "We need to start taking oxygen now to flush the nitrogen from our system so we don't get the bends."

Like I said, it had been a while since I'd done this, but the protocol was coming back to me. I donned my mask, and Harper adjusted the oxygen flow.

He dug a watertight holster from my pack and looked up at me. "Right-handed, correct?"

I nodded, and he strapped the firearm to my right thigh, adjusting it so I could reach it without bending over.

Harper explained each item as he added it to my body. Not that I wasn't grateful for the blade strapped to my left thigh and the M4 slung across my chest, but by the time he was through fishing things out of the bag, I was convinced he was Santa Claus and the pack was his magic bag. I hoped like hell they kept their promise to fish me out as soon as I hit the water because there was no way I could swim with all the extra weight strapped to me.

I was feeling a lot like an anchor when Lancelot turned toward me. He lifted his mask, gave me a thumbs up, and said, "Badass."

I acknowledged the compliment with a thumbs-up and forced myself to relax. He and the others wore twice as much gear. I'd done this before but never with this much weight. Harper suited up, and, soon, the team was lined up behind a huge netted bundle they said was our transportation from the drop zone to the boat—provided we, meaning I, didn't sink to the bottom of the ocean before we, meaning I, got in it.

The last item Harper had for me was a communication device so we could keep in touch once we made it to the boat. While he accessorized my badass outfit, we went over the mission plan. Since my plan went something like this—get on the boat, disable the computer system, and kill the bastard doing this if he resisted—I'm glad someone else was thinking this through.

"Any idea what kind of resistance we might meet?" he asked.

I shrugged. "Not a clue. Could be a handful of guys, could be they're packed in the boat like rats."

"We have to assume they're prepared to protect the technology at all cost."

"I'd be surprised if they aren't. This is a game changer, and they know it."

"Then we'll be careful not to sink the boat before you secure the computer." He flashed me a bright smile. "Just kidding."

And I didn't think he had a sense of humor. I returned his smile with one of my own, grateful his little joke lightened my mood.

"Much better," he said. "We've got this."

I placed the receiver in my ear.

"Good?" he asked.

I nodded, and the lieutenant turned away. His voice sounded in my ear. "Everybody check in."

One by one, the team members confirmed they were online. Harper turned to me. "Sloan?"

"Yeah, I'm here."

He turned to face the rear of the plane. "Approaching the drop zone. Hold on."

I grabbed my tether strap and held on for dear life as the cargo door slowly opened, leaving a gaping hole in the rear of the aircraft. My brain knew it was a controlled maneuver, but my pilot heart skipped a beat. The last thing any pilot wanted to see was a hole in their aircraft, especially at thirty-thousand feet.

Before I could take a deep breath, Harper reminded me to count to ten before he fell forward into the abyss, and it was my turn to face death.

I waddled to the edge. I counted six tiny dots representing the team I was depending on to keep me alive. My internal clock told me it had been longer than ten seconds since Harper dove from this very spot. The jumpmaster, an Air Force corpsman, pointed at his watch and signaled for me to get a move on. I'm sure he wanted to shut the cargo door and forget he'd ever seen us. In fact, I was certain those were his orders. If we succeeded, our names would never be linked to this mission. If we failed, there was no mission. Period. The plane was out on a training run, end of story.

Against my better judgment, I spread my arms wide and leaned forward until gravity took over.

Liam Donovan
Gulfstream G650
Sunday 04:00 Zulu (14:00 ChST)

"**I**'m going to have to tell them eventually."

"No need to start a panic at this point," Captain Davis replied. "If they haven't noticed the loss in altitude, why point it out?"

"They'll notice soon enough," Wilkerson added. "We'll have plenty of time to prepare them for a crash landing."

"Shit!" Liam resisted the urge to drive his fist through the cockpit's back panel. He'd always been the kind of person to step in, to do something. He'd recognized the personality trait early on when he'd gotten into fight after fight in defense of his friends who had been victims of the local bullies. Every fight he lost, and there had been plenty when he was nothing but a kid, had driven him to hone his skills, so by the time he'd made it to high school, his reputation preceded him. No one messed with Liam Donovan—or his friends—lest they suffer the consequences.

Someone was messing with him now, and knowing there was absolutely nothing he could do about it was driving him nuts. Much more of this, and he'd be as crazy as his passengers.

"How long before they reach the boat?" Davis asked.

"I have no idea." Another thing trying his patience. Megan Sloan was one of the most competent intelligence agents he'd ever worked with, but she'd been more than a colleague. Until he'd screwed everything up by sleeping with a bimbo in San Diego. Finding out had sent Megan into a tailspin, and he couldn't help but think the breakup of their relationship shortly before the mission in Iran had had some bearing on the outcome. They should have spoken up—asked to be replaced on the team, but, afraid to expose their personal relationship, neither one had said anything. They'd gone forward, and—he could speak only for himself—he'd known they weren't in the right frame of mind. He remembered being pissed at her for not giving him another chance, and pissed at himself for screwing it up in the first place. If he hadn't been castigating himself at every turn, he might have recognized the warning signs along the way. As it was, he'd messed up the mission, and though he knew it was wrong, he'd left two of his team for dead and gotten the hell out of there before he lost more men.

Leaving Megan in a desert hellhole had been the hardest thing he'd ever done, and the least honorable no matter what their orders had been. Megan wasn't some weakling who needed him to keep the bullies away, but the one time she'd needed him, he'd let her down.

Still, she'd been the first person he'd thought to call when his present assignment turned into the flight from hell. She hated him, and rightfully so, but she had more honor in her little finger than he'd ever possessed. After emerging from the desert, wounded but miraculously alive, she'd continued their mission in the only way she could.

Few knew of The Drone Theory task force. He'd learned of it by calling in favors in the intelligence community. Anyone who knew Megan was pumped for information regarding her whereabouts. Thus, he'd followed her career these last few years and instantly knew she was the one person uniquely qualified to get him out of his present predicament.

She'd do as ordered, though, which meant he and his high-profile charges were a distant second in priority to recovering the technology. Technology his team had failed to recover in Iran. No one was saying it, but he knew it was true. Someone had gotten their hands on the drone technology and built on it.

He'd heard through the grapevine Megan blamed herself for the failed mission that had almost cost her everything. Heading the task force was her way of atoning for past sins. This was her second chance. She wouldn't fail. He knew her. She'd do whatever it took to complete the mission—or die trying.

He glanced at his watch. "How long can we stay in the air?"

"Couple more hours, tops." Wilkerson had been keeping close tabs on the fuel situation, calculating consumption by hand since they had zero confidence in any of the gauges.

"At this rate of descent, what comes first? Running out of fuel or a hard water landing?"

"Water landing. No doubt about it."

"Great. Just great."

Major Megan Sloan
North Pacific Ocean 750 miles NW of Guam
Sunday 06:15 Zulu (16:15 ChST)

Shit! I'd never been a strong swimmer, but, weighed down with all this equipment, I didn't have a chance. Moments before my flippers touched the surface a voice sounded in my ear. "Ditch the chute! Ditch the chute!" My hands were already on the release latches, so I did as instructed and freefell the last few feet into the water. As I sank below the surface, I fought the panic slamming my heart against my ribcage and shifting my lungs into overdrive. Then, by some miracle, I was rising fast. Scissoring my legs, I worked my arms to speed up the process. My head popped above the water and, through my watery goggles, I saw two men hanging over the wall of the Zodiac, arms outstretched.

"Gotcha!"

It wasn't pretty, but they managed to haul my ass into the boat. Before I was fully situated, we were on our way.

"Here, let me help." It was Angel, I think. He helped me ditch the goggles and the breathing apparatus. It all went overboard.

I hoped to God someone knew where we were going because we were in the middle of nowhere, surrounded by ocean.

"Sit back and relax, Major." Angel wrapped my hand tight around a grip molded to the top side of the boat. "And hang on. Water's rough."

"How long?"

I wasn't sure if he heard me or just anticipated my question, but he was quick with an answer. "Fifteen minutes."

I nodded my thanks and turned my attention to mentally preparing for the fight ahead, and I had no doubt there would be a fight. I wasn't stupid enough to believe this was the perpetrator's end game. There was more at stake here than a plane full of American politicians. You didn't mess with the United States and not expect retaliation.

I noticed the change in the vibration of the powerful but almost silent motor a second before the change in our speed registered. We slowed to a crawl. Beside me, Angel directed my attention to a speck on the horizon. It flickered in and out of sight as waves rocked the boat.

Hallelujah. It was real.

"We should be able to get closer," Lancelot said. "Everyone, look alive. We have no way of knowing what kind of surveillance they have on board. If we can see them, we have to assume they can see us."

Satellite photos had revealed the usual array of antennas for a seagoing vessel, plus one stupidly large satellite dish, which was both comforting and concerning. At least they weren't using military-grade surveillance to detect approaching craft, but a yacht that size would come equipped with a decent radar setup which might or might not pick up something as small as our Zodiac.

Admiral Reese had used the term ghost ship. Situated far out of the usual shipping lanes, even with their transponder turned off it was unlikely a cargo ship would run over them. They were the ocean-going version of a needle in a haystack. If not for the transmission Jude had intercepted and traced to their location, we might never have found them.

"They could have anything from physical lookouts posted on the decks to some sort of technology we know nothing about," I said.

"She's right," Harper said. "We approach with caution. You see anything on deck, Kid?"

Kid lay prone in the bow, his face pressed to the butt of a rifle mounted on a tripod and resting on the inflated edge of the Zodiac. It made me seasick just to look at him. I don't know how he managed it, but his focus hadn't wavered since we'd been underway. "Nothing stirring, sir. No movement on the bridge. If I didn't know better, I'd think the damned boat was abandoned."

"Guts?"

"Nothing, sir. Like Kid said, looks abandoned."

"We all know it isn't, so don't let your guard down. They're there, somewhere. When we board, do not assume we'll be taking them by surprise."

"Expect the worst, and you won't be disappointed." This from Lancelot who, up until now, had been lounging in the middle of the boat like we were out on a pleasure cruise. I'd seen it before. Some soldiers were like live wires dancing on wet pavement before a mission. Others were like cobras coiled in a basket, calm on the outside but prepared to unleash holy hell at a moment's notice. I didn't want to be the one to poke the coiled snake, but the people who knew him best had no problem.

"Advice from your wedding day?" Cookie asked, earning a chuckle from everyone, including Lancelot.

"Nope. Don't you Neanderthals read? Words of wisdom from Helen MacInnes. She wrote spy novels, back in the day."

"One man on the stern," Guts said. "Looks like he's taking a smoke."

"Want me to take him out?" Kid asked.

"Not yet. Wait until my signal." Harper steered the boat on a steady course toward the floating nest of evil.

The sighting ramped up the tension in the boat. Even Lancelot checked his weapons. I went over the plan in my mind. Kid would take out anyone standing on the deck before the first team, Cookie and Angel, boarded the boat. Lancelot and Guts would be right behind them, securing the open deck in the opposite direction. As soon as the two teams gave the all-clear, I would board with Kid and Harper on my six. The four-man forward team would clear a path for the rest of us to make our way through the boat in search of the computer center and the person controlling the Gulfstream.

The yacht became a distinct shape on the water then, slowly and silently, a solid wall of black as we crept closer. Kid's target had moved out of sight. There was no way of knowing if he'd gone inside or had taken up a post beneath the canvas canopy stretched over the aft deck. We'd know soon enough.

Harper's hand was steady on the tiller as we crept closer and closer. Silent, like the deadly serpent he was, Lance coiled to strike. I moved to my knees, my hands instinctively touching the weapons strapped to various parts of my body. Assured everything was where it was supposed to be, I forced air in and out of my lungs.

I hadn't heard anything from my crew on the USS *Ronald Reagan* who were under orders not to contact me unless the status of the plane changed, so when Angel began fidgeting with his communications gear, I sensed the whole no-news-is-good-news cliché had been shot to hell. An image of Liam's smiling face flashed in my mind, one from the days when I believed in those smiles, and, for one blinding split second, my breath hitched and the pain in my abdomen threatened to sink me straight to the bottom of the ocean as I imagined a world without him in it.

With a nudge to my shoulder, Angel drew my attention to the satellite phone in his hand. "Admiral Reese, for you."

As I pressed the phone to my ear, I felt the Zodiac slow. "Admiral?"

"Donovan notified us, and our surveillance confirms, they've changed direction again, and their losing altitude."

"What's their heading now? Can they land?"

"Nowhere to land but in the water. As for their direction, they should pass right over your location soon."

"How soon?"

"If they maintain their present airspeed, less than an hour."

What the hell? "Thanks, Admiral. Tell them we've got the boat in sight and to be prepared to take control of the aircraft at any moment." Handing the phone to Angel, I clicked my comm device on. "Times up," I said. "Looks like they're going to ditch the plane right on top of us."

The Zodiac took a leap forward, its nose rising out of the water as we sped toward the yacht.

Harper's voice pitched low sent a shiver down my spine. "MacInnes also said, 'Civilization is a perishable commodity.' It isn't going to perish on our watch."

"The water is getting closer." Deputy Secretary Cho looked away from the window, a mask of panic on her face. "We're going to crash into the ocean!"

Her announcement drew everyone else to a window, and when they'd all come to the same conclusion, pandemonium broke out. Liam didn't need his partner, Mike, to stick his head in the cockpit to tell him what he could hear with his own ears.

"Hey, man. They're going batshit crazy back there."

"Yeah, we can hear it up here." Liam stood, stretching the kinks out of his muscles. Jump seats were made for elves, not grown men. "I'll see what I can do. Going apeshit won't help them survive when we hit the water."

"I tried to calm them down, but the Cho woman keeps running her mouth. She's got the entire delegation stirred up."

"Fantastic." Liam clamped a hand on Mike's shoulder. He still looked pale from the stomach bug he'd been battling since Hawaii. He'd only recently come out of the forward lavatory to declare himself on the mend. Now this. "Have a seat. If we get control of the plane again, these guys are going to need all the help they can get to pull this thing out of this descent."

"What do I do? I don't know shit about flying planes."

Liam waved a hand at the array of buttons and switches across the ceiling. "If it buzzes, beeps or flashes, reset it. Davis and Wilkerson will do the rest."

"I can do that." Judging from the lack of confidence in the man's voice, Liam wasn't so sure, but he had no choice. Mike had little suc-

256

cess getting the passengers to listen to anything he had to say, so it was up to Liam to restore calm.

"I'll be back in a few. Stay alert, guys." At their rate of descent, Davis calculated they had around twenty minutes before they hit the water. Megan and her team had better hurry up.

Standing in the forward galley, Liam surveyed the situation. General panic was the description he'd use in his report—if he ever got a chance to write it. Everyone, save one, was out of their seat. Some had their faces glued to the oval-shaped windows. Others stood in the aisle, looking like rats searching for a way out of a rapidly flooding sewer pipe. Amid all the chaos, one person sat perfectly still in her seat—Senator Shelby Conrad. Though she sat next to a window, her eyes were cast down, her hands folded in her lap. She was either the coolest cucumber in the batch or too frightened to move. Either one was okay with him. It was time to scare the shit out of the rest of them and gain some order in the cabin.

"Sit down and shut up!" He singled out the ones he knew by name, pointing to empty seats and staring them down until, one by one, they complied. "Fasten your seat belts." He walked through the cabin making sure everyone had followed his instructions.

"As you have discovered, we are in a slow descent. At this rate, we'll hit the surface in about twenty minutes—unless Major Sloan and her team manage to disable whatever system is controlling our aircraft. The last report from Admiral Reese said Major Sloan and a SEAL team out of Guam have located the boat and will engage the enemy as soon as possible." Hands braced on his hips, Liam fixed his gaze on the escort plane visible through one of the windows. He took a deep breath and continued. "Major Sloan is one of the best. She'll recover the technology and disable it. You can count on her."

Senator Hastings leaned into the aisle so he could make eye contact with Liam. "But can we count on her disabling the system *before* we end up in the ocean?"

He sure as hell hoped so, but he couldn't give any guarantees, so he said, "If it comes to ditching in the ocean, listen to Charlie and Jeannie. Do everything they say, and you'll increase your odds of survival."

With those words, he turned and headed to the cockpit. Time was running out. If they didn't regain control soon, they'd all be tucking their heads down and kissing their asses goodbye.

Kwon Seul-ki
North Pacific Ocean 750 miles NW of Guam
Sunday 06:30 Zulu (14:30 ChST)

Seul-ki glanced up from the computer screen he'd been studying for the last few hours. The sound of heavy, rapid footsteps and raised voices in the passageway outside his small cabin had broken his concentration. He listened, heart pounding. Had Supreme Leader finally decided he was of no more use? Were Choi's loyal soldiers preparing to come for him? To finally put an end to his misery? If so, they'd better hurry. Did they know what he'd done? Did they know he'd changed the direction of the plane? At this very moment, it was descending rapidly on a collision course with their boat.

There was nothing his guards could do to stop it. They could kill him, but he was the only one who could change the settings, and he had no intention of doing so. It was time to end this game Choi Minho played.

Over the last few hours, he'd made enough deliberate mistakes any hacker with average skills and equipment, much less the United States government, should have been able to track the signals to his location. But as time had gone on, he'd lost faith in the Americans finding them and putting an end to this, so he'd taken matters into his own hands, redirecting the Gulfstream.

His stomach cramped at the idea of taking more innocent lives, but the plane was the only weapon he had.

The door burst open, and General Pak, an automatic weapon slung across his front, stepped in. "You are not to leave this room," he said, his gaze raking the small room, for what, Seul-ki had no idea.

He was always alone except for the lone guard who kept watch over him. "Where is your guard?"

Seul-ki shrugged. "Why? What is going on?"

"It is none of your business," Pak said. "Get back to work. Supreme Leader does not pay you to ask stupid questions."

He doesn't pay me at all, Seul-ki thought as the general slammed and locked the door behind him. There was more shouting and footsteps pounding up the staircase adjacent to one wall of his room. Sitting heavily into his desk chair, he listened to the activity on the upper decks. The sound of gunfire reminded him of the times the soldiers had practiced firing their weapons, except those sessions had been in measured, controlled bursts, not this continuous and random spacing of shots. He made out the sound of the big gun mounted near the bridge. He'd only heard it once before and knew it could only mean one thing. The Americans had come.

He smiled.

It would all be over soon.

Major Megan Sloan
North Pacific Ocean
Sunday 06:30 Zulu (17:30 ChST)

We had the setting sun behind us, and, as far as I could tell, the giant flaming orb was the only advantage we had. They were going to ditch the plane right over our heads unless we pulled off a miracle pretty damn quick. Every minute we were out here brought the passengers and crew of the Gulfstream closer to disaster. I frantically tried to calculate the odds of the pilots pulling the plane out of its descent seconds before impact, but there were too many unknowns to make any kind of judgment. How experienced were the pilots? How would they react under extreme pressure? What was the rate of their descent and their airspeed? Did they have enough fuel left to pull off such a maneuver and still find dry ground? I was no expert on the Gulfstream 650. I couldn't even begin to guess how the plane itself would perform under that kind of stress. All I knew for sure was we were out of time. We had to get aboard the yacht and disable the computer system holding the plane hostage.

We were closing in on our destination fast. How Kid maintained his perch in the bow of the Zodiac was beyond me, but he and his weapon were our first line of defense. As we got closer, I was struck by the size of the boat. It hadn't looked this big in the satellite photos. With its dark hull and helipad, it resembled a research vessel more than a private yacht. It wasn't the biggest or fanciest yacht out there, but it was bigger and fancier than the average boating enthusiast could afford. Jude had dug up specifics—nearly 150 feet long and weighing almost 700 tons, with more than a dozen staterooms, not counting crew quarters and public rooms. It'd be a bitch to search even if we had all the time in the world, which we didn't.

According to Jude, the boat could accommodate around sixty people at one time. I doubted there were sixty people on board, but it was a possibility. The seven of us facing off against that many in close quarters gave me pause, but when I'd voiced my concerns to the team earlier, they'd nearly laughed their asses off. Six SEALs against possibly sixty North Korean troops? Not a problem.

I was betting my life and the lives of countless others on the courage of my companions. I sure as shit hoped my confidence wasn't misplaced.

The first shots missed us by a mile. I didn't know if it was intentional, a warning, or if the shooter couldn't hit the broad side of a barn with a cannon. We were the only things out here, and, though it seemed like we were flying across the water, any decent marksman should have been able to hit the Zodiac, at the very least. At worst, pick us off one by one.

"Did you see where the shots came from?" Harper's question was directed at Kid.

"Yep. Surface mount near the bridge. Hold 'er steady for a sec, and I'll take care of him."

Kid fired a single shot. Harper swung the Zodiac wide, away, taking us out of range again. Binoculars held to his face, Cookie reported, "One down. They're coming out of the woodwork now. I count five. Make that six."

Shit. At this rate, we were never going to get on the boat.

"Weapons?" Harper asked.

"Automatic. Old shit. Maybe Chinese surplus."

In other words, unreliable, but still deadly.

"You ready, Lancelot?"

Ready for what, I wondered. He was still lying in the middle of the Zodiac, playing with his weapons. Only now I could see he still had his oxygen tank and was donning his mask. "Can you get a little closer, sir?"

"Coming around. Fire at will," Harper ordered as he powered the Zodiac toward the yacht. We were taking some serious fire, all of us lined up on the starboard side, returning the favor. I counted two down. When I glanced around, the bottom of the boat was empty. At my startled expression, Harper smiled and took us out of range again. "Lancelot is the best we have at close work. He'll keep 'em busy for us." To Cookie, he said, "Let me know when the first one goes down and I'll bring the boat around to the swim deck. By the time we dock Lancelot should have the situation in hand."

If I didn't know better, I'd swear these guys were having fun. We zigged and zagged, getting closer, then zoomed out of range, all the while my companions took pot shots at the men on the yacht. Kid whooped and hollered as he took out another one.

I counted four still shooting at us. It was only a matter of time before one of them got lucky and actually hit something. We needed to end this cat-and-mouse game and get on board the yacht.

Cookie glanced at his watch. "Bring her in, LT. Lancelot should be breaching any second now."

As if on cue, Lancelot's voice came in loud and clear. "Boarding now. Draw their attention toward the bow then get your asses over here before more of these cockroaches crawl out of hiding."

"Roger that." Harper swung the Zodiac around in the other direction.

The maneuver drew the remaining shooters away from the aft deck, their flight making their aim even less accurate. There was no use returning fire. At the speed we were going, I'd be lucky to hit the yacht, much less one of the shooters. Not so for Kid, who got off a round. I saw one of the remaining three drop. It was the split-second when the other two were distracted by their fallen comrade that allowed us to shoot under the extended bow of the boat. In seconds, the Zodiac was tied up at the swim deck, and, on Harper's command, we hauled ass onto the yacht.

Major Megan Sloan
North Pacific Ocean
Sunday 06:40 Zulu (16:40 ChST)

With Lance already on board the yacht, our plans shifted to accommodate the change. Guts and Kid were first out, followed by Cookie and Angel. LT was next, with me bringing up the rear.

Per our original plan, we split up. Team one, Angel and Cookie, took the port side, team two, Guts and Kid, took the starboard to assist Lancelot. Once this deck was secure, Kid would join up with me and LT to form team three. The plan was for team one to secure the upper decks while teams two and three made our way down.

I had no idea where we would find our target, but odds were the setup would be below the main deck. If Jude was right, all this guy needed was a laptop and clear sky for the satellite connection, which meant he could be anywhere on the boat. We'd barely made it down the first set of stairs when the muffled *pop-pop* of gunfire sounded from above. I held my breath until Angel's voice came through the comm. "Two down. Deck two clear. Heading up to the bridge."

Harper gave the two mic-click signal acknowledging the message. The five of us proceeded through what appeared to be a lounge area. The furniture had seen better days. The place reeked of cigarette smoke and stale food. A quick glance revealed overflowing ashtrays and dishes crusted with the remains of meals past. I'm no Suzy Homemaker, but the place made my skin crawl.

I moved forward, following the three-man team ahead of me, Lancelot on my six.

Like every boat I've ever been on, this one was built to take advantage of every available inch of floor space. The passageway lead-

ing off the filth-strewn lounge was so narrow we were forced to proceed single file. Guts was our lead guy, followed by Kid. As usual,
I was sandwiched between LT and Lancelot who was watching our
six. There was no need for stealth, they knew we were here, so Guts
and Kid kicked in any doors not already standing open. So far, all
we'd seen were once stately staterooms as well-kept as the lounge we'd
passed through earlier. Not a soldier in sight.

You know what they say. If it appears too good to be true, it
probably is. Our search was too easy. It didn't take an enormous
crew to pilot one of these things, but it did take a crew. Someone
had to tend the engines, steer the thing, and cook the food. Apparently, dishwashers and cleaning staff were optional. Apart from the
welcoming committee and the two Angel and Cookie encountered,
we'd yet to see a single person. Something wasn't right, and I hoped
we figured out what it was before it bit us in the butt. Confirming
I wasn't the only one with concerns, Harper's voice came across the
comm, "Look alive, stay alive."

The passageway ended with another set of stairs which, according to the deck plans I'd seen, would take us to yet another deck lined
with bedrooms forward, with the kitchen occupying most of the aft
section. Crew quarters were down another deck along with the engine room and the power plant.

We split up again. Harper, Kid, and I went to the far end of the
hallway. On LT's silent signal, we began kicking in doors, working
our way to the middle. Like the deck above, the rooms were empty
and well lived in.

"Where are they?" Guts asked.

"Maybe it's a ghost ship," Kid said.

"They're here," Harper assured. Then into our comm, he said,
"Cookie? Angel? Where are you?"

"On our way, LT," Angel responded. "Upper decks are clear.
Communications inoperable."

"Good work. Get your asses down here."

Lancelot and Guts remained at the top of the stairs while the rest of us regrouped in the least filthy of the rooms to discuss our next move and wait for the rest of our team to arrive. It wasn't long before Angel and Cookie joined us.

"What's next?" Kid asked.

"The good news is, there aren't sixty people aboard," Harper told them. "The bad news is, however many there are will likely be at the bottom of those stairs. Doesn't matter if there are two or twenty, they have the advantage. They know we're comin' and all they have to do is wait and pick us off as we descend the stairs."

"We need a diversion," Guts said. "Let's throw a flashbang down there. That'll buy us enough time to get down the stairs."

Harper nodded. "Anybody got a better idea?" We all shook our heads. "Let's do it. Guts, since it's your idea, you get the honor of throwing the grenade. I'll go down first. The rest of you follow." He pointed to me. "You're last."

I nodded my agreement. Their job was to get me to the computer system controlling the plane, not get me killed. They were taking a big chance, but I didn't have a better idea. Even if the enemy recognized the grenade and had time to divert their eyes and cover their ears, the noise and bright light in quarters this close would disorient the enemy long enough for a few of us to make it down the stairs. From there, it would be every man for himself. As we lined up along the passageway, I checked my weapon. I hoped I wouldn't have to use it, but there was no guarantee this would work. If I ended up being the last man standing, I'd have no choice but to try to blast my way to the source of the satellite signal.

LT was first in line. Guts would fall in behind him after he tossed the grenade down the stairs.

"On the count of three," Harper said, giving us fair warning to protect our vision and hearing.

Major Megan Sloan
North Pacific Ocean
Sunday 06:50 Zulu (16:50 ChST)

By the time I opened my eyes, LT had disappeared down into the smoke billowing up the stairwell. Our only chance at success was to take advantage of this brief moment of surprise.

"Stay close," Guts said as he followed Harper into the unknown.

As my foot connected with the top step, I heard the distinctive *tap, tap*, of an M16 followed by the thud of a body hitting the floor. The element of surprise was officially gone. The smoke cover had dissipated, leaving us exposed and trapped in the passageway. The wise thing to do would be to retreat and try to flush more of the bastards out, but we were running out of time, and my team knew it.

LT signaled us forward. Using the Navy SEAL version of sign language, Harper issued orders. On the count of three, we moved as one, drawing fire from the end of the hallway. I followed LT into a room. At first glance, it was some sort of office with a small desk along one wall and shelves along another, but then I saw it—a connecting door tucked in the rear corner, half-hidden by a small partition. My best guess was this was meant to be the captain's suite at one time but had taken on a new purpose. Outside, Guts and the others were still exchanging gunfire with the guys at the end of the hallway. My spidey senses told me whatever they were guarding was worthless. What I'd come for was on the other side of that door.

Using hand signals, LT and I came up with what would have to pass for a plan. The door wasn't wide enough for both of us to go through at the same time. He wanted to go first, but I shook my head. I'd been on this case since the beginning. The takedown was mine. After a few seconds, I won the stare down. LT moved to one side of the door. I took up position on the other, plastering myself against the wall. He held up three fingers.

Right hand on my M16, I placed my left on the door handle. On the count of three, I sucked in a breath and shoved the door open. Leading with my rifle, I burst into the room beyond. LT barreled in behind me. We swept the interior for the resistance I would have expected and came up empty. A young man, hands raised, sat in front of a bank of computer monitors perched on a makeshift desk. An open laptop computer sat to one side.

Heart pounding, I motioned with the tip of my rifle. "Stand up! Move!" If this was who I thought, he understood and spoke English as well as I did. To prove my point, he rose and stepped away from the electronic setup. LT clicked his throat mic and reported in.

"Target acquired. First room on the left. Get your asses in here."

"Roger that," Guts said. "Just finishing up here."

My prisoner fit the description I'd been given. Mid-twenties, short for a man, around five-foot-six with a slight build. He wore what I suspected was the standard uniform for hackers world-wide—worn jeans, a T-shirt, and tennis shoes—all American brands.

"Shut it off," I said, indicating the computer with a wave of my rifle.

He shook his head. "It's too late."

"I said, shut it off!"

Guts burst in, his gaze quickly taking in the situation. "Grab what you need and get the hell out of here. There's a plane headed right for us. We've got to get out of here."

"You sorry son of a bitch!" I slammed the hacker against the wall and pressed the tip of my rifle under his chin. "Guts, LT!" I yelled over my shoulder. "Get the computer. Now!"

"Yes, ma'am."

"How do we break the connection?" I asked. "How?!" Behind me, Guts and LT were yanking cords free from the various USB ports. "It's a Korean language keyboard," Guts said.

"Shut the damn thing off," I said over my shoulder.

Guts swore. "The power button has been disabled. It won't shut off."

When the hacker pressed his lips tight, I shoved the muzzle deeper into his jaw. "So help me God, I'll blow your head off right here if you don't tell him how to disable the program."

"It doesn't matter. We're all going to die. You're too late."

"As long as the plane is in the air, it's not too late." For the briefest of seconds, I saw a flicker of something in his eyes. "Disable, it and we'll get you out of here. Give them a chance, Seul-ki."

"Get a move on," Harper called from his position near the door. "Bring the computer and come on."

"You can disable the program. I know you can." I was getting to the kid. His eyes darted back and forth from my face to the computer. I lowered my voice so only he could hear me. "You don't want it to end like this, Seul-ki. The people on board that plane don't deserve to die."

"I don't deserve to live," he said.

"No, you don't," I agreed, "but you're going to because I'm not leaving here without you. Do what's right. Give them a chance to live."

I was down to counting heartbeats. Behind me, Harper cursed a blue streak. Guts was rock solid at my six. Nerves of steel as we both stared the hacker down and waited for him to reach the only conclusion we'd find acceptable.

"He's not going to do it," Guts said.

I searched my prisoner's eyes, now filled with tears of resignation. Guts was right. This guy had made up his mind. He wanted to die, but he wasn't doing it on my watch. "Screw you," I said before I stepped away, signaling for Guts to take my place. "Get him out of here. I'll get the computer."

Guts called for backup while I pulled out the waterproof bag I'd brought along. Before I closed the laptop, I tried the only thing I could think of. It was a trick Jude taught me once—something programmers used to find glitches in the code they've written. Using all ten fingers, I went "monkey" on the keyboard, randomly typing gibberish in an effort to "confuse" the program.

Angel's voice came through the comm. "Get out of there. Now! The plane is coming right at us!"

"Roger that," I said into the mic. "Get him out of here. I'm right behind you," I said to Guts as I shoved the laptop into the bag and sealed it shut. Harper was waiting for us in the passageway.

"Move!" he said as he urged me to follow Guts and Seul-ki up the stairs. We made it out to the main deck. Off in the distance, I could see the Gulfstream flanked by F18s. We'd come too far, come too close to success to give up now. I shoved the computer into Harper's hands.

"Take it and go!"

"Not without you."

"Go," I said and sprinted for the ladder leading up to the bridge.

Major Megan Sloan
North Pacific Ocean
Sunday 06:55 Zulu (16:55 ChST)

"**S**loan!" Harper yelled. "Get your ass over here!"

My foot slipped on the ladder, causing me to bang my shin on the unforgiving metal rung. Pain shot up my leg, but there was no time to process it. All I could think about was Liam and the others on the plane. The laptop had been disconnected, but the connection with the plane hadn't been broken. There was only one explanation. Wi-Fi. I had no idea where the router was, and I didn't have time to look for it or to beat the information out of our prisoner. My only chance to break the connection was to disable the satellite dish sending the signals to the plane.

"Damn idiot," I mumbled as I made it to the helipad and sprinted for the ladder attached to the side of the bridge. I should have had one of the guys disable it earlier. There was no time for self-recrimination. The plane was growing bigger and bigger. I could make out the wings of the sleek aircraft now. In a few more seconds, I'd be staring into the eyes of the pilots if I didn't get a move on.

Shoving the sick feeling in the pit of my stomach aside, I climbed like my life depended on it.

"You're out of time, Major!" Angel shouted in my ear. "Get off the boat! Now!"

I could see the antenna array. I scrambled up onto the roof of the bridge. Up there, what was only a gentle roll with the waves down below was exaggerated one-hundred fold. I tried to stand but couldn't find my footing. A wave crashed into the boat and sent me skidding on my ass to the edge of the roof. I grabbed for anything to keep me from flying off and managed to snag the base of an antenna. Giving up the idea of standing, I swung my legs around and kicked out at the parabolic satellite antenna. I managed to make contact with the bowl, but that wasn't going to do it. I stretched, trying to connect with the center structure. I'd never felt vertically challenged before, but, for once, I wished I was taller.

Giving up on disabling the workings of the antenna, I kicked out at the base. These things were directional. If it's not pointed in the right direction, the signal being sent will miss the satellite completely. All I had to do was tear the antenna loose from its moorings.

"Shit!" I could barely touch the base, much less dislodge it. The Gulfstream was close enough I could hear its engines screaming as it hurdled closer and closer to the water. God, what the people on board must be going through!

"Shoot it!" Harper's voice was in my ear. "Shoot the damn thing!"

I'd dropped my rifle at the bottom of the ladder. I fumbled for the 9mm strapped to my right thigh and took aim. The first few shots went wide. I braced myself and tried again, emptying the clip into the satellite dish. As the last brass hit the fiberglass roof, I prayed I'd done enough damage. Rolling to my stomach I clutched the edge of the roof and came face to face with the plane.

"Come on! Come on!" I chanted as the plane bore down on me. Only the best of pilots could pull a plane that size out of a freefall, and only if they had complete control of the plane. I had no idea if these pilots were good enough or even if they had regained control of the avionics.

"Shit!" Angel's voice filled my ear. "Get off, now, Major!"

"Jump!" Harper screamed at me.

It was too late for me to jump, and we all knew it. All I could do was hold on and pray the pilots on the plane were up to the task. Even if they were, there was no guarantee the plane itself wouldn't break apart under the stress.

"Come on. Come on. You can do it." Refusing to look away, I repeated the mantra as if saying it out loud would somehow help the flight crew pull off a miracle.

Maybe it was my imagination, but it looked like the nose of the plane was edging up. "You got it. Come on. Come on. Pull it up."

It wasn't my imagination. The nose was higher than it had been, but was it enough? They were only seconds from impact. I couldn't look away. If this was how I was going to die, I'd look it straight in the eye and die with a curse on my lips.

My heart hammered against my ribs. I gripped the chrome railing and, at the last possible second, instinct kicked in. I pressed my face into the roof of the bridge and prayed for a quick end this time, because, once again, I'd failed.

Liam Donovan
Gulfstream G650
Sunday 06:56 Zulu (16:56 ChST)

Come on. Come on.

Liam barely constrained his need to do something, anything, as he watched the tiny speck grow larger and larger with each passing minute. Ever since they'd been able to make out the boat on the ocean's surface, he'd somehow known it was *the* boat, the one originating the signal controlling their aircraft. Having it confirmed by Admiral Reese only added to his need to do something tangible to end this. But as the image took on more definition, he began to understand the concept of impotence. A prisoner of some unknown entity, his hands tied. All he could do was sit and watch death approach at an alarming rate.

"Nothing yet?" he asked.

First officer Wilkerson glanced over his shoulder. "Does it look like we have control?"

"Sorry." Liam cursed inwardly. None of this was the fault of the flight crew. They were as much prisoners of this situation as he and the other passengers.

"Just be ready to take care of the BUSes. We'll have our hands full pulling her out of this dive." Captain Davis had been white-knuckling the yoke for the last ten minutes.

Liam, on his knees where he could access the switches on the center console as well as the ones overhead, nodded. "Ready," he said, aware he was the only person on the plane not wearing a seat belt. None of them were going to survive a water crash at this speed, especially if what his gut was telling him turned out to be true. Unless something changed, and fast, they were going to take out the boat on their way down. There wasn't a seat belt in the world capable of saving him.

He glanced at the satellite phone resting in a cup holder on the center console. The line was still open. He could pick it up and demand an update, but what good would it do? Megan and her team were doing their best. If it wasn't good enough, they'd all pay the ultimate price for failure.

"Donovan! Donovan! Are you there?"

Liam grabbed the phone. "Donovan here. What's going on, Admiral?"

"Sloan has secured the technology and has the operator in custody."

Hearing Megan was okay released something inside him, but as quick as the reprieve came, it was replaced by a gut-wrenching certainty. "They've got to get off the boat. We're headed right for it."

"They're aware, Donovan. They're exfiltrating now."

Liam recognized the statement for what it was—code for, "They're abandoning the second mission priority—disabling the signal controlling your aircraft."

"Roger that." He swallowed hard. "And thanks, Admiral."

"Godspeed, Donovan."

The line went dead. Liam's hand tightened on the hard plastic until the pain in his fingers forced him to ease off.

"Someone's on top of the bridge," Davis said. "What the hell? Are they crazy?"

Liam leaned forward, the image taking on more definition as the seconds screamed by. "Batshit crazy," he said. "It's Major Sloan." He'd know her silhouette anywhere.

"What's she doing?" Wilkerson asked.

"Disabling the signal." His gut clenched. Damn her! The woman had been ordered to abandon the mission, but there she was—a petite Amazon hell-bent on doing the impossible. Just as she'd done in the desert, but, this time, there'd be no miraculous resurrection.

"Time's up!" Davis said. "We're going down too fast."

"Be ready," Liam warned. "She's gonna do it." *Or die trying.* He kept the obvious statement to himself, watching helplessly as she gripped the chrome railing and kicked out at the satellite dish he could easily make out among the array of antennas atop the bridge.

Come on, Meg. Come on.

They were close enough he could almost feel her frustration at not being able to defeat the mounting bracket holding the dish in place. For the span of a heartbeat, he thought she'd given up, and he silently willed her to get off the boat. *Move, dammit! Get off the boat!* She'd have a much better chance of surviving if she was in the water when they hit the yacht. He'd been responsible for almost getting her killed once. Being the actual instrument of her destruction this time made him want to puke.

He refused to look away, as if his gaze could somehow give her powers she didn't have or, at the very least, get her off the top of the bridge. He sucked in a breath when a wave rocked the boat, almost sending her tumbling into the water, but, at the last second, she grasped the low railing and managed to remain on the roof. She was determined to die today, and there wasn't a damned thing he could do about it.

Megan, he silently pleaded with her as her image grew larger and more distinct.

Letting go of the railing, she rolled to her back. He saw the muzzle flashes. Bits of debris flew into the air as she unloaded the clip into the satellite dish then flopped onto her belly again.

Beep. Beep. Beep.

"Holy shit!" Davis yelled. "She did it!"

The electronic sound drew Liam's gaze away from the yacht beginning to fill the cockpit windows. "What's happening?" he asked.

Before the words were out of his mouth, he felt the change in the plane. Davis and Wilkerson responded to the change immediately, yanking on the yokes.

"Shut it off," Davis said over his shoulder to Liam. "Shit, Todd." Liam took in the control panel. Lights were flashing all over the place—red warning lights accompanied by alarms. Both pilots were fully engaged in pulling the nose of the plane up. Liam began resetting switches and pushing buttons while, out of the corner of his vision, he watched the inevitable take place. The boat and surrounding ocean rushed at them at dizzying speed.

Then he saw her. Megan. Prone on the bridge roof, and, for a heartbeat, he felt the heat of her gaze lock with his. His breath caught in his lungs. He blinked...and she was gone. In the next breath, the nose of the plane collided with the tallest of the boat's antennas, ripping it from its moorings.

"Come on. Come on, baby! Climb! Climb!" Davis yelled.

Major Megan Sloan
North Pacific Ocean
Sunday 07:00 Zulu (17:00 ChST)

"Holy shit! Sloan! Major! Are you okay?"

It wasn't the voice of an angel whispering in my ear, but it was the only angel I wanted to hear. I clicked on my throat mic. "I'm still here, Angel."

"Damn, that was a close call!"

"Tell me about it." I could still taste the exhaust from the plane's engines as it flew over me, taking the rest of the antenna array with it. Peeling my hands loose from the railing, I rolled over onto my back. The pain in my abdomen was real enough that I felt around for shrapnel. Coming up empty, I opened my eyes. In the distance, the Gulfstream was slowly climbing to a safe cruising altitude.

I was still catching my breath when the boat shuddered beneath me.

"Major!" Angel shouted in my ear. "Get off the boat! Now!"

Another shudder nearly tossed me over the edge. *Shit.*

"She's going to blow sky-high, Major. Get off!"

Ignoring the pain in my midsection, I shimmied to the ladder and slid down to the helipad the way I'd seen the sailors do on the *Ronald Reagan*. The boat was listing to starboard, so I scrambled to the port side and flung myself off. Midair, the concussion slammed into me. Flying bits of flame and debris flew past me. I hit the water like the proverbial cannonball. Dead weight as the ocean swallowed me up.

Liam Donovan
Gulfstream G650
Sunday 07:02 Zulu (17:02 ChST)

"**S**he's climbing!" Wilkerson shouted. "God damn, she's climbing!"

Liam felt the lift, and the view out of the windscreen confirmed it. The horizon was slowly but surely changing. Where there had been mostly water with a sliver of open sky now lay mostly sky.

"Do we have enough fuel to make it to Guam?" Davis asked his first officer.

"Give me a second."

Liam wiped sweat from his eyes and stumbled into the jump seat. He'd had close calls before, but nothing came close to this one. His thoughts immediately went to Megan. Had she cheated death again? Or had their close call with the yacht been too close?

Mike appeared in the cockpit door, his face ashen, a bead of sweat trickling down from his left temple. "What happened? Are we flying again?"

"Everything's under control up here," Liam said. "Right?" He threw the question to the pilots.

"We might make it to Guam," Wilkerson said. "Climb to forty-five thousand and stay there."

"Why so high?" Mike asked.

"We consume less fuel at the higher altitude," Davis said.

"Got the heading," Wilkerson said.

Liam stood, ushering his partner toward the passenger cabin. "No need to alarm the delegates any further. Let's just tell them we're headed to Guam. At this point, what they don't know won't hurt them."

"Can we make it?"

Liam shrugged. "If Wilkerson says we can, I'm inclined to believe him. He knows this plane better than I do."

Mike nodded. "They did a hell of a job pulling us out of that dive."

"They sure did. Let's remind our passengers they're in good hands."

The look of relief on the delegates' faces almost made Liam rethink his decision not to tell them about the fuel situation. Was it fair to let them think all was well, the danger over? Perhaps not, but there wasn't anything to gain by giving them the truth, either.

They'd already begun discussing how this episode would impact their negotiations when Jeannie, the forward cabin steward, tapped him on the shoulder. "There's a call for you on the satellite phone."

"Thanks, Jeannie." He scooted past her in the narrow galley. "By the way, you and Charlie did a great job today." While the passengers had been going apeshit, the cabin stewards had remained calm. They'd done their best to instill reason in the others, but they'd simply been no match for the dominant personalities on board.

"We tried."

"Don't worry about it. You did good." He'd be sure to tell someone they'd displayed bravery and decorum above and beyond the call of duty. He sure as hell couldn't say the same for most of the passengers. With the exception of Shelby Conrad, they'd all displayed some level of insanity during the crisis. And these were the people charged with negotiating a nuclear arms agreement for the United States? If this situation wasn't screwed up, he didn't know what was.

Wilkerson spoke into the satphone. "Here he is, sir. Thank you, sir. I'll pass your comments along to Captain Davis."

Liam accepted the phone. "Donovan here."

"Thought you would want to know Major Sloan is okay." Admiral Reese went on, describing her harrowing dive into the water seconds before the explosive charges the North Koreans had used to blow the yacht to bits. How many times had she cheated death today? Two he knew of for sure. Probably more since she'd boarded a yacht filled with North Korean soldiers. If she'd been a cat, she would be running short on lives. As a human, she was living on borrowed time.

The need to strangle her with his bare hands warred with the desire to hold her close—to protect her.

"Thanks for letting me know. She's an amazing soldier. We owe her our lives."

"I can't argue either statement, Donovan. We're returning to port. Come see me before you fly back to the States. I'll buy you a drink."

"Thank you, sir. I'll look forward to it."

Liam stared at the phone for a minute before setting it in the cup holder that had become its home over the last few hours. Outside the windscreen, the sun was setting on the longest day of his life. Thanks to Megan Sloan, he was alive to see it.

"It's been a hell of a day, gentlemen," he said.

"Hell of a day," Wilkerson agreed.

"Let's not do this again," Davis said.

President Shane Gilchrist
White House Situation Room
Sunday 07:05 Zulu (03:05 EDT)

Shane Gilchrist stood as the video monitor on the opposite wall went black. He took a minute to catch his breath, letting his gaze rest a moment on each of the silent faces gathered around the table in the White House Situation Room. As the action had played out on the satellite feed, he'd considered his options. He could go public. Let the world know what Choi Min-ho had been up to. Or he could keep his cards close to his chest and see what he would do next.

He turned his gaze on DIRNSA Admiral Richard Sherman. "How sure are you they didn't get word out before the team boarded the boat?"

The Director of the National Security Agency replied, "As sure as we can be. We've been monitoring all cell communication as well as the satellite connection ever since we isolated the source. It's safe to assume we took them by surprise and they didn't have time to report the assault."

Gilchrist nodded. "I hate to assume anything, but in this case, I'm going to make an exception." He took a deep breath and let it out. "So...assuming Choi Min-ho has no idea we are in possession of his weapon of mass destruction, I'm inclined to keep this our little secret for now. As of this moment, we're putting a lid on this."

His gaze landed on Secretary of State Harman Adams. "Contact Deputy Cho as soon as they land in Guam. The summit will go on as planned. No one is to even hint we know about this technology. No one is to mention the detour this plane took. Make sure every last one of them understands this is a matter of national security and everything is classified Top Secret."

"Do you think that's wise, sir?" Brett Loren, his chief of staff asked. "This news could result in a big boost in your approval ratings. Not to mention put Choi Min-ho in his place in regard to the nuclear arms negotiations."

"I don't give a rat's ass about my approval ratings, and you know it. This is high-stakes poker, and we have an ace up our sleeve no one knows about. Now's not the time to play our ace. We need to act like we don't know anything and wait and see what happens. If this was Choi's only device, then he's screwed, and he knows it. If not, he'll deploy again, only this time we'll know what to look for." His gaze landed on DIRNGI Robert Cooper. "Am I right, Bob?"

The director of National Geospatial-Intelligence nodded. "We know what to look for, sir. If he deploys another device, we'll shut him down."

"Before he ditches another plane in the ocean?"

"Yes, sir."

"Which brings me to another question. He turned his blue eyes on Henry Rotham. "Where are the other planes, Henry? The task force recorded several missing planes over the last few years. I want to know what happened to them. Did they sink them in the ocean, like they tried to sink Global 2455? Or did they land them somewhere? If they landed them, what happened to the passengers?"

The director of the CIA shifted in his seat. "I'll put every available resource the agency has to answering those questions, sir."

"Rosemary." Gilchrist addressed the director of Homeland Security. "Your department will take charge of the technology."

A chorus of protests rose from the occupants of the room. Apparently, everyone wanted to get their hands on the device Sloan and her team had recovered.

"Simmer down, everybody. DHS has the most to lose here. We can't have planes dropping out of the sky, or the public will hang the TSA out to dry. So here's what we're going to do. DHS is going to be in charge of the device. Anything they find out about it will be shared with anyone with a need to know. Submit your requests for information, in writing, to Rosemary."

Henry Rotham spoke up. "We want to question the prisoner."

"Stand in line," Stephen Butler, secretary of defense said. "The DOD is better equipped to interrogate him."

"This is the United States. We're turning him over to the FBI. I don't want anyone saying we applied undo pressure on a prisoner."

"He's an enemy combatant," Butler argued. "We should treat him as such."

"My mind is made up," Gilchrist said. "We're done here." They all stood as he moved to the door. Hand on the door handle, he turned to face them. "Remember. Not a word of this leaks, not even to your most trusted aides. Let's keep a lid on this and see what Choi does next."

Choi Min-ho
Pyongyang, North Korea
Sunday 08:00 Zulu (17:00 KST)

A t the abrupt interruption, Choi looked up from the zinc mine production report he'd recently received from Hamgyeong-nam-do province. "What is it?" he asked his secretary.

"Supreme Leader, your scheduled phone call from General Pak has not come through. Should I try to contact him?"

"Yes! Immediately!"

Choi paced his office, waiting for the much-anticipated phone call. Some of his best soldiers were aboard that boat. They knew their jobs. They would not fail at their mission to protect the technology at all cost. Yet, he'd received no communication from them regarding any problems. This was not good. He'd counted on detaining the delegation from the United States in order to prove who had the upper hand in the nuclear arms negotiations. Without the plane and the people on board, he had nothing to bargain with.

The American maggots had turned the world against him. Even countries he'd considered allies had expressed concerns about North Korea's nuclear program.

The secretary returned, his face pale, his voice shaking. "Sir, no one answered. I tried several times. Should I continue?"

Maybe something had happened to the satellite phone. Dead batteries or some other malfunction. There had to be a good explanation for Pak not calling. "Summon the technician at once! I'll speak with General Pak on the video connection."

Nearly an hour later, with no results via the video connection Choi used to speak with the hacker, he had no choice but to think the worst had happened. He called for the head of his intelligence-gathering agency and demanded the man direct a satellite at the last known coordinates for the yacht. In anticipation of this latest mission, Choi had ordered them to the new spot northeast of Guam in the North Pacific. They'd been anchored in the same spot for several months with no report of any kind of problem with the vessel. Could some kind of mechanical problem result in a catastrophic failure of the boat? Or was it as simple as an electrical problem preventing them from communicating with him? No electricity meant no satellite signals. And no satellite signals meant he'd also lost control of the American aircraft.

General Kwon entered the office behind Choi's flustered secretary. "It's a pleasure to serve you, Supreme Commander," he said, bowing low to show his respect.

"I have coordinates." He held out a slip of paper. The general took the paper without looking at it. "I need eyes on that spot immediately. Can it be done?"

"I'm certain, sir."

"Good," Choi said. "No one is to see what is there but me. do you understand?"

The man who was charged with running a very effective intelligence community didn't blink at the order. He was used to Choi demanding satellite surveillance of various places within the borders of North Korea and around the world. "I'll have the video feed sent directly to the monitor here in your office."

"No delays, Kwon. This is a matter of national security."

By the time the satellite imagery came through, the sky had gone almost as dark as Choi's mood. He'd heard nothing from the boat. Nothing! Heads would roll if they'd lost control of the aircraft. Choi stared at the dark monitor, at first thinking Kwon had sent him footage from the wrong coordinates, but as the satellite zoomed in on the water, one small dot of flickering light caught his attention.

It took a moment for him to realize what it was—a piece of burning debris!

Stunned, he collapsed in his chair, his gaze fixed on the spot where his yacht was supposed to be. Not just his yacht, but the most secret weapon on the planet!

What had happened? It must have been sudden, or Pak would have reported a problem and requested assistance. Had the Americans figured out what was happening and tracked the satellite signals to the boat? He dismissed the thought as ridiculous. If they'd suspected he had hijacked their delegation, he would have heard from them. President Gilchrist would never turn down an opportunity to push his agenda against North Korea to the rest of the world.

As the thought of all he'd lost sank in, a rage like he'd never known before swept over him. Abruptly rising, he swept the video monitor off his desk. It landed on the floor, the glass screen shattering on impact. The door opened, his secretary bolting in with his personal guards on the man's heels.

"Are you okay?" he asked, taking in the debris scattered across the floor.

"No. I am not okay." He pointed to the mess he'd made. "Clean this up. I'm going to my rooms. Send me one. One of the Americans this time." They were ugly with their white skin and pinched faces, but tonight he had a need to screw the United States any way he could. Stepping past his stunned secretary, he felt the power rising in him again. He might have lost one battle, but there were other ways to win the war.

EPILOGUE
Major Megan Sloan
Naval Base Guam
Sunday 08:00 Zulu (18:00 ChST)

"**O**ur ride's here."

I followed Lancelot's outstretched arm to see a bright speck in the darkening sky. It seemed like forever since these guys fished me out of the water, but in reality, it hadn't been long at all. Pieces of flaming debris were still floating on the water—a safe distance away now. I was cold and wet, and, having cheated death twice in the last few hours, I was more than ready to call it a day. "I hope we're in time for cocktail hour."

"You did good work today," Harper said. "Drinks are on us tonight."

"Thanks. I've got to deliver the package to the right people." I nodded toward the plastic-shrouded laptop. "And hand him"—I pointed to Seul-ki who was handcuffed to a hand grip on the side of the Zodiac—"over to the proper authorities. Whoever that might be."

"Take your time," Lancelot said. "It's a standing invitation."

"Any word on the plane?" I asked Angel.

"Landed at Andersen with fumes to spare. A few people had to be treated for anxiety, but they're all alive. Thanks to you."

"It was a team effort," I said. "Couldn't have done it without you."

As I had surmised while sitting in the Zodiac, figuring out who had jurisdiction over the technology and the prisoner was nothing short of a disaster it took days to unravel. Ultimately, the Department of Homeland Security won the custody battle for the computer, but only after agreeing to allow various other agencies access to whatever information could be extracted from the hard drive. The FBI came out on top in regard to our prisoner, assuring no one would violate Seul-ki's civil rights.

"What civil rights?" I asked. He wasn't a citizen. Hell, he was an enemy combatant who'd refused to cooperate upon capture. If not for the extraordinary skills of a couple of pilots, and one damned well-built aircraft, the bastard would have added the passengers and crew of the Gulfstream to his murdered list.

The president, I was told, had high hopes Seul-ki would provide the United States with valuable information he could use to force more international sanctions on Choi Min-ho's regime. I doubted the hacker would talk or if anything he had to say would be enough to bring about any kind of change in the world. He had been a pawn in a deadly game—allowed to know only enough to do his assigned task. Nothing more.

According to Colonel Rodgers, The Drone Theory Task Force had already disappeared from existence. The agents on loan from various agencies had been reassigned, and those who had been recruited specifically for the task force, like Jude, had been absorbed into the vast intelligence machine. Once my presence on Guam was no longer needed, I was to report to Colonel Rodgers' office at the Pentagon for further assignment.

Just great.

"You've got a phone call, Major."

I nodded at Angel. In the week I'd been here, my SEAL friends had graciously made room for me in their world. I have a cage to call my own with a cot to sleep on, and a footlocker set on blocks doubled as storage and a desk so I could complete the reports I knew would disappear into the ether almost as soon as I turned them in. "Thanks, Angel."

The only office in the place belonged to Lt. Harper and housed the only landline. Since he preferred to spend his time with his team members, the office was rarely occupied. It was up to whoever was passing by to answer the phone when it rang, so, needless to say, not many calls got through.

I settled into the hard-as-a-rock desk chair and, after picking up the receiver, pushed the flashing red button. "Major Sloan."

"Megan."

My heart did a somersault then settled somewhere in my throat.

I hated that Liam's voice still had any kind of power over me. Maybe it always would. "It's good to hear your voice." No lie there. He was alive, and though I didn't wish him dead, I'd gladly have killed him with my own hands. Maybe that was why he was the last of the passengers on the Gulfstream to contact me.

"Good to be here to be heard," he said. "Sorry to take so long to call, but it's been kind of crazy."

He didn't need to elaborate. The nuclear arms summit was underway, as scheduled. Not a single word had been said regarding the hijacking of the American delegation. The reasoning behind the decision to keep our mission under wraps was way above my pay grade and—like most things government and military—classified as none of my business. People like me were the help. Nothing more. I used to be okay with that, but this mission had messed with my thinking

"How's the summit going?"

"Who knows? Security is tight. No one leaves the table without an armed escort. You should see the hallway outside the restrooms when they take a break. Looks like a black suit convention."

I smiled at the image. "Don't you mean, cheap black suit convention?" I'd heard the Secret Service paid better than most federal law enforcement agencies, but they didn't pay *that* well.

"You know what I'm talking about, then." His chuckle reminded me of a time when we laughed at each other's jokes. Ancient history.

"I do. What's next for you?"

I could almost see his broad shoulders shrug. "Who knows? I'm supposed to accompany the delegation home. My presence has been requested at the Pentagon. Colonel Rodgers' office. You know what he wants?"

Hell, no. "Sounds like they've got another assignment for you."

"That's my best guess. What about you? What's next?"

"No idea." Truth. I knew one thing, though. I'd resign before I'd work with Liam Donovan again. *Been there. Done that. Have the scars to prove it.*

"Well...I just wanted to say thank you, and sorry for the close call."

If I closed my eyes, I could still hear the roar of those engines and taste their exhaust. "I understand you were in the cockpit."

"Yeah, Davis and Wilkerson needed all the help they could get. Once they had control again, warnings were going off all over the place. I reset stuff while the two of them leveled the sucker out."

"I can only imagine." I'd spent countless hours since my return to dry land imagining the chaos in the cockpit as the three of them rushed to gain control of the aircraft.

"Look, there's another reason I'm calling."

If I'd had spidey-senses, they would have been tingling. "What other reason?"

"The delegation is going home day after tomorrow. They want to give you a ride home."

"Tell them thanks, but I'm going to be here for a few more days. Tying up loose ends with the team. There's a C17 stopping over on its way home from Japan next week. I understand I've got a seat on it."

Truth was, I didn't have a clue how I was getting home, or when, but I'd build my own wings out of duck feathers and Super Glue before I'd wing it all the way to D.C. in the same plane as Liam Donovan.

"Is that so?" He always could tell when I was lying through my teeth. Too bad I hadn't developed the same ability where he was concerned. I could have saved us both a lot of misery.

"Screw you, Liam."

"See you in D.C.," he said with a laugh.

I hung up on him.

Not if I see you first.

AUTHOR'S NOTE

Fiction: something feigned, invented, or imagined; a made-up story.

Status: MISSING is a work of fiction. However, parts of the story are true or based on truth.

On March 8, 2014, Malaysia Airlines flight MH370, while en route from Kuala Lumpur to Beijing with 227 passengers and 12 crew members aboard, *did* go missing over the Indian Ocean,1 and I, by no means, intend any disrespect toward their memory.

Following the initial reports that MH370 had gone missing, people around the world held their breath as officials tracked the plane's flight path using satellite signals sent from the twin jet engines to their manufacturer, a standard feature to track flight hours and address maintenance issues. Thousands of man-hours and hundreds of millions of dollars were devoted to the search. After many months of extensive searching revealed no sign of the aircraft, the hunt was abandoned and the plane and everyone aboard was considered lost at sea. To this date, only a few pieces believed to be from the plane's fuselage have washed ashore on islands in the western Indian Ocean.

The manner of MH370's disappearance spawned any number of conspiracy theories. Everything from alien abduction to hijacking to pilot suicide was considered. *Status: MISSING* is based on my own theory, which I shared with anyone who would listen, that the plane had been hijacked by someone on the ground using drone technology. In a final report issued in July of 2018 regarding the incident, Malaysian officials stated, "No matter what we do, we cannot exclude the possibility of a third person or third party or unlawful interference." Head investigator, Kok Soo Chon, told reporters, We are not of the opinion that it could have been an event committed by the pilot."

In another interview, Tun Dr Mahathir, former prime minister of Malaysia has suggested the plane might have been hacked and controlled remotely. "The technology is there. You know how good people are now with operating planes without pilots. Even fighter planes are to be without pilots," he said.2

In my story, Agent Sloan blames herself for a failed attempt to recover Top-Secret drone technology she, and the American intelligence community, believe has been adapted to hijack airliners while in flight. Truth: Military (armed) and intelligence gathering drones, UAV's (unmanned aerial vehicles), are remotely flown by trained pilots, sometimes from thousands of miles away. Truth: The CIA did lose an RQ-170 Sentinel drone in Iran, near the Afghanistan border in December of 2011.3 Iran issued differing accounts, first saying the drone was shot down then later saying the Iranian military hacked into the aircraft's control system. U.S. officials claim there was a malfunction that led to the stealth plane straying across the border where it eventually crashed. Reportedly, no attempts were made to physically recover or destroy the technology. Agent Sloan's failed mission is purely straight out of my imagination.

Connecting the dots between a lost drone and cyber-hijacking was less of a stretch than I initially imagined. Fly by Wire4 technology is the standard for commercial aircraft these days. Computers and electronic switches have replaced manual flight controls, reducing weight, conserving fuel, and improving safety—unless a writer with a vivid imagination decides to create a scenario where a plane is remotely hijacked. Can it be done?5 The answer is—maybe.6 Tests have been done that seem to suggest it is possible and government officials are aware of the danger.7

Have I played fast and loose with the facts? Perhaps, but remember, this is a work of fiction. I'm allowed to make things up. In the mid-1800s, Jules Verne imagined an electrically powered submarine and a 'projectile' that carried people to the moon and back. More recently, *The Jetson's*7 television cartoon featured a robotic maid, a robotic vacuum cleaner, a flat screen television, and a tanning lamp, to name just a few. Do you recall the laptop computer in *2011: A Space Odyssey*? And the list goes on.8

To sum it up, one pilot I spoke to said this, "If it hasn't been done already, someone is working on it."

Thanks for reading *Status: MISSING*. Agent Sloan is out on her next mission as we speak. As soon as the details are declassified I'll give you a full accounting of her activities. Subscribe to my newsletter[1] for updates on her missions.

Reviews are the life-blood of authors. Please consider leaving one.

D W Maroney
www.DWMaroney.com[2]
www.facebook.com/dwmaroney_author[3]
Twitter - @DWMaroney
Goodreads[4]

---

1. http://eepurl.com/gdHqpH

2. http://www.DWMaroney.com

3. http://www.facebook.com/dwmaroney_author

4. https://www.goodreads.com/author/show/18841960.D_W_Maroney

Footnotes

1 https://en.wikipedia.org/wiki/Malaysia_Airlines_Flight_370

2 https://nypost.com/2018/07/31/mystery-of-mh370-only-grows-after-final-report-into-disappearance/

3 https://www.nytimes.com/2011/12/08/world/middleeast/drone-crash-in-iran-reveals-secret-us-surveillance-bid.html

4 http://www.davi.ws/avionics/TheAvionicsHandbook_Cap_11.pdf

5 https://www.cbsnews.com/news/airplane-computer-systems-can-be-hacked-report-says/

6 https://www.newsweek.com/flight-airplanes-can-now-be-hacked-ground-cyber-expert-warns-962420

7 https://www.aviationtoday.com/2017/11/08/boeing-757-testing-shows-airplanes-vulnerable-hacking-dhs-says/

8 https://www.buzzfeed.com/kasiagalazka/science-fiction-things-that-actually-exist-now

9 https://www.cnn.com/2018/03/21/health/gallery/sci-fi-inventions-that-became-reality/index.html

Glossary

ABU – Airman Battle Uniform (camouflage uniform worn by Air Force personnel)

ACARS – Aircraft Communications and Reporting System

AFISR – Air Force Intelligence, Surveillance, and Reconnaissance

BUS – Electrical switches

EDT – Eastern Daylight saving Time

C-130 – Four-engine turbo-prop military transport airplane

C-17 – The workhorse of the Air Force. Cargo plane with four-turbofan engines designed to transport cargo and personnel.

C2 – Navy's twin-engine, high-wing cargo aircraft whose primary function is OCD (onboard carrier delivery) of supplies, mail and passengers.

ChST – Chamorro Standard Time – also known as GST – Guam Standard Time

CIA – Central Intelligence Agency

CO – Commanding officer

CYA – Cover your ass

DFW – Dallas/Ft.Worth International Airport

DHS – Department of Homeland Security

DIA – Defense Intelligence Agency

DIRCIA – Director of the Central Intelligence Agency

DIRNGI – Director of National Geospatial Intelligence

DIRNSA – Director of National Security

DOD – Department of Defense

FAA – Federal Aviation Administration

FBI – Federal Bureau of Investigation

FFDO – Federal Flight Deck Officer – Volunteer Federal law enforcement officer commissioned by the TSA. (Can be a pilot or member of the flight crew) Their purpose is to defend the flight deck against criminal violence and air piracy.

FLY BY WIRE - Replaces the conventional manual flight controls of an aircraft with an electronic interface. FBW technology converts the movement of flight controls to electronic signals transmitted by wires. Computers determine how to move the actuators at each control surface to provide the ordered response.

GEO Satellite – A geosynchronous satellite has an orbital period the same as the Earth's rotation period so it remains permanently fixed in the exact same position in the sky.

Gitmo – Guantanamo Naval Base, Guantanamo Bay, Cuba

Global Hawk – Unmanned surveillance aircraft built by Northrup Grumman

GPS – Global Positioning System

Guard Frequency – 121.5 MHz Radio frequency used for civilian aircraft emergencies. Also known as IAD (International Aircraft Distress) or VHF Guard

HST – Hawaii Standard Time

ISR – Intelligence, Surveillance and Reconnaissance Aircraft

IT – Information technology

KST – Korea Standard Time

LAX – Los Angeles International Airport

LEO – Law enforcement officer

MIT – Massachusetts Institute of Technology

MP – Military Police

NCO – Non-commissioned Officer

NGA – National Geospatial Intelligence Agency

NSA – National Security Agency

NTSB – National Transportation Safety Administration

PACOM – U. S. Pacific Command

PBE – Personal breathing equipment

SAR – Search and Rescue

Satphone – Mobile phone that connects to orbiting satellites instead of land-based cell towers.

SEAL Team – Sea, Air, and Land Team – Navy Special Forces – part of the Navy Special Warfare Command

SECDEF – Secretary of Defense

TSA – Transportation Safety Administration

UAV – Unmanned aerial vehicle – also known as a drone

WFO – The FBI's Washington Field Office in Washington, D.C.

WKT – Wake Time

Zero-Day Bug – A computer software vulnerability that has yet to be discovered.

Zulu – Military time zone Z – also known as GMT (Greenwich Mean Time) – and more recently UTC (Universal Time Coordinated or Coordinated Universal Time.) All of these are or have been used to reference time at the zero meridian (Longitude 0). Zulu time is the time standard used by the military and in aviation and weather forecasting.

50459173R00182

Made in the USA
Middletown, DE
25 June 2019